WITH...

Rose Gold

"When it comes to naming names, Walter Mosley knows no peer. . . .
Endlessly entertaining." —*The New York Times Book Review*

"The Rawlins books have always borne their author's unique, visionary
stamp. Rawlins himself is at the heart of the series' appeal: a well-read
autodidact and man of action, father of found children and spouse to
no one who sometimes sees his double life divided between the land
of law and the underworld." —*The Wall Street Journal*

"[Full of] rich social fabric, rendered in well-observed details of skin
color, speech, dress and, of course, neighborhoods. This is the triumph
of each Easy Rawlins story—documenting this changing panorama of
a city where the migration of Southern blacks, eager to claim it as
their new world, is constantly remaking the city as it remakes them."
—*Los Angeles Times*

"[Mosley] never lets us forget that we're all human, we all make mistakes, we're all flawed. And he does it with flair . . . unmatched by his
contemporaries." —*The Toledo Blade*

"Impressive. . . . Easy's experiences and insights perfectly mirror the
turbulent [era]." —*Publishers Weekly* (starred review)

"Mosley has few peers when it comes to crafting sentences, and he's
woven some beauties into this swift-moving yet philosophical story
that does more for illustrating an iconic period than hours of docu-
mentary film could. This Easy Rawlins novel harks back to the great
early days of the series." —*Booklist* (starred review)

WALTER MOSLEY

Rose Gold

Walter Mosley is the author of forty-three books, most notably thirteen Easy Rawlins mysteries, the first of which, *Devil in a Blue Dress*, was made into an acclaimed film starring Denzel Washington. *Always Outnumbered* was an HBO film starring Laurence Fishburne, adapted from his first Socrates Fortlow novel. A native of Los Angeles and a graduate of Goddard College, he holds an MFA from CCNY and lives in Brooklyn, New York. He is the winner of numerous awards, including an O. Henry Award, a Grammy Award, and PEN America's Lifetime Achievement Award.

www.waltermosley.com

Also by Walter Mosley:

Rose
GOLD

An Easy Rawlins Mystery
WALTER MOSLEY

Vintage Crime/Black Lizard
Vintage Books
A Division of Penguin Random House LLC
New York

FIRST VINTAGE CRIME/BLACK LIZARD EDITION, JUNE 2015

The Library of Congress has cataloged the Doubleday edition as follows:
Mosley, Walter.
Rose Gold: an Easy Rawlins mystery / by Walter Mosley.
Pages cm
1. Rawlins, Easy (Fictitious character)—Fiction.   2. Private investigators—
California—Los Angeles—Fiction.   I. Title.
PS3563.O88456R68 2014   813.'dc23   2014012936

Vintage Books Trade Paperback ISBN: 978-0-307-94979-0
eBook ISBN: 978-0-385-53600-4

Book design by Michael Collica

www.weeklylizard.com

Printed in the United States of America
10 9 8 7 6 5

For Amiri Baraka

Rose Gold

Back then, Moving Day in L.A. was a phantom holiday that occurred, for many Angelenos, every other month or so. In the 1950s and '60s, when the rent was dirt cheap, people moved to be closer to a new job, away from an old lover, or when it seemed that a fundamental change of life was in order. Sometimes the person moving would not only change the numbers on his or her door but also the name on the mailbox, the used car in the driveway, and even the style of clothes they donned to walk out and meet the day.

Now and then the move was not merely aesthetic or convenient but necessary; like when a bill collector, lawyer, or the law itself was hot on the temporary tenant's trail. At a time like this the migrant lease-holder would make sure that the new domicile was inside the border of a different unincorporated town or municipality of L.A. County. That way the law offered few systems to track his whereabouts. A man could actually avoid dunning or even arrest by merely moving across the street.

In the case of a necessary move, the rental émigré would load up a truck in the middle of the night and go with no fanfare, or notice to the landlord.

This was not the case with my midmorning migration.

My daughter and I were moving, that Sunday, from Genesee at Pico to Point View just a few houses north of Airdrome; not more than eleven blocks. This was a necessary move that was not due to any legal or monetary bureaucracy.

Five months or so earlier I had almost died. At that time I had been involved in a case that put my home in jeopardy, and so I had sent my daughter to stay with her brother at a friend's place, temporarily. I resolved the case but then drove my car off the side of a coastal mountain. Whether this accident was due to a subconscious death wish or just bad luck is uncertain, but I was in what the doctors called a semi-coma for the better part of two months.

During that time a squatter named Jeffrey had taken possession of the empty house on Genesee. With the help of my friend Raymond Alexander, Jeff was put out. This was not a gentle eviction and I worried that Feather, my adopted daughter, might one day be home alone when the squatter returned for revenge.

And so I sold the Genesee house and bought a new, larger place on Point View. I might have ranged farther but that September, Feather was going to enter the seventh grade at Louis Pasteur Junior High and the new address was just a block away from there.

And so some friends—LaMarque Alexander (Raymond's son), Jesus (my adopted boy, now a young man), Jackson Blue and his wife's associate Percy Bidwell—helped Feather and me load our belongings into a rented truck and drive it over to the new door.

I would have hired a moving company but recently, within the last week, the city had seen fit to inspect all five of the rental properties I owned and demanded I fix structural problems, perform a termite extermination, and in one place they even required that I install a new heating system. It would take every cent I had, and then some, to pay for the improvements, so I rented a truck from my old pal Primo and called on my friends to lend a hand with the move.

Feather set herself up in the entranceway of the rare two-story residence and directed the men where to deposit the bureaus, tables, beds, boxes, and chairs. My daughter had light brown hair and skin. She was tall for twelve and lean, not to say thin. She was becoming an accomplished long-distance runner as her brother, Jesus, had been, and was fluent in three languages already. Neither she nor her brother had one drop of blood in common with me, or each other, but they were my kids and we were family.

"Uncle Jackson," Feather said from the front hall, "that little table goes in Daddy's room upstairs. He uses it for his desk."

"Upstairs?" Jackson exclaimed. He was around my age, mid-forties, short, jet black, and skinny as a sapling tree. "Girl, this table might look little but the wood is dense, and heavy."

"I'll help, Uncle J," Jesus said. My boy was pure Mexican Indian. He was no taller than Jackson Blue but his years of working his own small fishing boat had made him strong.

Jesus got behind the table, taking most of the weight, and Jackson groaned piteously as he guided it up the stairs.

"This is a really nice house you got here, Mr. Rawlins," Percy Bidwell said.

He was almost my height, a brassy brown, and good-looking. His hair had been processed into tight curls. I always distrusted men who processed their hair. This was a prejudice that I realized was not necessarily justified.

"Thank you, Percy. I like it."

"Jewelle said that you haven't moved in years. I guess this house was just too good to pass up. Must've cost quite a bit for a place this big in this neighborhood."

I also didn't like people asking about my business. Percy was racking up the negative points on my friendship register.

"Do you work for Jewelle?" I asked.

"No." He seemed almost insulted by the question.

Jewelle MacDonald had come from a real estate family and on her own had amassed an empire of apartment buildings and commercial properties. She was even part owner of a major international hotel that was being constructed in downtown L.A. Jewelle was barely out of her twenties and married to the onetime roustabout, now computer expert Jackson Blue. It was no insult to ask if Bidwell worked for her. She had sent him to help Jackson, after all.

"Jewelle told me that if I wanted to get in contact with Jason Middleton," Percy said, "that you were the one who would do that for me."

His sentence structure told me that he thought that *I* was somehow under the direction of Jewelle; that all he had to do was mention that she had asked for something and I would make that something happen.

I turned away from him and called, "LaMarque!"

"Yes, Mr. Rawlins?"

The lanky twenty-two-year-old loped from the truck to my side.

"Where's your father?"

"He had to go back east on business."

Business for Raymond, more commonly known as Mouse, was high-end heists with the strong possibility of brutality and bloodshed.

"So he sent you to take his place?" I asked. I could feel Percy Bidwell starring daggers at my back.

"Mama did. When you called to ask for Dad to help, she send me."

"How long you been back from Texas?"

"Nine days."

"You outta all that trouble now?"

"I ain't in no gang no more," he said, looking down a little sheepishly.

EttaMae, LaMarque's mother and Raymond's wife, had sent the young man down to Texas to work on her brother's farm for a while. She did that to save the lives of the gang members who had tried to claim him as one of their own. Raymond would have killed them all if she hadn't interfered.

A car pulled up to the curb just then. It was a dark Ford with four male passengers. Most cars in Southern California transported a solitary driver, a couple, a double date, or a family. Four men in a car most likely spelled trouble if there wasn't a construction site somewhere in the vicinity.

"Well," I said to LaMarque while watching the men confer, "you get back to work and I'll give you twenty dollars to go home with."

"Yes, sir," he said. Etta had taught the boy his manners.

LaMarque ducked his head and ran back to the truck.

"Mr. Rawlins," Percy Bidwell said.

"Yeah, Percy?" I was watching the men as they prepared to disembark.

"About Mr. Middleton."

"What is it you want with Jason?"

"That's private," the young man said.

"Then you better just call him up yourself and leave me out of it."

"I don't know him."

"And I don't know you."

"Jewelle told me to tell you to call him."

"You don't tell me what to do, son, and neither does Jewelle."

The four men were out of the car by then. They were all white men, tall, and burly. Three of them wore off-the-rack suits of various dark hues. The eldest, maybe fifty years of age, was dressed in a dark-colored, tailored ensemble that was possibly even silk.

The leader began the stroll up the slight incline of my lawn.

"Easy," Jackson warned from an upstairs window.

"I see 'em, Blue."

"Is it all right?"

"I hope so."

"Mr. Rawlins," Percy was saying, trying once again to impress his will upon me.

"Either get back to work or go home, Percy," I said. "I got other things on my mind right now."

2

"Mr. Rawlins," the headman said as he approached the front door of my new home.

My new home. How did this stranger know where to find me on Moving Day?

"Yes?" I said darkly.

Percy was headed back toward the truck. Jesus put down a hassock he'd been carrying and gazed up at us.

"Roger Frisk," the white man said, holding out a hand.

I say *white* but Frisk's skin was actually ruddy pink in color, a mottled salmon.

"Do I know you, Mr. Frisk?" I asked, refusing to take the proffered hand.

When the slighted hand darted under the left-side breast of my visitor's elegant jacket, I wondered if I should tackle him. After all, he looked like an upscale hood. But I couldn't imagine some fool driving up in a car, walking to my front door, and then shooting me in broad daylight on a Sunday.

The hand came out with a white business card between its fingers.

I stared at the card like a NATO sentry watching his Russian counterpart handing a note through a chink in the Berlin Wall.

"I'm the special assistant to the Chief of Police," Frisk said.

I took the card. It said the same thing.

"So?"

"I need to speak with you, Mr. Rawlins."

"A cop named Frisk?" I replied.

He smiled and gave me a quarter nod over a shoulder roll.

"It's Sunday and I'm in the middle of a move," I said. "I can come down to your office say Tuesday afternoon."

"Maxwell!" Frisk commanded while staring me in the eye. His eyes were green like those of a pet cat that my long-dead mother had, named Speckles.

"Yes, sir," one of the suits responded as he ran from the sedan up to his boss's side.

"You, Sturgeon, and Moorcock help Mr. Rawlins's friends finish off the move."

"Yes, sir."

The yes-man in the dark brown suit waved at his fellow cops, pointing toward my twenty-five-foot moving truck. Before I knew it, they were climbing into the back and pulling out furniture and boxes. I suppose I could have stopped them but there were over one hundred boxes of books alone left to move—and the heaviest furniture was yet to come.

"That's very nice of you, Special Assistant Frisk," I said, "but it's still Sunday and I don't know you from Adam."

"The police department needs your help, Mr. Rawlins."

"That may be," I said, "but I feel no compunction to help them. You know my relationship with the constabulary is tenuous at best."

I used the upscale language to show Frisk that he couldn't run roughshod over me, but he just smiled.

"Be that as it may, Mr. Rawlins, I think you will find that it is in your own best interest to concern yourself with our needs."

"Look, man. I don't know you. Send Melvin Suggs over here and I will discuss whatever concerns you have with him."

Suggs was the only Los Angeles cop that I trusted. He was white but he had always been fair with me.

"Detective Suggs is on an extended leave of absence."

"Wounded?" I asked.

Frisk shook his head in such a way as to let me know that my police contact was in trouble with his masters. This in itself was no surprise to me. Melvin was too smart, in a basic human sense, to last forever in the morally bankrupt LAPD. But the fact that he had been put on leave without me having any notion of it was the cause of a familiar pang.

This distress was based on the fact that people in L.A. often disappear without anyone noticing. Months, sometimes years later you found yourself wondering, whatever happened to so-and-so? By that time there would be no sign of their passage even for the most seasoned investigator.

But modern-day alienation wasn't my problem right then.

"Excuse me," one of the cops-turned-mover said as he carried two heavy boxes of books marked *Encyclopedia* past me and his boss.

"Look, Mr. Frisk," I said as we shifted onto the lawn. "Today I have this move and after that I have building citations against my properties for code violations. I don't have the money to pay for the upgrades, exterminations, and fixes and so I'm going to have to do most of it myself."

"I'm in the chief's office, Mr. Rawlins," Frisk said easily. "Every day I'm on the phone with the mayor or one of his top officials. Any city ordinance can be relaxed, even wiped away. At the very least I could make it so that your problems with the city can be put off until such time that you can afford to attend to them."

Roger Frisk didn't strike me as being an immediate threat, but he was a danger. Whenever top men left their homes on a weekend to lend a helping hand to a black man, there was danger in the air. I didn't know how this hazard might show itself but I was hell-bent on avoiding it.

"It's not just that," I said, trying to sound reasonable. "Other expenses have come up over the past month, and I have to make some serious money if I want to keep ahead of the curve. Pro bono work for the city won't get me where I need to be."

I wasn't lying. Unknown to me or my daughter, a counselor at her elementary school had given her name to the admissions office of the prestigious private school Ivy Prep. This counselor, a Miss Timmons, had sent Feather's test scores and grades to the school, and so we had received a letter of acceptance without even applying.

Feather was ecstatic. Ivy Prep would put her education on a whole new trajectory. She could consider Harvard or even Oxford for college.

And all it cost was a mere thirty-five hundred dollars a semester plus books, uniforms, travel, and special events.

"We understand that you have to make a living, sir," Frisk said in a respectful tone. "There is an independent party that is willing to pay eight thousand dollars for you to take on a missing person's case, and there will be a twenty-five-hundred-dollar bonus for the satisfactory completion of that situation."

I was speechless for at least thirty seconds. No policeman had ever offered me money—and I had been stopped, rousted, beaten, and caged by a thousand cops in my years on and near the street.

A black-haired, charcoal-suited cop walked past carrying a red-lacquered Chinese box across the threshold of my new home. I had owned that chest for more than twenty years.

"Well, Mr. Rawlins?" Frisk asked.

It occurred to me that if Melvin was off the force I'd need a new contact. Frisk seemed like a possible candidate.

"What happened with Melvin?" I asked. I really wanted to know, but this was also a test. I didn't expect to be told the actual circumstances, but even if he held back what had really happened with Suggs, it mattered to me how Frisk answered.

"Detective Suggs was discovered to be in a relationship with a woman that he'd arrested a few months earlier," Frisk said. "There was no proof of wrongdoing but the department gets very suspicious of liaisons of that nature. He's under a heavy review. If he quits, the department will drop the investigation; if not, he might be facing jail time."

It wasn't unusual for a policeman to show up unexpectedly at my door, maybe even surprising me with a request, but Roger Frisk went beyond surprise—his candor was stunning.

Melvin had admitted to me that he'd been seeing a woman named Mary whom he'd arrested for passing counterfeit one-hundred-dollar bills. Before that bust and without exception, Melvin had been an unkempt and messy dresser. But when he told me about Mary he was wearing a white shirt and a pressed suit that had nary a grease stain. His shoes were shiny and his teeth bright.

Love will spruce up the most disheveled bachelor; like an undertaker would do after that bachelor gets shot in the back.

I'd worry about my friend at another time. Right then my attempt to avoid any meaningful conversation with the special assistant had been scuttled by his offers and his honesty.

"There's a Cuban diner over on La Cienega," I said. "We could go over there if you want."

"Perfect," Frisk said. "I love Cuban food. I'll even drive."

3

Arturo's was on the east side of La Cienega, two blocks south of Pico. It was a classic American diner with a facade made from chrome and glass. The parking lot had white-lined slots for six cars and only three of them were occupied. Frisk pulled his dark Mercury Marquis up between a sky blue Pontiac station wagon and a red Chrysler truck.

When he got out of the car he surveyed the street by moving his head from side to side. He was a careful man in a land where most so-called white men took their security for granted.

The restaurant comprised one long counter that sat eight and had a small window for takeout orders. Arturo was somewhere behind the window and Manny, a sparsely whiskered man with black eyes and wearing a bright white T-shirt and pants, worked the counter.

"*Hola*, Señor Rawlins," Manny hailed. The pale-skinned counterman was in his middle years, somewhere between thirty-five and fifty. He looked both suspicious and friendly, an unstable combination but, I felt, acceptable in the service profession.

"Manny," I said. "This is Roger Frisk."

"Welcome," Manny said.

Frisk surprised us both with a barrage of Spanish in reply. He was very comfortable with the language and Manny responded with verve. I recognized odd words but I was no linguist. When I was a child I spoke Creole French, but that language was now mostly lost to me.

There was an older Spanish couple sitting at the two stools farthest from the street, next to Arturo's service window. They were drinking beer and eating homemade potato chips from a blue plastic basket.

I moved to the red vinyl stool overlooking La Cienega. Frisk followed slowly, still chattering away with Manny.

When we were both seated I interrupted, saying, "Two deluxe *mix-tos* and twelve to go. Also you can add two sweet plantains and four orders of beans and rice."

"How is Feather?" the counterman asked.

Whenever I ordered plantains he knew it was for her.

"She might be going to this fancy private school if I play my cards right."

"I'll ask my wife to pray for her," Manny said. "Café con leche?"

"For me," I said.

"Me too," Frisk added.

Manny went through a crevice into the back to submit my order.

"You come here a lot?" the pink cop asked.

"So what can I do for you, Mr. Frisk?"

He smiled, glad to be getting down to business at last.

"You ever hear of a man named Foster Goldsmith?" he said.

"Goldsmith Armaments," I said, "International. I read the papers."

"They got a major research facility out past Arcadia."

"Uh-huh," I said.

Manny brought our coffees. Frisk thanked him in Spanish.

When the server moved off, Frisk said, "Old Stony Goldsmith is a regular contributor to Sam Yorty's campaign fund. He's also involved with many city projects; after-school programs, charity donations, he even plans to build a new wing at L.A. Hospital."

"A regular robber baron."

Frisk didn't like that jab. At least, I thought, he had some kind of value system.

"Goldsmith is a very important citizen in City Hall's eyes," he said.

Then our pressed sandwiches came. I was hungry and took a bite before commenting.

"Goldsmith has a problem?" I asked.

"America has a problem," Frisk said. "With all these hippies, anarchists, communists, and criminals, we have to keep a close watch on our democracy if we want to stay being free."

This was a new topic of conversation between white men and black in America. There was a time, a time I could remember, when Negroes were not considered full citizens. Patriotism was not expected from us; and, in return, the majority of our people were denied the vote.

While times were slowly changing, my memories remained. But I didn't feel like arguing with Frisk. If he actually believed what he was saying there would be no changing his mind. Though I suspected, by the way he was talking, that he was just mouthing these catchphrases. He was a pragmatist saying the words that his superiors liked hearing.

"So Goldsmith has a problem?" I asked again.

"He has a daughter."

"And she has a problem or she is a problem," I surmised.

"She's a student at UC Santa Barbara."

"Beautiful place."

"A hotbed of revolutionaries."

I took another bite of my Cuban sandwich. The pickles were what made it special. And Arturo used real Swiss cheese that gave it that sour tang.

"I thought you needed my help," I said.

"I do. The mayor does."

"Are you working for the mayor or the cops?"

"The police force answers to City Hall."

"Since when?"

"Goldsmith has a problem," Frisk said. "His daughter."

"And what can a man like me do to relieve his distress?"

"It's my job to find her and make sure that she gets home."

"Runaway, missing, or kidnapped?" I wasn't in the mood for niceties.

Frisk didn't answer immediately. He pondered my question, leading me to wonder if he was making up a reply.

"It's uncertain," he said at last.

"I'm listening."

"Rosemary, that's the Goldsmiths' daughter's name, has been missing from her dormitory for at least the last two weeks. No one has seen her."

"Boyfriend?"

"A man called Foster telling him that if he ever wanted to see his daughter again that he'd have to come up with, with . . . a great deal of money."

"How much money?"

"I'd rather not say."

"So it's kidnapping," I said.

"Maybe. You see . . ." Frisk paused, trying to pull together the delicate skein of the tale. "Rosemary has been involved with various revolutionary and anti-American groups. It could be that one of them has actually abducted her, but she could also be in league with the people that called."

"But you don't know."

"The call came from a pay phone at a gas station in West Los Angeles. She'd been missing for days before the demands were made."

"What does her father think?"

"He isn't sure. The last time he spoke to his daughter she was railing at him about his part in delivery systems dealing with napalm and the war; that and other things."

"What other things?"

"Just leftist banter. She's been brainwashed by communists and sees her father as some kind of monster."

"That could be a big problem," I agreed. "You wouldn't want to report a kidnapping and find out that the supposed victim is really an extortionist in disguise."

"He doesn't want his daughter going to jail."

"I understand the problem, Mr. Frisk, but what could I possibly contribute to the investigation? I haven't been to Santa Barbara in a while and I don't know anyone up there."

The special assistant to the chief of police was tapping the index-finger fingernail of his left hand on the green tiled surface of the counter. He was staring hard at me as if, after all of this, he was wondering if I was the right man for the job.

"Because of that call we think that the trail might be down here in L.A.," he said at last. "We have reports that Rosemary has been seen in Los Angeles with a man named Mantle, Robert Mantle."

"Battling Bob Mantle?"

"You know him?"

"I've seen him fight. I don't think he ever won a round but he made it to the final bell in every match I ever saw, bloody as a slaughtered hog but still on his feet. I haven't seen him for a while."

"He got hit too much and they banned him from the ring. We thought if you could get next to Mantle maybe he could point the way."

"What's their relationship?"

"That's not clear."

"Do you know where I could find him?" I asked.

"If I did I wouldn't be talking to you, now would I?"

"I thought maybe you needed a man like me to talk to Mantle because he might trust a brother." If I was being hired as a Judas, I wanted him to say it out loud.

"If I knew where he was I'd ask him myself."

"So you're looking for this Rosemary Goldsmith," I said.

"Yes," Frisk agreed, "but we need you to find Mantle. He's the key to finding the girl."

"That may be," I said, "but I'd like to talk to her parents before I go out looking for him."

"That wouldn't be a good idea," Frisk advised.

"Why not? They're the ones who'll be paying me, right?"

"Rosemary's parents are separated. The call was to him. All communication with either the mother or the father must be done through my offices."

Something about his officious tone made me wary.

"I'd like to see your LAPD ID," I said.

"What?"

"You heard me, man. Show me some ID or we can end this conversation right here."

"You saw my card."

"Anybody could print up a fancy card. I need something with a picture on it. Something I recognize. I don't know you, Mr. Frisk. You could just be playin' me."

Frisk didn't like my demand. He hesitated while I took another bite out of my sandwich, but finally he produced a wallet from his breast pocket and took out a laminated card with his picture, rank, and police affiliation stated clearly.

"Sorry about that," I said, "but you know there's a lot of people out there like to pull the wool over your eyes."

"Will you take the job?"

"I need two thousand dollars for expenses and four thousand down on my fee. You get the client to give me that and I will be on the job first thing in the morning."

"The money will be delivered to you later today," he said.

The fact that money was no object was the best reason I had for passing up the case. Nobody ever put down 50 percent up front— unless they were desperate; and desperation went hand in hand with danger.

"What about those city inspectors?" I asked, pushing my bad luck.

"I'll make a call tomorrow."

"I should say no, but I got too much in the hopper to turn my back. You have the client send me the money and I'll do my due diligence."

Frisk smiled and put out that hand again.

Though reluctantly, this time I shook it.

4

Frisk went out the front door of the restaurant and down the aluminum stairs while I paid Manny for our lunch and the brown paper bag filled with food for my workers.

"That man a friend of yours, Mr. Rawlins?" the short Cuban waiter asked.

"Potential employer."

"When I used to be in the Cuban army I was a sentry for El Jefe."

"Castro?"

"Sometimes the Russian KGB would come to talk about their secrets. They had dead eyes and only came after dark. Your friend looks like he could be one of them."

"He's a cop."

"Oh," the amber-skinned man said. "That's why."

"Thanks, Manny," I said. "See you soon."

On the short drive back to my new home Frisk addressed me as my employer.

"You should check out Benoit's Gym. Mantle does odd jobs there," he said. "They might be connected to this."

"Benoit's down on Crenshaw? The one run by Hardcase Latour?"

"That's it."

"What do you mean, *connected*?"

"Nothing definite," Frisk admitted. "It's just that he spent a lot of time down there before the girl went missing."

"When's the last time anybody saw Mantle?"

"Almost two weeks."

"You got a picture of him and the girl?"

By then we were pulling up in front of my place.

Frisk's pockets were chock-full of information. This time he pulled out a small leatherbound notebook with two photographs between its leaves. One was a reduced mug shot of Bob Mantle. He was holding a number card in front of his chest and sneering at the camera. Bob wasn't a handsome man but even through that frown and broken nose he looked friendly. Dark-skinned like me, with a buzz cut and generous lips, he might have been twenty-eight, twenty-nine at the time of the arrest.

The girl's picture was more pedestrian. Smiling and pretty, she was not yet twenty, sitting at a restaurant table among friends. Through the window behind her was a fleet of docked yachts at some marina where the rich congregated. Her hair was brown and her skin pale and clear. She was attractive in a sexless way. Her hazel eyes had intelligence and depth. I imagined that she questioned everything those eyes lit upon.

There was something odd about the photograph: It was printed, not developed. Maybe, I thought, it had been cut out of a yearbook and pasted to a stiff paper backing.

"An odd couple," I said.

"Find him quickly, Easy, and that'll lead to her. That's the best scenario we can hope for."

The special assistant's men had put a deep dent in the moving truck's cargo. Two of them had doffed their jackets, one even loosened his tie. I brought the bag of sandwiches to the back of the van and called everybody out. They seemed to like the food. Feather took hers, along with an order of the plantains and one serving of beans and rice, to the kitchenette. The table and chairs were already set up there and she was a proper child.

The cops were grateful but quiet. Using plastic dinnerware that Manny provided, they ate quickly and went back to work. Frisk, for his part, went to the car and sat alone thinking official thoughts and planning his future.

After lunch we all, with the exception of Frisk, threw ourselves into the move. Percy Bidwell stopped trying to pressure me and even Jackson did a halfway decent job. By two o'clock everything was out of the van and in the house or the garage out back. Feather had organized the process so that every box and piece of furniture was in the room where it belonged.

The cops left. Frisk didn't talk to me again. I was a soldier and he a passing general. I hoped his elite planning included the money I'd asked for.

I found Jesus in the backyard studying the high redwood fence that separated me from my neighbors.

I walked up behind my son and put a hand on his shoulder.

"A lot bigger than what we're used to," I said.

"Not as big as that house Auntie Jewelle had us in."

"But we didn't own that."

"It's real nice, Dad."

My son. When I found him he was the pet of a child molester who believed he was untouchable. The pedophile was long dead and Jesus had become a man that any nation would have been proud to call citizen.

"Benita still wants to go back to school?" I asked of his common-law wife and mother of his child.

"She says that if she's a registered nurse we could make enough that we could buy our own place."

"What school?"

"SMCC has most of the courses she needs. She just has to bring in enough to help pay for Essie and the rent."

Essie, my de facto granddaughter, was still a baby.

"I think I can give you enough to pay for the first year," I said. "After that . . . we'll see."

Jesus wasn't a big talker. He smiled and nodded. We'd be on the same page ten years after my death.

"Hey, Jackson," I said to one of my oldest friends in the master bedroom on the second floor.

He was sitting on a padded walnut chair, sifting through a box of books.

"You read all'a these, Ease?"

"Most of 'em. Why?"

"No reason," the little black man said. He sat up and crossed his legs.

Jackson was wearing stained canvas painter's pants. His white T-shirt was torn in three places and even though it was a size small, it hung loose from his shoulders. He was the right-hand man of the CEO of the largest French insurance company in the world, but he was still a child of poverty, afraid of his own shadow.

"What's with this guy Percy?" I asked.

That shadow passed over Jackson's face. "Why?"

"I don't know," I said. "He seems to feel like he deserves special attention."

"Jewelle send him," Jackson said, avoiding my gaze. "He graduated from UCLA in business or somethin'. He's working in her office, lookin' for somethin' better."

"Does she expect me to help him?"

"If she did she'd tell you so." Jackson stood up and walked past me out the door.

I followed him into the hall and watched as he jounced down the stairs. I had seen Jackson through many phases. He had been a thief and a coward, a con man and a liar, but I had never known him to be rude through any of that.

I might have questioned him further but LaMarque was coming up the stairs as my old friend descended.

"I'm gonna leave, Mr. Rawlins," the young man said.

Reaching for my wallet, I asked, "How long your father said he'd be gone?"

"Three weeks."

"He still call in?"

"Every two or three days he call Mama and me."

I handed him four five-dollar bills.

"Tell Etta to say hey to him for me."

"Okay, Mr. Rawlins, I will."

By four that afternoon all of my helpers had gone. Jesus drove the truck back to Primo's garage in East L.A. Jackson, Percy, and LaMarque took off in separate cars and Feather was behind a closed door putting her room in order.

Frenchie, the little yellow dog, was in there with her. We had left him in the car while moving. But as soon as we were done Feather brought him in and let him sniff around the new premises. When he got a whiff of me he looked up with a quizzical expression on his canine face. He was remembering, I believed, the days when he hated me. But that was over now and so he yipped a greeting and went on with his nasal investigations.

The upstairs of my new home was made up of a round hall and three bedrooms: two large and one small. Feather had apportioned me the largest of the boudoirs while she claimed the smallest. The middle chamber was to be used as a library and study room.

I told Feather that I didn't mind taking the small room but she said, "The parent should have the biggest room and, anyway, Bonnie might move in to live with us again one day and then it would be a bedroom for two."

Bonnie Shay had been my girlfriend for much of Feather's life. For a while there we had broken up and then I almost died. Now we were trying to find our way back together again. I couldn't seem to get my emotions straight around Bonnie. I didn't love anyone else. I didn't want anyone else. But when we were together I felt like a citizen of a defeated nation with no right to hold my head up.

I went downstairs to the huge living room. A latticed picture window took up most of the front wall and looked out onto Point View. The living room of our Genesee home was one-sixth the size and so there wasn't nearly enough furniture to fill it. I sat on our toy sofa and wondered if there was really money on the way from Roger Frisk.

No more than ten seconds later there came the chime of a three-toned doorbell that I'd never heard before.

5

She was tall for her age, Asian (probably Japanese, I thought), with tawny skin and a mouth that spent more time laughing than eating. She was skinny as only a child can be and her black hair hung down past her shoulders.

"Mr. Rawlins?" the girl said. Her bright green one-piece dress barely made it down to the middle of her bandy thighs.

"Yes?"

"I saw you moving in but my father said to leave you alone until you were through working."

"Um," I said. "So how can I help you?"

"Is Feather home?" She looked worried, like a tourist trying to find a toilet in a country where she didn't speak the language.

"Yeah," I said, moving to the side. "Second floor, it's the first door on your right."

The frown transformed into a grin and she ran up the stairs with an awkward, fetching gait.

I heard knocking and then the girls screaming at the top of their lungs. For all of Feather's maturity, she was just another kid among her school friends.

I could hear their feet clomping around through the ceiling as Feather showed her guest the features of her new room.

Walking back to the couch, I was accompanied by small echoes of my own footsteps in the mostly empty space. Behind me came the scratchy clicking of the little yellow dog's claws. He had come down-stairs to avoid those banging feet and loud squeals.

"Come on and sit with me, dog," I said.

I sat and he leaped up next to me. We perched there side by side while Feather and her friend laughed and screeched overhead.

"This is my friend Peggy Nishio," Feather said half an hour or so later. "We took algebra together in summer school but I didn't know she lived right across the street. They just moved there a month ago. Can I go over to her house for dinner?"

"Is it okay with your mother?" I asked Peggy.

She frowned and nodded.

"Okay," I said, and the girls ran for the front door and out.

Frenchie stood up, alert at the sudden departure. I scratched behind his ears and he settled down again.

I wanted to walk around the house making a mental list of what I had to do and buy for the place. But Roger Frisk's visit kept interrupting. Ever since the accident I'd had a declining interest in being a private detective. But what else could I do? I was a black man with a sixth-grade education. I could read as well as many college graduates and I knew math from working on building projects. I had no degree, however, no certification. On paper I was qualified to wash dishes or sweep floors, not nearly enough to afford Feather's Ivy Prep tuition.

I thought of old Marley in *A Christmas Carol*. He dragged the chains of his mortal life behind him like some slave that had escaped with the manacles still attached to his wrists and ankles. I was free but every step was a challenge. I was my own man; but that man owed his soul to the company store.

When the doorbell chimed this time it was like an old friend.

The man standing there on the front porch was a dandy with some heft to him. He had the mannerisms of a small man, delicate and precise, but he was beefy. While he had the poise of a fop, his flinty eyes and hard jawline spoke of trench warfare replete with mud, blood, and shit.

"Mr. Rawlins?"

"Uh-huh."

"Tout Manning." I was happy that he didn't offer to shake hands. "Roger Frisk sent me."

"Well," I said reluctantly, "come on in, I guess."

I led the big man into the living room and offered him the couch. I took the upholstered maroon chair that was designed to look like a plush seashell throne.

"Just moved in?" he asked. Tout Manning's suit was somewhere between gold and green in color. It had stingy lapels and only two buttons. Despite the color it was a professional-looking ensemble—almost a uniform.

"Today."

"That's something. Sorry to have to bother you in the middle of all that."

"How did you find me?"

"Frisk."

"How did he find me?"

"Sent the Three Stooges around your old neighborhood asking about where you might be."

I had told a woman, Grace Matthews, who lived across the street from my Genesee home, that I was going to move closer to Feather's school.

"That's a whole lotta legwork just to find me."

"You're an important man, Mr. Rawlins, Ezekiel."

We went silent for a few moments. That's when Frenchie began to bark at Tout. It was as vicious a complaint as a three-pound dog could make. Tout turned his head to contemplate my intelligent pet, and then the man bared his own teeth and growled.

Frenchie yelped and ran from the room.

"Nice dog," my guest said.

"As I understand it, Rosemary Goldsmith has been missing for quite a while," I replied.

"That she has."

"So why is it all of a sudden so important that you get me on the search party?"

Instead of answering, Tout Manning reached into his breast pocket and came out with a thick brown envelope. He leaned over to hand the packet to me.

Swaying back again, he said, "Sixty one-hundred-dollar bills. That's what you asked for, right?"

"Are you a cop?"

"I work in Mr. Frisk's office."

"What does that mean exactly?"

"It means that from now on I'm your official contact with Mr. Frisk. There's a piece of paper with my phone numbers in among the hundred-dollar bills. Office, home, and answering service. Call me if you need anything."

"I need something now."

"What's that?" Tout asked. He crossed his right leg over his left.

"Information. Is there a criminal case against Mantle or what?"

"There might be a criminal aspect to the case," Manning admitted. "Whether that shadow falls on Bob or not is unclear. All you have to remember is my phone number. No matter what you come across, legal or illegal, you are to call me first. I don't care if there's blood on the ground, you call me and leave the regular cops out of it."

"What if somebody is dead?"

"I'm the contact. You're working directly for the Chief of Police."

"What if I don't like that situation?"

"What's not to like? You're in the inner circle now, Ezekiel. Nobody can lay a hand on you."

"Do you think Mantle is holding the girl against her will?"

"Who knows? You find Mantle for us and we'll tell you who did what."

I didn't like Tout Manning, my dog didn't like him.

"Yes, Mr. Rawlins?" Tout said. "Is there anything else you need to know?"

"What if I gave you back your money and your phone numbers, Mr. Manning? What if I told you that I don't want to have anything to do with this mess?"

"You just moved, Mr. Rawlins. Here you are in your nice new house and everything. You wouldn't want to have to do that again so soon. But if you don't do what Chief Parker and Mayor Yorty want, that'll be the only choice you have—to move and move far. Because you know working stiffs like you and me have to do what we're told. I mean even your little dog knows that much."

Oddly his threats soothed my nerves. I was used to men in authority trying to intimidate me. It almost always meant that they had something to protect.

"Are there any other crimes or infractions that you want Mantle or Rosemary for?" I asked.

Manning looked surprised for a moment and then he smiled.

"There might be a robbery or some mayhem here and there," he said. "You know the colored brothers are always close to that line. If it's not them it's their cousins and if it's not their cousins it's their mothers' other sons."

"What I need to know, Tout, is if there's going to be some armed zealot aiming his gun at the back of my head while I'm knocking on the wrong door."

That actually got my police liaison to laugh out loud.

"No, no, no, Mr. Rawlins. You're safe. That's why Mr. Frisk came to you. Nobody is going to look twice at a black man asking about his buddy." Tout got to his feet. "If you have any more concerns just call me. If you can't get me directly I check into the answering service every hour or so; if you tell them that it's an emergency they'll call me."

He walked toward the door and I followed.

"See you, Ezekiel. Don't forget—call me and only me if you find anything or need anything."

He walked down to the curb and climbed into a cranberry-colored Volkswagen. As he drove off I thought that I would never have imagined a big, dangerous man like that in a tiny tin Bug.

6

I stood there in the open doorway thinking that I might be in over my head and deciding that I should put in a screen door so that my new house could catch the breeze without inviting in a battalion of flies.

Maybe my life needed a screen door.

The little yellow dog clicked his claws on the tiled floor of the entranceway, pacing and whining about too much change too quickly. I picked him up and he stopped his complaint. Together we went back into the sun-flooded living room. I sat on the sofa and the dog curled into a ball on my lap.

There was a young woman out there named Rosemary Goldsmith, the daughter of a weapons manufacturer. Along with Rosemary was a black ex-boxer named Mantle. . . .

I'd seen Battling Bob Mantle maybe five years before. He was fighting a welterweight contender named Juan Díaz. Mantle had been outclassed from the first minute of the first round but he kept on coming. He threw fists and elbows, and shoulders in the clinches, at Díaz. For ten full rounds Mantle flailed at the Mexican hopeful. Díaz won nine rounds on the judges' cards, and that was still a favor to Mantle. I thought at the time that Battling Bob fought like a man who believed he was a boxer but was not. His resolve was so strong, however, that it took all of Díaz's will and great skill to defeat him.

The little yellow dog was asleep. I placed him gently on the cushion next to me and walked to the long, well-appointed kitchen, where Jackson Blue had connected my phone.

The heavy black phone was set on two phone books on the white and red tiled kitchen counter.

Benoit's Gym was listed in the Yellow Pages.

The phone rang eight times before someone answered.

"Benoit's."

"Yeah," I said tentatively. "Is this Benoit's Gym?"

"Ain't that what I just said?"

"Uh-uh, I mean, yes. I'm calling for, um, let me see, I'm calling for a Bob, Robert Mantle."

"You takin' his boxin' class?" the man's voice asked. He was black, probably from the eastern South—Charleston would have been my bet.

"Yes," I said. "Yes I am."

"He's not here."

"I wanted to, um, to take his class. You know, I want to get in shape and I always liked boxing. My cousin Shawn takes karate but I don't like all that kicking."

"Bobby's beginner class is at ten in the morning Mondays, Wednesdays, and Thursdays. If it's your first day you need to have real boxer's trunks, not no swimmin' suit, and regulation eight-ounce gloves. If you don't have the right trunks and gloves Bobby won't let you take class, he won't even let you watch."

"Okay," I said in a gentle voice that wasn't mine.

"It costs eight dollars a class up front. You could come tomorrow. You don't have to have all that stuff because Bobby's away and Tommy's teachin' his class. Tommy lets you wear sweatpants or swimmin' trunks. He don't care what you look like, only how you fight."

"That's too bad. I heard that Mantle was a good teacher."

"I don't know where you heard that," the voice told me. "Tommy Latour could fight rings around Bobby. That's how they met—when Tommy was kickin' Bobby's ass in a ring in Las Vegas."

"That's Hardcase Tommy Latour?" I asked, maybe a little out of character.

"I gotta go, man. Be here before ten with eight dollars and Hardcase will teach you how to spar."

"Thank you."

The gym worker hung up without telling me good-bye. I wasn't bothered, however.

Outside the big kitchen window grew a spindly, fourteen-foot pomegranate tree. That and the master bedroom's bathroom's huge bathtub were two of three major factors in me buying that house. I loved having real fruit growing in my yard. There was a lemon tree out back.

I was a country boy at my core. If I didn't think the neighbors would go crazy I would have dug up the front lawn and put in a vegetable garden. I might have built a chicken coop in the backyard and replaced my fire-engine red speedster with a donkey or mule.

I knew that I wanted off the Goldsmith case, because of my daydreams. I always had rural thoughts when I wanted to get away from troubles. Black Southerners didn't leave the farm for the lure of the big city; we left because of grinding poverty and the oppression of racism that was so pervasive it was like the heavy atmosphere of a much larger planet.

I had taken one step into the conundrum of the missing rich girl. If it was any other job I could have still backed out. But Tout Manning was right. I couldn't say no to the mayor's minions. They might have been his creatures, they might have been indentured while I was a free man—but they were like hunting hounds, and I was either going to point out the prey or fall victim to their snapping jaws.

I couldn't quit the job but I could pretend that I wasn't on it, at least for one night.

I walked upstairs and wandered around the rooms.

Feather's bed was already made and there was a multicolored throw rug between it and her maple desk. I could see in her neatness my attention to detail.

Years before, on Saturday mornings, she, Jesus, and I cleaned up the little house we shared. We worked all morning and then had French toast with real Vermont maple syrup for brunch.

Feather was looking forward to designing our new space. For her it was like an unfinished work of art: a musical composition or sculpture; a big house to make into a home before she moved off to Harvard or Oxford and grew into a stranger that I would love because of this present-day past together.

The phone interrupted my maudlin thoughts. It rang six times before I made it down to the kitchen. Frenchie joined me there.

"Hello?"

"Easy?"

"Hey, Jewelle, what's happening, girl?"

"Nothing, I mean, just the usual. Jackson said that the police came by today and helped you move?"

I laughed, remembering how Jackson was a master storyteller second only to Mouse.

"They wanted me to work for them and I said I had to finish moving."

"Did Percy Bidwell come along?"

"Yes he did," I said.

"And?"

"Did you tell him that I would introduce him to Jason Middleton?"

"I said that he could ask you but it was up to you what you did."

Middleton was an influential investment banker from an old California family. That family had a black servant named Mattie. Mattie had a daughter named Loretta. Jason had hired me to prove that Loretta wasn't in on a burglary at his home. The police thought it was her. Mattie did not, and Jason, in spite of better judgment, had fallen in love with the handsome daughter.

It all worked out. The police ended up arresting Middleton's younger son's college roommate. Mattie, and her daughter, moved to Boston to work for Middleton's eccentric sister, and I had a favor that I could cash in whenever I wanted.

"What did Percy say?" Jewelle asked.

"He practically told me that you expected me to make the introductions."

"I didn't. You know I wouldn't do that."

"I didn't think so. Do you need me to do anything?"

"No, Easy, no. I'd just like you to talk to Percy. If you think he's worthwhile you can introduce him to Middleton if you want."

I had once seen a report that the FBI had made available to the public. Due to national safety and other constitutional concerns, over 80 percent of the file had been blacked out. That document was loquacious compared to the editing Jewelle was doing on the explanation of her involvement with Percy Bidwell's needs.

"I told the cops that I couldn't work on their project because of the money I needed over those city infractions," I said, partly to get out of prickly talk about Bidwell and Middleton.

"And what did they say?"

"They gave me six thousand dollars and said that the city would give me more time."

"You know, Easy"—Jewelle sounded more like herself on the safer grounds of business—"it was odd about those inspections."

"Odd how?"

"Usually the city sends its inspectors out in force when they want to collect fines and whatnot. You know I manage hundreds of units and you were the only one they targeted."

"That is odd."

"Yes it is."

"Can I do anything else for you, J?" I asked again.

"Will you let Percy call you if I promise he won't be rude again?"

"Sure," I said instead of the *no* I felt.

7

We got off the phone quickly because Jewelle felt bad asking me for favors. Under different circumstances I would have stayed on the line with her, trying to imagine that my life wasn't about to spiral out of control.

Between Frisk and Tout Manning, Battling Bob Mantle and Rosemary Goldsmith, I was about to go way out into the deep end of the pool; far enough to find salt water, jagged stones, and circling sharks that didn't have a moral compass I could comprehend.

I was sitting at the rectangular table set in our new octangular dinette. Three walls of that room had big windows in them. It was a house built for light. The table was too small for the space but it's what we had. I sat there looking at the grain in the cherrywood, trying to find therein a map that led away from the difficulties of my life.

When he heard about my money problems Jackson had offered me a job at Proxy Nine. The French insurance giant had promoted his career; he thought that it could do the same for me. I would have been the American security chief with a high-five-figure salary and hours that fit my sleeping habits. It was better money than I made as a PI. I would have been treated with respect and there was little chance that I would ever be in physical danger.

I should have taken that job but it would have meant that I would no longer be among my people—the transplanted black folk that had moved from the South looking for dignity. Jean-Paul Villard, the president of P9, was a good man, a French freedom fighter in the war against the Nazis. I liked him but I wasn't looking for a boss. . . .

"Daddy?" Feather had come in while I retraced my hapless journey through an unpredictable life that was, once again, on an unerring course.

"Hey, honey, what you have for dinner?"

"Spaghetti and meatballs with green salad and chocolate-chip ice milk for dessert," she said. "It was good."

"What's your friend's name again?"

"Peggy."

"She seems nice."

"What's wrong, Daddy?" Feather sat in the chair opposite me. "Are you mad that I left you instead of staying to help?"

"No," I said. "No. This is your new home. You need friends on the block."

"You wanna watch some TV with me?"

"Sure."

I got the little portable Zenith from a box in the upstairs library and set it on a wooden chair in the echoey living room. I made popcorn sprinkled with sugar and drenched with salty butter. Feather and I ate the snack while watching *Voyage to the Bottom of the Sea* starring Richard Basehart and David Hedison on channel 7. After that she watched *The F.B.I.* with Efrem Zimbalist Jr. while I read the newspaper. When that show was over, Feather was asleep and so I carried her up to bed. She was too old for me to undress her, so I just took off her tennis shoes and threw a blanket over her.

Then I went downstairs to watch the Smothers Brothers on channel 2. I liked their antiwar, liberal sentiments. There was a new America coming; a nation where people like Roger Frisk and Sam Yorty wouldn't be making the rules—at least that seemed like a possibility at the time.

I was in my old car flying off the side of a cliff over the broad Pacific. It was night but the lunar light was almost as strong as a sun. My car was hurtling down and yet the fall was taking forever. The reflection of the moonlight traveled like lightning across the rippling surface of the ocean, which was coming toward me like some kind of superior life-form that fed off the souls of men.

I was terrified of death and bored with the fall.

I considered lighting a cigarette but somehow this seemed like sacrilege.

The water was less than a foot away. Between the looming impact, the voracious light, and drowning, my death would be both exquisite and excruciating, absolutely final and oddly dull. I looked out through the shattered windshield determined to experience every moment of my demise. I could see, in minute lunar-lit detail, the corrugated surface of the ocean. . . .

In the dream I was completely calm. But when I opened my eyes, terror crept over my heart.

Feather was saying, "Daddy, I'm making breakfast. You have to get up."

I sat up from the sofa gasping, expecting my mouth to be filled with brine.

"Are you okay?" my daughter asked.

It's funny, the things you see when you feel Death's hand clutching at your chest.

I saw the outline of the faux fireplace in the wall and wondered if there was a real hearth hidden behind the plaster facade. Feather, I noticed, was wearing her old jeans with a baby blue T-shirt and red Keds. This was one of her uniforms for whenever she had a physical job to do.

The sun was at midmorning somewhere outside the big window.

"I need a cigarette," I said.

"I thought you were quitting."

"I did. Then I started again."

I took three drags off of a king-size Pall Mall in the backyard.

By the time I got to the table, Feather was serving French toast, maple smoked bacon, and buttered grits that were just the right consistency. There was coffee and a dish of canned Del Monte fruit cocktail flanking the breakfast plate.

"You got a job I don't know about?" I asked after tasting the strong French roast.

"Peggy's mom and dad run a sewing shop with people from their family downtown. I told her that you showed me how to sew and I did some for her mom. They said I could come down with them and work for two-fifty an hour. Can I?"

I was already dressed, so we finished breakfast and walked across the street to a moderate-sized ranch-style house.

A friendly, somewhat Americanized Japanese woman answered the doorbell. She was wearing a calico dress and smiling. Her skinny daughter was standing against the far wall of the sitting room we entered through. When Feather ran to her they clasped hands and giggled.

"Mrs. Nishio?" I said, extending a hand.

She smiled, shook, and almost bowed a little.

"Aiko," she said.

"Easy," I said.

"I'm Jun," a man grunted.

I looked from the pear-shaped, olive-colored face of the Japanese hausfrau to a doorway that framed a broad and short man wearing a dark work suit that was not designed in the West. The coal gray jacket was long-sleeved and might have been a shirt. He wore a light blue shirt underneath. The loose pants were the same color as the jacket. Only his tennis shoes were from this continent.

"Pleased to meet you," I said, reaching out. After our perfunctory handshake I said, "Feather says that you offered to let her go to work with you today."

"She's a good seamstress," the little powerhouse of a man rumbled. He brought to mind a low mountain that was also a sleeping volcano. I liked him.

"I wanted to make sure that she wouldn't be a bother."

"She helped with the dishes last night," Aiko said.

There was a volume of homespun philosophy under that utterance. Feather understood the difference between frivolity and work. She was welcome because she knew what to do when.

"When will she be home?" I asked.

"Twelve forty-five," Jun Nishio said. "She's twelve so we will only let her work four hours."

"Sounds fine," I said.

Aiko smiled and Jun grunted favorably.

"Have a nice day, honey," I said to my daughter.

"Love you, Dad."

8

The bright red 1965 two-door Plymouth Barracuda looked like a crimson canine tongue with a lightning bolt tattooed along its side. The unlikely car lolled in the driveway. I stared at it a moment, thinking for the hundredth time that I should trade it in for a more appropriate conveyance that fit my profession. But I had a soft spot for the modern-day gangster car. My friend Primo gave it to me after the accident. I drove that electrified tongue from the shadows of death back into life.

I was getting sentimental with age.

Benoit's Gym was across the street from the May Company department store on Crenshaw. It was half a block long and deep, a bungalow that would fly apart if a small tornado ever passed through.

There were no windows but the front door was open.

It was hot inside even at nine in the morning.

There were three rings in the center of the single room that the gym encompassed. Leather-helmeted men were battling in each one. The six heavy bags were all occupied, as were the dozen or so speed bags that took up the back wall. There were jump-ropers, shadowboxers, sit-up partners, medicine ball circles, and enough sweat to slake the salty thirst of ten thousand flies.

Some men were yelling instructions while others grunted either in pain or from the exertion of inflicting damage, and everywhere was the concussive sound of blows being delivered and received.

This was where aimless young men came to hone their rage to a fine point of violence in an attempt to shed the skin of poverty, hatred, and fear. Poor men of every race had taken this journey. Most of them fell along the wayside, becoming the stepping-stones of the few that conquered.

In a corner, behind a battered ash desk, sat a man poring over a ledger. I assumed this was the man who took in money and pointed the way and so, inhaling the strong scent of human toil, I walked up to the blunt-faced concierge.

"This where I check in?"

His skin was a light molasses-brown, and his eyes had some green to them. It took me a moment to register that he was wearing coppery wire-framed reading glasses. His lumpy, battered face denied everything but the pain it had survived. Sixty or more, that face had seen a hundred thousand punches coming and avoided maybe two.

"What you doin' in here, main?" he said. "You ain't no trainer and you too old to get in the ring."

"Charlie Tinford," I admitted. "I hear Bob Mantle got an exercise class on Mondays."

"Buster," the man said.

Buster stared at me, wondering about words I had not uttered. Boxers get a sense of people from their bodies and expressions. He was sizing me up.

"Why?" he asked.

"Why what?" I replied even though I knew what he was getting at.

"Why you wanna take Bobby's class?"

"Tryin' to get back in shape," I said. "My girlfriend, Gina, been lookin' at younger men lately. She's only twenty-seven and still thinks a man is mostly just physique."

I shouldn't have used that last word, it made Buster wince.

"Physique?"

"Muscles."

He didn't believe what I was saying but the gym wouldn't pay its bills by turning money down.

"Eight dollars," Buster said.

I had the wad of ones folded in my pocket. I handed it over and watched him count the bills—twice.

"Bobby's gone for a few weeks but Tommy Latour is teachin' his class," Buster said after the money was safely in a gray metal box in his bottom drawer.

"Is this Latour any good?" I said as if I might have to ask for my dollar bills back.

"You never heard of Hardcase Latour?"

"Should I?"

"He fought Carmine Basilio in an exhibition fight. He didn't win but he didn't get knocked down neither."

Charlie Tinford was placated by this and nodded to say so.

"That's Tommy over there with the big dude on the heavy bag," Buster told me. "You could change anywhere and then ask him where you go."

"Don't you have a dressing room?" Tinford asked.

"The whole place is a dressin' room. Your locker is that gym bag in your hand."

I was ready, in my gray sweats and navy blue T-shirt, to take my class and covertly interrogate the general populace concerning the whereabouts of Battling Bob Mantle.

"Mr. Latour?" I said to a gold-colored man who was holding the heavy bag for a dark-skinned heavyweight banger.

"Yeah?" Latour said, still concentrating on holding the bag steady.

"Charlie Tinford. I'm gonna take your ten o'clock class."

That's where things began to go wrong, right there at Benoit's Gym, before any bloodshed, bullets, or treachery. There was something about my tone; I heard it myself. In an instant I knew that I hadn't taken this job seriously enough.

Tommy Latour turned his handsome face to regard me upon hearing the lie crouching down in the tall grass of my words.

"Hold up, Ebenezer," he said to the heavyweight. "Go get Rod to spot you."

"Yes sir, Mr. Latour," the young hopeful replied.

It was questionable whether Tommy even heard his young apprentice. He was staring at me with deep concentration.

"Tinford?" he asked.

I should have walked out of there. My best course would have been to go home and pack my belongings, take Feather and move to another state. I knew that but I was stubborn. I was like a man in free fall who still thought he might grab hold of something and save himself.

"Yes, sir," I said with a smile. "Charlie Tinford reporting for duty."

"You was in the army, Charles?"

"European theater."

"And now you wanna box?" He nodded and smiled like a coyote having laid eyes on an unwitting hare.

"Noooooo," I assured him. "I just wanna get in shape is all."

"You look pretty fit. How much you weigh? One eighty?"

"Six pounds more than that."

"Why don't we get in the ring?" he offered. "Class don't start for an hour and I could see where you fit in."

"You fought with Carmine Basilio," I argued.

"You got twenty-five pounds on me," he replied, "and I'll go easy on you."

"How much does Bob Mantle weigh?" I asked; I shouldn't have but I did.

Latour grinned at my faux pas, making me wonder about the ESP of high-level sportsmen.

"You know, I don't think you belong here, Charlie," Tommy said. "If I was you I'd leave before somebody kicked my ass."

I looked around then. Six or seven hard-looking boxers had stopped their exertions to stare at me. Maybe the name *Rod* was a code word between Hardcase and the young giant Ebenezer. It didn't matter. It was time for me to go.

I picked up the gym bag wondering if I might get hold of my revolver before someone could hit me. I decided against confrontation and strode toward the open door, willing my feet not to run.

I climbed into my Barracuda, my emotional gauge set somewhere between elation and panic. My breathing was heavy and uneven.

For maybe five minutes I sat there.

I thought of Tout Manning assuring me that I was safe because I would be a black man among black men. The fact that I took Tout's words as truth made me laugh; a white man telling a black one that he was safe because of his skin. For a minute or so I luxuriated in the solace that I'd avoided a beating. Then my windshield shattered. The explosion and shower of glass were accompanied by three almost festive pops of gunfire.

9

"Uhuru Nolicé!" someone shouted as I was being showered by a hail-storm of sandlike shattered glass.

Uhuru Nolicé. That's what the man yelled before the tires on the street squealed and a gold Ford Fairlane fishtailed away. *Uhuru Nolicé.* I know the words now but right then they were an unintelligible cry of anger and retribution.

Immediately I patted my chest, shoulders, and arms looking for the bullet wounds that I wouldn't have felt for a minute or two.

No blood.

No blood but there was a license plate: California yellow with black characters. I didn't get all six numbers but the first four were AXI 2.

Not bad under fire.

I got out of the car to inspect the damage. My legs were a little wobbly.

The windshield had been made from safety glass. Primo put it on all his cars because his beautiful young cousin, Rafaelita Marquez, had been in a minor accident but she was scarred for life because of shards of broken glass.

Across the street Tommy Latour, Buster, and half a dozen other boxers were standing on the curb, watching me.

A siren wailed in the distance.

I knew I wouldn't get far with a busted-out windshield, so I leaned back against the hood intending to wait for the predatory howl to reach me.

"Mistah?" An elderly woman was approaching me. She had a white handkerchief in her left hand.

"What can I do for you, ma'am?" My tone was mild, seemingly unconcerned.

"You bleedin'."

"No." I really didn't believe it.

"From your face."

She touched her left-side cheekbone with the handkerchief hand. I did the same with my fingers.

There was blood. Not too much but more than a razor cut you get shaving. I took the handkerchief and pressed it to my face. Only two months before, a gangster named Keith Handel had shot me in the same place. That too was a grazing wound. I wondered if this gash was due to a bullet or a sliver of flying glass.

"Thank you, ma'am," I said.

She nodded but at the same time glanced up the street. The siren was getting closer. My benefactor started moving away.

"Your handkerchief," I said.

"You keep it, honey," she told me. Then she turned and walked as the police pulled up to the curb behind my car.

Other sirens could be heard in the distance. I stood up straight, pressing the cloth to my cheek with one hand and holding the other where it could be seen.

The cops were both men as was the custom back in those days; white men—that was standard practice too. One was older and graying while the other was black-haired, young, and athletic. Both men had their pistols drawn.

The older cop's eyes were as gray as his hair. I wondered idly if his eyes might have been darker like his partner's when he was young and hale.

"What happened here?" the older cop asked me.

"What happened? Somebody shot out my damn windshield!" I wasn't really angry but a cool head in a situation like that only raised suspicion.

"Why?"

"I have no fucking idea."

"Watch your language, son."

Son. Forty-seven years of age, thirty-nine of them on my own, and the policeman I paid my taxes for called me *son.*

"You mean 'sir'?" I said.

"What?" he wanted to know.

"Sergeant," the younger cop cried. He had gone into the gym bag next to my seat and found the .22-caliber pistol within.

"Put your hands on your head," the sergeant commanded.

"I'm bleedin'," I said.

"I said put your goddamned hands on your head!"

"Watch your language, son," I reminded.

He grabbed the wrist of my bandage-bearing hand and twisted it down behind my back. The other cop ran to us with his handcuffs out. He pulled the other hand behind my back and clapped on the cuffs.

Other police cars were coming. That was better for me. If I didn't resist and there were lots of cops around, there was actually less chance of a severe beating.

I shouldn't have mouthed off to the officer, I knew that much. But I was making all kinds of mistakes out there on the street, and on the job too. It was like I didn't want to be me anymore.

A crowd was gathering as two more cruisers converged on my car. Looking among the faces in the throng, I saw the woman that had told me I was bleeding. I was still bleeding. I could see it in her eyes. And then it dawned on me. . . . I had been thinking that her coloring was a delicate rose-gold blend; that was the name of my quarry—Rosemary Goldsmith, Rose Gold. This free-floating association told me that I was in a minor state of shock.

"Sit down!" the older cop ordered. He pushed me against the department store wall and I squatted to keep from getting knocked over.

"What you doin' to that man?" a male voice shouted.

There was rumbling from the crowd but by then there were four more cops on the scene.

"Get his ID," the gray-haired cop told his young counterpart.

"Stand up," the young man said as his partner talked to another cop. He was holding the pistol his partner had found in my bag.

The young cop patted my hips but found nothing because I was still wearing sweatpants.

"Where's your wallet?"

"In the bag you took my gun from."

"Sit down."

After the cops got me settled they had a powwow. One called in on his radio while the others discussed, with implied sagacity, the crime scene of my car. This conversation went on so long that Hardcase Latour and his boxing cronies got bored and went back into the gym, leaving only the bespectacled Buster to report on the progress of the arrest.

"You're in deep shit," the older officer said.

"Language," I reminded him.

"Stand up," he ordered.

I complied.

"You're going to prison over this gun," he said with a grin.

I just stared at him.

One of the cruisers had gone off, possibly looking for the shooter. The extra two cops left were searching my lolling tongue of a car.

"Who tried to kill you?" the older cop asked.

"I don't know."

"Was he on foot?"

"It was probably two of 'em," I said. "One driving and the other to shoot."

"What kind of car?"

"I didn't see."

"Where'd you get this gun?"

"Pete's Gun and Ammo on Sixth downtown. Cost eighty-nine fifty."

"Don't get smart with me, son."

"You looked in my wallet, man. You've seen my driver's license, my investigator's license, and my carry permit. The gun hasn't been fired and there's no other weapon in my car. What else do you need?"

"The driver's license and the gun permit have two different addresses on them," he said like an ex-convict at a South Park picnic bench claiming checkmate in a pickup chess match.

"Roger Frisk," I said. I should have waited until they brought me to the station but I wanted to rub my connections in the gray cop's face.

"What?"

"Call Roger Frisk in Chief Parker's office. Call him and he'll tell you where I live at."

"Fuck you."

I just smiled. If we were in a back alley I would have lost a tooth or two but on a busy street on a Monday morning in 1967 he showed a little restraint.

"What about Frisk?" he asked.

"Nuthin' else in the car," one of the other cops called.

"Ask Frisk about me and he'll set you straight, young man," I added.

"Sit down!" He needed to exert some control.

I squatted again and waited. The four cops that remained talked and took turns glancing in my direction.

My rose-gold savior had moved on with much of the crowd. Buster had abandoned his post. Finally one of the cops got on the radio.

Forty-five minutes later I was a free man. They even returned my gun.

10

Tout Manning had told me to contact only him, but I hadn't committed his number to memory and the slip of paper with his digits was in my wallet. Nothing I could do about that.

Eighteen blocks away, still on Crenshaw, there was a used-car lot called Foley's. It consisted of a tiny bungalow constructed from aluminum and glass surrounded by a parking lot the dimensions of a city block that was crowded with junkers from the last fifteen years or so.

"What happened to your face?" the forty-something bottle-blond saleswoman asked when I approached her.

"I was drivin' down the street not two miles from here just past the May Company and a Bekins movin' truck changed lanes in front'a me. The next thing I know my damn windshield shatters." I was seething but not because of what I was saying. "I don't know. Must'a kicked up a big rock from its back tire or somethin'."

"That's terrible," she said, but I picked up another message.

"I know it is but I don't have time to waste on that. I got a job interview in San Bernardino at two. I gotta get a new one."

"Job?" she asked, frowning at the wound.

"A new car," I said, "so I can get the hell out there and get the new job."

The woman, I didn't catch her name, was once beautiful, very much so. She was still quite handsome. Her cheekbones were high and her eyes were cornflower blue. She might have, at one time, been a model or an aspiring actress. I imagined that men had, when she was in her twenties, sought her out, offering things that turned her head enough to break some women's necks. This parking lot was the last place she wanted to be. In her eyes the cut on my cheek was more interesting than all the used cars in the world.

"Do you need a first-aid kit?" she asked.

It sounded like the first line of the second paragraph in a cheap romance novel.

My nostrils flared and once again I wondered at my state of mind.

Southern California was, and still is, like a drug. It is both mind-altering and addictive. You could walk outside twenty days out of twenty-one into balmy air where no one noticed you or cared what you did. In a place like that a middle-aged black man and white woman—he from the Jim Crow South and she who was once sought after by millionaires—could shack up and get naked, shedding their histories, even their ages. They could be young again, skin on skin in each other's arms, and no one would give them a second thought.

Her lips parted. I glanced at the bungalow, wondering if the ceiling-to-floor windows had blinds.

"No thanks," I said, answering her offer of first aid. "I got to get out there."

Her disappointment was palpable but she knew about making money, that's why she worked on this car lot.

"This Dodge here," she said, gesturing lazily, "is the best we have on the lot for cheap."

It was a 1961 Super D-500, dark maroon in color. There were no dents but the paint had dulled in spots. It was a perfect car for a man in my profession. I figured that even if I lost the tempo of being a detective I should at least drive the right car.

"Even trade?" I said to the woman who might have been the love of my life for a week or so.

Her grimace turned into a grin.

"Why the hell not?" she said.

When I got to Motor and Pico I pulled to the curb and took in a deep breath. At some point, I wasn't sure exactly when, I had lost the thread of my chosen profession. I was off-kilter. Hardcase Latour heard it in my words, saw it in my gestures. It had marked me as the target for an unknown assassin on a city street.

I rubbed the middle finger of my right hand across the scab that had formed on my cheek. For some reason I sniffed the tip of that finger. There was no odor but I was reminded of the strong scent of garlic.

My mother kept a garlic patch behind our shanty shack in New Iberia, Louisiana, when I was a child. Sometimes I'd go out there in the afternoon while my mother was cooking. I'd pull out a bulb, break off a section, and bite into it. The garlic was so strong that it would burn my mouth. Tears came from my closed eyes but I didn't cry out. My father said that garlic was too strong to eat raw. He couldn't do it but I could.

I'd bring the rest of the clove to my mother because she was always using garlic in whatever meal she was cooking.

"I got this for ya, Mama," I'd say, gleefully aware that I had bested my old man and no one even knew it.

That memory was all I needed. I took another deep breath and I was back in alignment. Like the junker I was driving, I was both new and seasoned.

I came to a cube-shaped apartment building, slathered in violet-tinted plaster, on Sutter Street toward the southern border of Culver City.

Three stories high, the building housed five apartments, one unit covering the first floor and four smaller living spaces making up floors two and three.

Melvin Suggs lived in the bottom unit. Next to his front door was a staircase that led to the other apartments.

Melvin's door had an official eviction notice nailed to it.

I knocked.

It was a lovely August morning. The jays and robins, sparrows, and a few pigeons flitted and waddled, sang and searched for food.

I knocked again.

A large cockroach was staggering around the white concrete path that led to Melvin's door. A young sparrow swooped down and grabbed one of the insect's hind legs. The tug-of-war between them was a drama of the highest order. This was life and death in its rawest, most naked form.

After half a minute of struggle the sparrow let go of the roach's foot, hopped over the bug, and pecked at its head. The roach scuttled halfway into the overgrown lawn, where its nemesis clamped its beak on his leg again. They seemed to be of equal strength, but the sparrow had youth on its side where the huge cockroach gave the impression of old age.

The fight made me nervous. I wanted to protect the roach.

The roach made it a few more millimeters into the brush. The sparrow was flapping its wings furiously.

I might have moved to scare the bird off but I heard the door coming open behind me.

"Rawlins?" a familiar gruff voice said.

I didn't want to turn away from the drama but I had my own struggles to be concerned with.

Melvin was maybe five-nine, four inches shorter than I, but we weighed the same. He wasn't so much fat as bulky, with a squashed face, lovely doe-brown eyes, and powerful hands. He was wearing blue-striped boxer shorts and a gray T-shirt with a dozen tiny tears across the front. His basic brown hair had a few more strands of gray than at our last encounter. The unruly mop was getting longer and he hadn't brushed it yet that day. The only concession he had made to civility was to step into a pair of dilapidated brown slippers.

"Mornin', Melvin."

"How'd you know where I lived?" he asked.

"Guy named Gilly used to make bottled water deliveries in this neighborhood. He's a friend of a friend who knew I knew you. You're famous among the brothers, Mr. Suggs. The only white cop we know of that would never call us a nigger."

He glowered at me. "Why are you here?"

"I heard you were in some kind of trouble."

"What the hell does that have to do with you?"

"My source told me that you were facing jail time if you didn't resign."

"Who said that?" Suggs asked the question as if the notion was ridiculous.

"Roger Frisk."

Suggs's shoulders dropped half an inch and his mouth went slack.

"I don't believe it."

"I never lie to you, Melvin. You're my favorite cop."

"So? What do you want?"

"I was thinkin' maybe we could help each other out."

"How can you help me?"

"My father told me when I was a boy," I said, " 'Ezekiel, when you're in trouble the first thing you look for is somebody that wants to help you. Because that want alone is half the way home.' "

Suggs was built like an oaf but that rough exterior was blessed with a razor-sharp mind. He knew that I represented at least a chance at hope.

He grunted and snorted like that old cockroach might have done while rooting through the garbage. There was a predator yanking at his leg and he needed a miracle no matter where it came from.

"Come on in, Easy," he said. "You know the doctors are saying that too much sunlight might give you cancer."

11

Suggs's living room was in shambles. It consisted of a blue sofa, a dark red stuffed chair, and a four-foot-square coffee table that was light brown and frosted, like a maple-glazed cake doughnut. There were half a dozen white boxes from Chinese takeout on that table. On the other side of the room, across from the blue sofa, was a portable TV on a folding pine chair just like the temporary setup my daughter and I had the night before. There were socks and shoes, T-shirts and underwear, newspapers, books, and even a .45 revolver strewn upon the tan carpet.

A thin layer of dust covered everything and there was a sour tang on the air.

"Have a seat, Easy," Suggs said.

Walking to the red chair, I heard the carpet crunch under my feet.

"You want me to make you some instant?" the gruff cop offered.

"No thanks, Melvin, I already had my jolt this morning."

I sat down and put my hands on my knees.

He stared at me for a few seconds. I imagined that I was his first guest in many days. He was trying to recall how to be a host in his own home.

"Why don't you sit, Melvin?" I said.

He regarded the sofa for a moment before sitting down at the end farthest from my chair.

"Dodgers lost last night," he said. "Back east somewhere. I said when Koufax quit that they were in deep shit."

I knew men that had gone senile and forgotten their children's names but they could still reel off sports scores from a dozen years before.

"Why's the LAPD on your ass, Melvin?"

He jerked his head as if he'd been slapped.

"What'd they say?" he countered.

"That you hooked up with a woman you arrested."

He squinted at the words as if they were bright, cancer-inducing sunbeams.

Then he nodded and said, "Mary Donovan. Seven months ago. I arrested her for passing bad hundred-dollar bills at a fancy downtown clothes shop. It wasn't even my beat. I was covering for a guy had appendicitis. Just followed the numbers to her door in West Hollywood. Just followed the numbers."

"And you had a thing?" I asked.

On the wall behind Melvin I saw a line of tiny black ants that had discovered the trove created by his despair. He had been looking down upon the dirty carpet, but when I asked about his connection he raised his head, fixing me with a confused stare.

"I'm in love with her, Easy." These words tore from his throat. "I'm in love with her," he said again, "and she's gone."

He didn't care about the ants, the eviction notice, the police investigation, or even the possibility of going to jail. He probably hadn't bathed in a week, hadn't cut his hair in a month. Melvin Suggs, as cynical a man as I had ever met, was, maybe for the first time in his life, heartbroken.

At that moment I felt, keenly, that he and I were of the same race despite any color schemes.

"What happened?" I asked.

"I don't know." He shook his head. "One day we were drinking Champale on a blanket at Redondo Beach and the next she was gone."

Moving Day.

"She was gone and a week later I got suspended," Melvin was saying. "I hadn't been to work for days. They said that I was on forced leave without pay and subject to review for conduct unbecoming an officer. I wasn't even positive what they were looking for until you just told me."

"You knew that you let Mary off."

"I would have," he said. "I would have, sure, but I didn't need to. I couldn't prove intent. She'd taken a thousand dollars in hundred-dollar bills out of a downtown Bank of America three days before I busted her. Even a court-appointed attorney could have claimed that she got the boodle from the bank without knowing what it was."

"You think her disappearance had anything to do with your troubles?" I asked. I had to.

"No," he said, shaking his head like an old Roman general after his last defeat. "No. We were good together, Easy. I know her."

He slumped back on the sofa and stared out over the detritus of his coffee table.

The problem was him and possible charges by the police department. But all Melvin cared about was the woman that had probably betrayed him.

"I'm on a case, Mel."

"Yeah?" he said, not looking at me.

"Missing girl."

He grunted.

"You help me with that and I will find your Mary Donovan."

That got his attention. He looked up warily.

"How would you do that?"

"I'm good at what I do, Detective," I said. "They don't see me comin', don't know when I'm there, and couldn't tell you when I left. People so worried about my threat that they don't see the danger."

Suggs was a smart man who liked smart men. He was a fool for love but if you have to be a fool that's the best way to go.

"You can find her?" he asked, a child in his voice.

"Frisk said that if you quit the force, jail time would be off the table," I said.

"Fuck that. I didn't do anything wrong," he said. "Can you find her?"

"I can do my level best."

"What do you need from me?"

"Some police work and some personal things."

"What's the police work?" the cop asked.

"Roger Frisk came to my door yesterday when I was moving into a new place. He told me that he was looking for a girl named Rosemary Goldsmith, said that she had been in the company of a broken-down boxer named Bob Mantle. I tried to turn him down but he insisted. He finally persuaded me and sent a guy named Tout Manning to give me what I needed to move forward."

I went on to tell him about Benoit's Gym and the attack. I didn't waste time complaining about the police interrogation. We both knew that the game was hardball in the street.

When I was finished Melvin said, "Frisk is who he says he is. He's high up on the chart and there's nobody above him except the chief. I never heard of this Manning guy. But Bob Mantle . . . you hit a note with him."

"What kinda note?"

"The kind they tie to a dead man's toe."

I waited while Suggs put the story together in his head.

"Mantle has an alias," he said after a minute or so, "Uhuru Nolicé."

The senseless shout that accompanied the shots took form in my mind.

"He's suspected in the shooting death of a high-school vice principal in Watts," Melvin reported. "A guy named Emerson, I think. Then there's an armored car heist in Burbank, and finally a shootout that left three cops dead in Watts."

I knew about all three crimes. They were front-page news.

"They weren't connected in the papers," I said.

"No. The only connection was a telephone call and a letter, both to Bill Tarkingham at the *Herald Examiner*. The call claimed that the vice principal deserved death because he was a traitor to his people. About a week later a letter made of letters cut out from magazines was delivered to Tarkingham. It claimed responsibility for being the mastermind of the shootout. On the phone the caller said he was Uhuru Nolicé. The letter had that name glued to the bottom."

"What's that have to do with Bob Mantle?"

"When he was a student at Metro College he became politically active and started going by the name Uhuru Nolicé. He would dress up in African robes and give fiery speeches in the student union. Nobody paid any attention officially until the telephone call but by then he had gone underground."

The ants were still marching down the wall behind Melvin. Their relentlessness felt somehow daunting.

"Why didn't Tarkingham report on all this?" I asked.

"He told his editor," Suggs said, "but because there was no actual confession it wasn't considered newsworthy. After the letter his boss had a meeting with Chief Parker. They decided to hold back until the police could get a handle on the case. They didn't want to erode public confidence in the LAPD, and there was some concern that Mantle would be hailed as a hero in some parts of the colored community."

"He killed those three cops?"

"That's what the brass thinks."

"Why? I mean, it was a crank letter made from cutouts. Were there fingerprints?"

"I don't think so," Melvin said. He sat up straighter when talking about the details of his profession. "But there were details about the killings that were never in the news . . . and nobody outside of Tarkingham and Parker's office knew the name Nolicé."

"How do you know all this, Melvin? Aren't you on probation?"

"I got my contacts."

"And so what am I to Frisk and Manning? Like a sacrificial lamb or somethin'?"

"You are the man to go to if they want their finger on the jugular of the colored community."

I closed my eyes and brought my hands to the top of my forehead. I wished, irrationally, that I had not come to Melvin; that I had not heard about the killings and Uhuru Nolicé. But I knew that ignorance couldn't save me. Maybe nothing could.

"You got a cigarette, Melvin?"

"In the kitchen. I'll go get it."

He went through an arched doorway that had no door. I reached into my gym bag, into a secret sleeve under a Velcro strip that the police had missed, and came out with an envelope I had thought I might need before the day was up.

"Old Golds," Melvin said when he came back. He had pulled on a pair of jeans; I took this as a good sign on a bad day.

I handed him the envelope.

"What's this?"

"A thousand dollars," I said. "Consider that a down payment on us working together on the case."

"I thought you were going to find Mary for me."

"I am. But four murders, an armored car job, and a kidnapping trump a simple missing person. You pay the rent, hire a cleaning lady, and get a haircut and I'll be calling in about Uhuru-Bob."

Melvin lit my cigarette.

I inhaled the fumes, knowing for a fact that I would never die due to complications arising from tobacco smoke.

"You got a picture of your girlfriend?" I asked.

He pulled a wallet out of his pocket and took from it a Kodak snapshot of a pretty young woman with long brown hair and a smile that would have worked on any child or mark.

12

The drive from West Los Angeles down to South Central was like following a social science chart starting from working-class Culver City, where people thought they were middle class, down to the crime-riddled black community, where the residents were under no such illusions.

Maybe, I thought as I pulled up to the curb on South Central Avenue between 76th Street and 77th Place, it would be better falsely believing that you were living the good life rather than knowing you probably never would.

My office was on the east side of the street, on the third floor of a block-long building. The workspace was smaller than my new master bedroom but it was large enough for the extra-wide desk that sat with its back to a window looking over Central, and a blue sofa that was just the right size for a three-hour nap.

The first thing I did was change out of my gym outfit into regular clothes. Then I went to the window and looked down on the street. Midday pedestrian traffic had been on the rise since the riots. Employment was definitely down and hope, especially for black men, was pretty low too.

If I wanted a better class of client (that is to say, anyone with disposable cash) I should have moved downtown or west of there. But as I got older, experience with my people had become not only exhilarating but nostalgic. Every new black face I met was a hopeful long shot and at the same time I was reminded of experiences so broad that they seemed to cover multiple lifetimes. No amount of silver could buy the passions in an aging man's heart.

———

After my mawkish musings about the street, I sat down and pulled out the phone book. After that I dialed a number.

"Metro College," a man's friendly voice said.

"Records department please."

"We don't have a records department, sir."

"I need to talk to someone about a student you have who is applying to me for a job."

"The administration office is what you want, sir," the friendly, officious switchboard operator informed me.

The next thing I heard was another ringing phone.

"Student services," a mature woman said.

"Is this the administration office?" I asked. I didn't need to but I wanted to respond to the operator's obliquely condescending attitude.

"Yes, sir, it is," the woman said and I felt a little stupid.

"And who am I speaking to?"

"Miss Hollings."

"Well, Miss Hollings, my name is Jason Silver. I run a little mom-and-pop assembly shop on Robertson. Actually we're in an alley off Robertson, behind a hotdog stand. We put together toys and party favors that are prefabricated in Japan. That way, you see, the Japanese can say *Made in the U.S.A.* and still have some control."

"And?" the woman asked. "How can I help you?"

Her mild confusion was part of my design, like a transient element of a modern art installation.

"You have a student there named Robert Mantle. He's applying for a part-time position and he wrote on the application that he was in attendance at your college."

"I'm familiar with that name. I'm pretty sure he's one of ours."

"That's Robert Dallas Mantle who is studying political science and who lives on Slauson?"

"Let me see," she said. I heard the opening of a metal drawer and then the rustling of paper. "Oh, yes. I know Bob. He hasn't given a middle name and we don't have a course in poli-sci. here at Metro. Bob is a bookkeeping major and he lives on . . . let me check . . . yes, he lives on Hoover with his mother. Someone in our department met with him four weeks ago. He wants to transfer to a four-year school where he can major in dramatic arts but he's learning a trade first. What position are you hiring him for?"

"He applied for the production-line job but maybe I should put him on the financial side."

"He's a very good student," the woman confided, "and a very neat dresser, wears a suit and tie to class every day. That's why I thought I knew who you were talking about."

"He does?"

"Yes. Why?"

"When he came in here he was wearing some kind of Afro-dashiki thing."

"Oh." She hesitated. "I seem to remember that Bob *is* very particular about the clothes he wears."

"Define *particular*."

"Nothing bad, Mr. Silver. He just dresses for whatever it is he's about to do. It's an aesthetic."

"So if I change his job to bookkeeping he'll put on a suit and tie?"

"Probably. Is there anything else? I have to get back to my work."

The most important piece of information I got from Miss Hollings was that the police had not notified Metro College that their student was suspected of armed robbery, kidnapping, and murder. That was not standard procedure for the LAPD. Their penchant was to storm in with heavy boots and shotguns, knocking down doors and making threats.

What was it about Bob Mantle that had made them so circumspect?

I was considering that question when there came a tapping on my office door.

My inquiring mind dropped the police and their strange behavior and picked up on that soft knock. I hadn't seen recognition in anyone's face at Benoit's. It was unlikely that someone there knew my name, profession, *and* office address; unlikely but not impossible.

In that instant my life became a blues song. There I was, sitting in my own chair afraid to answer the door. That was another reason I kept my office in that neighborhood, because only the people down there understood the fear of everyday occurrences—like a simple knock.

This series of thoughts, contradictorily, lightened my mood. I smiled broadly, pulled the .22 from the gym bag, and called out, "It's unlocked."

The door came open framing a familiar countenance—EttaMae Harris, Mouse's wife and one of the three true loves of my life. She was wearing a simple shift that was decorated by pale blue and deep burgundy swirls.

I dropped the pistol back into the bag and jumped to my feet. Etta and I embraced halfway between my desk and the door.

She was a big woman, lovely and dark. We kissed lips, then leaned back and smiled for each other. Her face was round and proud. I felt like I was something special when she gazed upon me.

Behind her was a small white woman in a dark red dress. This woman was younger than either Etta or I. She seemed to be laboring under a great weight.

"Easy, this here is Alana Atman. Alana, this is Easy."

"Hello," I said.

"Hi."

We shook hands.

"Come on in."

I stepped to the side, allowing the women to come in and situate themselves in the visitors' chairs. I closed the door and locked it, then went around to my reclining office chair.

"Looks the same around here," Etta said.

"No reason to change. I'm sorry I don't have anything to offer you."

"That's okay, Easy. Alana and me already et and drank. At least I did. She haven't been too hungry lately."

I smiled, waiting.

"We got us a little problem," Etta said after an appropriate wait. "Raymond told me that you came down here pretty regular so I was gonna leave you a note. We called your home number but the answering machine wasn't on."

"I just moved," I said. "But you know that. Haven't attached the recorder yet."

"Alana here was married to a man named Fred Post."

"The plumber?" I asked.

Just the question brought a trembling smile to the white woman's thin lips.

"Yeah."

"I'm so sorry," I said to Alana. Fred had died of a coronary not long before I drove off that coastal cliff.

"Thank you."

"He was only forty years old, Easy," Etta continued. "You know they ain't no guarantees in this life."

"That's for sure."

"Fred was our plumber," Etta said by way of explanation. "That's why I know the family. He never charged us and sometimes I'd babysit for their child."

"Uh-huh," I said.

"Anyway, Alana and Fred have a son name of Alton. He's five years old, and the other day a black woman calling herself his auntie picked him up from kindergarten and took him away. His mother haven't seen him since."

"No idea who took him?" I asked Alana.

She tried to answer but only managed to shake her head and cry.

"We need you to find him," Etta said. "Alana went to the police but they hardly even listened. You know the only thing worse in their books than a black mother is the white mother of a Negro child."

"Etta," I said, "I'm kinda jammed up right now."

Instead of insisting she said, "LaMarque told me that you wanted me to say hey to Raymond."

There was a whole persuasive speech squashed down into that solitary sentence—and no room for argument. In my business I traded in favors. If I wanted her to talk to Mouse I'd have to find a missing child.

"Do you know Fred's family?" I asked Alana.

"Not too much," the sad woman said. "Fred was estranged from his people."

"Because of you?"

The arc of her nod was maybe a quarter inch.

"Have you asked them about Alton?"

"I spoke to his mother," Etta said, "Mathilda. She says they don't have him, that she don't have no idea who coulda took him."

"You believe her?"

"I don't know. She sounded upset."

"Did she ask you about the police?"

"No."

"You have a picture of your son, Mrs. Post?"

From a scuffed, blue vinyl purse Alana produced a felt-lined yellow wallet. From this she took a small Kodak snapshot of a smiling caramel-colored boy wearing a cowboy hat and a light blue T-shirt.

"Alton," she said as she handed the picture across my desk.

"Handsome young man."

"I loved his father, Mr. Rawlins." It was then that I discerned the twang of the South in her words. "I'm from Tennessee. My people would take us in but they don't understand Alton. They'd treat him like he was different, you know?"

I could see the sleepless nights in the dark circles under her eyes.

I stood up and said, "Why don't you lie down on the sofa a minute, Mrs. Post. Lie down and close your eyes. Etta can tell me what I need to know."

Maybe it was because it was a mature black man who reminded her of her dead husband that Alana relented and allowed me to lead her over to the couch. She lay down and I believe she was asleep before her head touched the cushion.

"That's a woman do anything for her man," Etta said. "She's a man's woman."

"You close with the family?" I asked.

"Raymond liked Fred. They used to gamble together from time to time."

"What was Fred's life like before Alana?"

"He lived with his mother after his first wife died. That's Mathilda, the mother. His first wife was named Nora. Mathilda didn't mind too much about Alana but her older sister Mona, who brought the family out here, was sad to see Fred go—especially with a white woman."

"You think she has the boy?"

"The woman they described at the kindergarten didn't look like her," Etta said. "I send Peter over to Mathilda's house with some flowers. I told him to pretend that he was deliverin' to somebody else. He did but he didn't see any children or children's things in the house."

"Peter still at your place?"

"That poor white boy ain't got no place to go, Easy. And he gives me a lotta help when Raymond's outta town."

"Fred have any other family?"

"Lots of brothers, sisters, cousins, grandchildren, and great-grandbabies, and then there's Mona Martin. Mona raised Fred's mother and all her brothers and sisters. She's the head of the clan."

"Anything else you could tell me?" I asked.

"No," she said, shaking her head and sneering at her ignorance. "Just that Alton's gone and my heart goes out to his mama."

In the country we traded favors for survival. When we moved up north we packed our country customs in with the pots and old photographs.

"I don't know when I'll be home, Etta, but I'm sure to be there after midnight."

"I'll tell Raymond," she said. Then she looked at her sleeping friend. "You know, I hate to wake her up. She haven't slept two hours since her boy been gone."

"You can stay here," I said. "Just lock up when you go."

"Thanks, baby. You be careful now."

13

I was walking down the western staircase of my building as a man was walking up. It was Percy Bidwell. At that moment he looked up, saw me, and reminded himself to smile.

"Mr. Rawlins."

We stopped there in the stairwell upon reaching a common stair.

He was wearing dark brown pants and a light brown shirt with buff-colored pointy-toed shoes. His processed curls were a little tighter and he smelled of cologne, just that much too sweet. There was a heart-shaped curve to his pursed lips.

I fought down the urge to slap him.

"Percy. I thought Jewelle said that you were going to call."

"She told me that I should come by and apologize in person."

"You're lucky you found me," I said, pointlessly. "I'm hardly ever even here."

"I dropped by your house first. Nobody was there and Jewelle had given me this address."

"I'm pretty busy, Percy. What do you need?"

"I already told you that."

The Goldsmith case along with Alana Atman's missing boy had cut my temper pretty short. I was about to go on my way, leaving the young man to consider his lack of proper civility.

"Look, Mr. Rawlins," he said before I could put my thoughts into action. "I'm sorry, okay? It's just that I'm kinda desperate. You know I got a business degree from UCLA, graduated magna cum laude. I been workin' for Jewelle at the real estate office but I'm educated for a job in high finance. You know most'a these investment firms won't even give me an interview. Jewelle told me that you could help set up a meeting with Mr. Middleton and maybe even ask him to consider me for a job. All I need is for him to take a look at me. My grades speak for themselves."

"So what?"

Percy could have had many responses to my two-word offensive. He might have been confused or hurt, maybe stunned. But the only emotion I saw in his eyes was indignation. How dare I, a dark-skinned, middle-aged black man, hardly removed from being a sharecropper, dismiss a young Negro who was educated at university and, with just a little help, was about to conquer the world?

"Wh-what?" he stammered.

"You studied business, right?"

"Yes." He actually sneered. "My degree covers accounting, economics, and investment finance."

"What does a business education tell you about a man giving away his property?"

"I don't understand what you're saying," he said in such a way as to make it sound like *You're not making any sense.*

"Let's say a man owns a house up the street from here but he lives in another house—owns that one too. Now somebody comes up to this man and says, 'Look here, brother, I got this new wife and a three-month-old child. I know you got a empty house up the street. Why don't you let us have that so we'll have a place to live too?'"

"I'm not askin' you to give me a house, man," Percy said, reverting into the defiant tone of our common upbringing.

"No? So Jason Middleton isn't worth nuthin' to you?"

"He is to me but what kinda job could he give you?"

"Just the fact that you ask me that question tells me that you not ready to meet Middleton. Just the fact that you don't see that if somethin' is valuable to you then that thing has worth everywhere tells me that you wouldn't know what to do with the introduction if I made it."

"You want me to pay you?" Percy asked, twisting his lips at the sour notion.

"I'll tell you what, Percy, you think about what I said, maybe talk it over with Jewelle, and then get back to me." I took a step down.

"Just spell it out," he said.

"Look," I said. "I'm not your mother, your father, your friend, boss, or professor. I don't owe you an answer or even one minute of my time. And if you don't know how to spell, that's not my problem."

I rushed down the stairs and onto Central before Percy could formulate any kind of reply.

Once on the street I realized that I was still moving headlong into my work instead of with forethought and guile.

I needed a phone book but I didn't want to run into Percy again or to wake up Alana, for that matter. I turned south on Central, walked at double-speed two and half blocks to 79th, and turned left. There, in front of Jolly's Liquor Store, I entered a phone booth that had survived from a previous era.

The white pages told me that Mona Martin lived on South Denker. By the address I knew that her place was somewhere around 103rd. So I walked back up to 77th, got into my new-used Dodge, and left Etta, Alana, and Percy to do whatever they did when I wasn't around.

It was a small house built in the French Colonial style. The porch was a series of planks lifted up from the grassy lot and going around the entire house. The sloping roof raised high above the home, and the walls, which according to custom should have been white, were instead painted gray with red trim. A weather-worn picket fence surrounded the place. A flimsy chest-high barrier like that would supply little or no protection. The only thing it would have been good for would be to keep a small dog from running out into the street. But there was no dog.

There was a For Rent sign nailed to one of the four front posts that pretended to hold up the eaves of the roof.

I sat there, parked across the street in my Dodge, thinking not about Mona Martin and Alton or Percy Bidwell and his inexplicable hold over Jewelle, but instead concentrating on Rosemary Goldsmith and how I could get out of any serious involvement with her and Uhuru-Bob Mantle.

I lived in L.A. and worked there as a kind of specialized investigator. I wouldn't make it very long if the police turned against me. I could certainly fail at making any progress in the case, but after taking money I'd have to do at least enough to make a convincing report. I was thinking of how I might get away with doing the least amount of work when I saw the rooster.

It was brown with orange and royal blue wattles and a bright red comb. The king fowl was strutting up and down the sidewalk in front of the Post house like Napoleon surveying the ocean surrounding his exile. The arrogance of that land-bound bird made me smile, putting my useless fears somewhere in the backseat of the musty car.

A detective's main job is sitting quietly and waiting. But that wait is not passive. The real detective is always aware and on guard, thinking about what it is he must do. I sat there trying to imagine how Melvin Suggs could help me while I helped him; how I could pretend to find a missing heiress and at the same time keep the windows from getting shot out from my new car.

I sat there only for three hours and forty-seven minutes; not long at all for a man of my profession to wait. The entire time that rooster marched in front of the picket fence, stopping now and then to peck at it. I figured that the bird sensed some kind of seed in the lawn beyond and was looking for a way in.

I was just wondering if I should go knock on the door when a young woman and a small boy and girl walked up to the useless gate.

The bird was startled by the approach and started squawking and flapping at the children.

"Get the hell outta here!" the young woman shouted and she kicked the rooster up in the air and over the fence.

Once on the other side the bird forgot his quarrel and started pecking frantically at the lawn.

The woman was wearing tight aqua-colored pants and a blue and red striped shirt, also pretty tight. She had a nice figure and dark skin.

She knocked on the door, maybe heard a question, and shouted, "Angela!"

The door came open and the young woman ushered the two obedient youngsters in.

I waited another thirteen minutes, got out and crossed the street, opened the gate, and went right up to the door. The rooster eyed me but was too greedy to stop his feasting. There was a button for the doorbell but I knocked instead.

Two minutes passed before I heard footsteps. Ten seconds more and a woman's voice said, "Who's there?"

"Ron Welch," I said with improvised roosterlike conviction.

"What do you want?"

"I'm here about the For Rent sign you got on the beam."

Mona Martin's wariness was on a ten-second timer. After the appropriate span she opened the door and looked out at me with the guarded instincts of a prey animal. It struck me that this would be a good time to practice my rusty detective skills.

Mona was short and wide, my age plus fifteen, and filled with stoppered-up passions. I could see that she liked to laugh and eat and probably to make love if the right man was to show up. But for all her hungers and desires she was a woman who was ready to defend her domain. The flimsy fence was just the warning. I bet that she had a pistol on a table next to the door—within easy reach.

"You want to rent this house?"

"My brother," I said.

"Then why ain't he here?"

"He's in Galveston, ma'am. Him and his wife and their three kids movin' up at the end of the month and I told him that I'd have a house ready."

"Mona," she said, identifying herself as Buster had done at Benoit's. She realized that she'd been standing in a defensive crouch and relaxed her shoulders a bit. "All you got to do is call the number on the sign. Mr. Harrington'll be happy to take your application."

"You see," I said as if I were pointing out a recurring theme to a longtime confederate, "that's what I mean. Real estate man needs a application and a deposit. He wants to look at my job history and Social Security number. He wants to call my boss and my old landlord. I don't need all that mess when you and me can come to an understanding right here."

"What kinda understandin'?" Mona was standing fully erect now. She was taller than I thought.

"How much you pay for this house?" I asked.

"One-eighty a mont'."

"Is he givin' you back your deposit?"

"No," she said petulantly. "He says that I ruined the insides because I painted the walls violet. It ain't purple or red. I didn't paint the walls black. It's just a nice light violet color but Harrington says that they got to paint the walls white again or nobody's gonna take it. Here I got to get back to Arkansas by the end of the mont' an' he holdin' me up ovah violet walls."

"You see?" I said. "The way I see it a man like that don't deserve no consideration. I could give you ninety dollars and you call him and tell him that you decided that you gonna stay. That way I could move my brother an' his family in an' by the time Harrington finds out they already be here. He got the deposit and we got a home with no mess, no background check, and no deposit."

"You say ninety dollahs but my deposit is one-eighty," Mona complained.

"You won't get nuthin' if you just move," I reasoned. "Arkansas you said?"

"Me an' my grandniece an' her kids goin' back home. It's too hard makin' it out here in California. I mean the pay's good if you can get a job but it's too damn expensive if you don't. And wherever you go you got to be workin' for white peoples. And you know they all just alike— lookin' down on you and smilin' at the same time."

"I tried to tell my brother that."

"Can't you make it one-twenty?" Mona Post asked. "You know those violet walls is nice."

"I could meet you halfway at one-oh-five," I said with some hesitation.

Mona Post stared into my eyes trying to gauge if she could squeeze five more dollars out of me.

I tried to look resolute.

At that moment we were interrupted by the rumble of little feet and childish laughter. The boy and girl had come into the room from somewhere behind Mona.

"You two be quiet," the exasperated younger woman was saying as she came in from another room. Noticing my presence, she gave me a sidelong glance. The children were snatching at each other and grinning. I still hadn't gotten a good look at the boy.

"Okay," Mona said. "One-oh-five."

I reached into my pocket and pulled out a wallet.

"Auntie Moan," the woman said, paying no attention to me. "Can I have two dollars to take them to see that cartoon movie?"

"Cain't you see me talkin', girl?" Mona Post said.

"Dahlia?" I said to the woman.

"Huh?" she replied.

"Dahlia, right?" I said. "You live over on Santa Barbara with Willie Boy?"

"My name is Angela, honey, and I right down the street on Wilton Court."

"You're not Dahlia Brown?"

"No."

"You sure?"

"My name is Cox."

"Damn," I said. "And you don't know no Willie Boy Sutton?"

"No, sir." She was beginning to like me.

"You got you a double in the world, girl."

"Mr. Welch," Mona said.

"Yes, ma'am?"

"One-oh-five."

"Oh," I said. "Yeah . . . I mean no. I can give you twenty dollars right now to show you I mean somethin' and I'll bring the rest in three days."

"That might be too late," Mona Post warned.

I looked away as if considering her words. But really I wanted to get a better look at the boy. He suddenly turned away from the girl, avoiding her playful pinches. It was Alton.

"You two stop that!" Angela shouted.

"All y'all be quiet!" Mona commanded, and the room went silent.

For a moment I considered just taking the boy. But Mona probably had a pistol near at hand and Angela looked like she could put up a fight.

"Sorry, ma'am," I said. I spread open the wallet and came out with two tens. "This all I got right now."

She took the bills and said, "Why I got to wait three days?"

"That's how long it'll take for my brother to wire me the rest." I turned to Angela and said, "That's a handsome boy you got there."

"It's my cousin's son," she said, "and my sister's little girl. I'm not married."

14

An hour later I was walking into the ultramodern ground floor of the main offices of the French insurance giant Proxy Nine. The setup hadn't changed since the last time I was there: four or five uniformed guards protecting a group of desks that clustered behind a waist-high, see-through emerald plastic wall where a dozen young white people sat making calls and answering phones, providing direction or turning undesirables away.

I walked up to the main counter, where a weak-faced, bespectacled young man in a maroon jacket and black trousers stood. He looked me up and down, deciding that my dark lemon slacks and square-cut green shirt, my black skin and advanced age of forty-seven, would have a hard time making their way past his post to the elevators beyond.

"Yes?" he said.

"Asiette Moulon, s'il vous plaît," I said in my best French. My best wasn't very good or extensive but it was enough to confound the expectations of the young white American.

"What?"

"I'd like to speak to Asiette Moulon." When he still didn't know how to reply I added, "She's the young woman sits on the other side of that red door right behind you."

The young man actually turned to check if the door was still there.

"Who are you?" he said, turning back again.

"Easy Rawlins."

"And what is your business?"

"She's expecting me."

On the way downtown I had stopped to call Jackson Blue. They patched him through on a ship-to-shore phone from Jean-Paul Villard's yacht, where, Jackson told me, he and the CEO were having a meeting with their Spanish counterparts. I had told him what I needed and he had Asiette prepare the letter.

Asiette was a young Frenchwoman who was once nice to me when her fellow receptionist tried to turn me away. I told Jackson and he told Jean-Paul. Asiette, I was given to understand, had been promoted the next day.

"I need to know what it is that you want," the sad-sack young man said.

Next to the red door was a window. Through that window I could see Asiette. She happened to look up and I waved.

"Don't do that," the young man said loud enough to alert a guard standing off to my right.

But I wasn't worried. Asiette smiled and got up, opened the bright red door, and came to the protective young man's side.

"Easy," she said. "I 'ave everything you need. Come, come."

She raised the plastic plank that barred the entrance and I walked through to her small office.

That was a transition period in American race and class relations. Only a few years earlier you could tell whether or not someone belonged by their clothes, gender, race, and age. At one time, quite recently, only white people, mostly men, in business attire would be allowed through the front doors of downtown offices. Those rules were slowly evaporating but they lingered in the memories, desires, and expectations of the old guard and their offspring.

"Easy," Asiette said, "it is so good to 'ave you 'ere."

The last time I'd seen the young receptionist she'd worn the modest sweater and skirt of a French shopgirl. Now she wore a formfitting dress designed to look like a peacock feather wrapped around her. She wore glasses now too.

"You lookin' good, girl."

She was slender, five three, with black hair, gray eyes, and skin that had come from an ancestry of white people many centuries in the making. Her smile was so intense that I thought she might have said yes if I asked her out for dinner—or a weekend in San Francisco.

But I was in enough confusion about romance and the girlfriend I already had.

"You got the letter?" I asked.

"'Ave a seat," she said, indicating the green visitor's chair positioned in front of her orange desk.

Her seat was yellow and she lowered herself into it with apparent pleasure.

"How's it goin'?" I asked, just to be social.

"I love it 'ere," she said. "Not some of the white people but there is so much more."

"I guess so," I said. "When you're raised here it kinda weighs on ya. You don't have much choice about who you like and what you are. Everybody thinks they know you before you walk in the door."

"You understand so much. Can we 'ave lunch one day?"

Asiette must have figured out that I wouldn't have asked the question.

"As soon as I'm off this job," I said, and I meant it.

She pursed her lips and picked up a bright turquoise paper folder from the desk. This she handed to me.

The folder contained a single sheet of paper. The two-sentence letter, on official stationery, was typed and read, *Mr. Goldsmith, This is my friend and associate, Mr. Ezekiel Rawlins. He has important business to discuss with you.*

It was signed by Jean-Paul Villard. Jackson told me that he had a stack of blank letters signed by JP just in case Jackson needed his approval to get something done when the boss was not around.

When he was a young man you would have been a fool to trust Jackson with two scrawny chickens, but once he'd entered the world of Proxy Nine he had proven to be both honorable and faithful.

When I asked him about this primal change he said, *I just give what I get, Easy, give what I get.*

"You got something I can put this in?" I asked the adoring office manager.

She handed me a white envelope. I folded the letter, licked the paste fold, and sealed it.

"You will really call?" Asiette asked when I stood up.

"I got a girl but that doesn't mean I can't have lunch with a friend."

I left her to speculate on my meaning.

From a phone booth on the corner I called Feather to tell her I might be home late.

"What you doin'?" my daughter asked.

"Trying to make your Ivy Prep tuition, girl."

15

The gate to Goldsmith Armaments International was at the end of a dirt lane that branched off from Cherry Flats Road up toward Mt. Bliss. That was out in Arcadia in the farthermost reaches of the Valley.

There were two armed guards in tan and blue uniforms standing by a sentry hut set in front of a high fence that was crowned with barbed wire. The guards had a definite military manner about them.

One sentry, a golden-haired, thirty-something white man approached my car. He looked like a poster boy for push-up enthusiasts.

I rolled down the window.

"This is private property," he said.

"My name is Ezekiel Rawlins," I said as a sort of reply.

The other guard had reached his partner's side. He was also white but had red hair and the beefy figure of a weight lifter.

"You'll have to turn it around," Red said.

"I have an appointment with Mr. Goldsmith," I countered.

This suspended conversation for a full fifteen seconds.

Finally I said, "Jean-Paul Villard of Proxy Nine called to schedule the meeting."

Mr. Push-up unbuttoned the leather flap on the holster that secured his pistol, while Red went back to the little hut to make the call.

Some minutes passed. This gave me time to scan the environs. The vegetation out there was brown as it almost always was in August. The dry desert air and the unrelenting sunshine dominated in the summer months.

"There's no Ezekiel Rawlings on the schedule," Red said, returning from the hut.

"No 'g' and did you call his office?"

"You aren't on the board."

"The appointment was made two hours ago," I argued in my most civilized manner. "Does your board get updated more than once a day?"

Red frowned. I was sure that this look was often a precursor to violence.

I shrugged and gazed out the windshield at the heat-blasted foliage.

Red went back to the hut while Mr. Push-up fingered the butt of his gun.

Five minutes more and Red returned.

"What do you have for Mr. Goldsmith?" he asked.

"I have to speak to him in person. That's what I was told."

"He's busy. So whatever it is you have for him you will give to me."

"No."

"What?"

"It's a simple word, man. Not worth repeating."

Red gave me that look again and then went back to the hut. His partner backed up a few steps to keep an eye on me and the path behind.

Fifteen minutes later a Jeep drove down from a sheltering stand of eucalyptus trees. Red and Mr. Push-up opened the gate for the military car to emerge. It carried four more men, three of whom were also in uniform.

I was asked by Red to get out of the car.

I did so peacefully. For some reason five armed guards and their tall boss in business attire didn't bother me. After all, I was the emissary of JP Villard, one of the most influential businessmen in the world.

"Rawlins?" the man in the gray business suit said.

"Mr. Rawlins."

"My name is Gregory Teeg. I'm security supervisor. What do you have for Mr. Goldsmith?"

"It's for Mr. Goldsmith."

"He told me to get whatever it is you have."

"You got a phone in the little outhouse over there, right?" I said.

"Yes."

"Then you get JP Villard on the line and ask him to tell me if that's okay. Because I work for him, not you—not Mr. Goldsmith either," I added, though, strictly speaking, this was probably not the case.

Teeg was a white man with dark skin and wavy, copper-colored hair. He was slender and used to having his way in the orbit of his world.

"If I have to call anybody, you will be the one to answer," Teeg said.

I didn't quite understand what he meant, so I said nothing.

"Well?" he asked after a minute or so.

"Well what, man? I told you—I have a message for your boss. Your boss, not mine. Now either you gonna let me in or you not."

I wondered, maybe for the first time ever, at that moment, what it would be like to live in a world where a goodly number of the residents didn't hate or fear me. Teeg and Red and Mr. Push-up would have liked to knock me down and step on my face. It didn't matter what I said or how I acted. If I wanted my way I had to accept their hatred. That fact had been such an integral part of my life that I had never really questioned it. Even then the question was toothless.

"Get in the Jeep," Teeg said, interrupting my silent, useless philosophizing.

"I'll follow you in my car."

"Get in the Jeep if you want to see Goldsmith." Then he said to one of the men that had accompanied him, "Give these two your access keys," referring to Red and Mr. Push-up.

The three men who came with Teeg took up the post and the two guards who had met me accompanied us in the roofless vehicle.

Beyond the stand of eucalyptus trees there was a hill. Through the hill was an earthen, minelike tunnel that delivered us to another more solidly built metal gate set in a wall of metal and concrete.

The Jeep parked with six or seven of its brethren in front of the wall. Teeg, Red, Mr. Push-up, and I got out.

When we walked up to face the barred metal gate, my heart started beating fast. I wasn't feeling fear, but somewhere in the primitive part of my brain I was preparing for conflict.

The gate rolled to the left and, on foot, we entered the adult wonderland of weapons manufacturing. It was a large field of concrete bunkers and dead earth. Here and there, men in uniform and men in light-colored smocks moved from one bunker to another. All the men were white, and there were only men.

A scent in the air told me that something was burning. In the distance was a mountain. My mouth was watering and there was sweat sprouting at the back of my neck. After a quarter mile of marching we reached a large concrete hut that was scarred by gunfire. The rounds of live ammunition had penetrated between eight and twelve inches into the obdurate stone hide. This wounded building was the size of a big tent in the army. It was thirty feet across and five yards high. The double steel doors that secured this space opened when Red and Mr. Push-up used their keys on either side.

The doors revealed a dark and cavernous space. We all stood there— looking in.

"After you, Mr. Rawlins," Gregory Teeg said.

It came to me that this monolith, more than anything else, resembled a crypt. I would have been afraid to enter had I not already died once that year. I took the step through and lights, very bright ones, came on on all sides. My escort crammed in around me. The only thing in the room was a stairwell with iron steps that led down, down, down.

Each tier had twenty steps and then you turned around for another stage. Every three stages down there was a door with a sign marking that portal's province. There were signs for PROJECTILES, CORROSIVES, EXPLOSIVES, COMBUSTION AGENTS, and even a door labeled POISON GAS. This last title angered me. I had seen thousands of bodies firsthand that had been treated with Nazi-manufactured Zyklon B gas. I didn't want to believe that I lived in a country that could imagine any use for that kind of technology.

All the weapons-oriented doors were made from metal that had been painted lime green. But the eleventh entrance down was double-doored mahogany with brass knobs and no sign. Using special keys again, Red and Mr. Push-up unlocked and opened this fancy portal. Mr. Teeg and I went through but the guards remained outside.

The room we entered had a high ceiling consisting of long fluorescent light fixtures and white soundproofing tiles. The floor was laid with emerald green and blood red linoleum, and the walls were made from concrete, painted deep green. It was a large room, thirty by forty, and empty except for a small desk on the opposite side from where we entered. The desk sat by a pine door no larger than the lid of a poor man's coffin.

Behind the too-small desk sat a balding white man who wore a nice dark suit. The man had glasses that were highly reflective. Even when we'd gotten to him I could only see his eyes in glimpses.

"Foster Goldsmith," Gregory Teeg said, gesturing at the sitting man. "Easy Rawlins."

"Hello," the man said. "What can I do for you?"

My heart was still pounding. I was acutely aware of how far down under the ground I'd come. I was in a very serious situation and still the men I was with were like little boys playing games.

"Why you want to insult me like that, brother?" I told the sitting man.

"Excuse me?" he said.

"It's the man on the other side of that skinny door I need to see."

"I am Foster Goldsmith."

"In this big empty room? At that small-assed desk? I don't think so."

"Give me what you have," the bespectacled drone said. Despite his appearance he did a very good job of sounding like he was in charge.

"My mother used to tell me that if I paid attention I would learn something each and every day of my life," I said. "She said that if I did that I would grow into wisdom like Methuselah or Moses. On this day it's your turn to learn that even though you see a black man standin' in front'a you, you shouldn't assume that he doesn't read the newspaper just like you do, that he hasn't seen pictures of old Stony many, many times. If you remember that fact maybe your children won't end up slavin' for mine."

"I am the man you seek," he said. That's the job he was being paid for right then.

"You had plastic surgery to make you bald and pudgy?"

"Send him in here, Mr. Crispin," a voice said over an intercom speaker. The spectacled man had been about to argue further but abandoned his lie when the order came through. He stood up and opened the slim pine door.

He didn't need to tell me where to go.

16

The room I entered was long and deep, brightly lit and jumbled. There were four very long worktables along walls that revealed no other door. The tables were strewn with tools, a wide variety of mechanical parts, grease rags, and guns in pieces and whole; there were rifle barrels, bullet clips, and telescopic sites mixed among oil cans and vises, toolboxes, and other metal items all having something to do with the mechanics of death-dealing.

Toward the back wall stood a huge asymmetrical desk that was made from metal and looked like some gargantuan gray and extinct member of the pig family. Upon the desk were blueprints, files, a few paper coffee cups that had soaked through along the seams, and at least a dozen telephones.

Behind this desk sat a man who was maybe sixty but solid. This man stood up as I approached.

Foster "Stony" Goldsmith might have also been constructed from steel. His hair, skin, eyes, and even his suit were all various shades from silver to gunmetal gray. His posture was solid and his hands soiled with the materials from his worktables.

"That's a whole lotta phones," I said.

"Makes you wonder why JP Villard didn't call me in person," Goldsmith said. "He has the numbers of four of them."

I took the envelope from my pocket and handed it across the broad back of the porcine desk.

He tore open the letter and read it closely. Then he looked up, suddenly intrigued by my presence.

"What could you possibly have to say to me?" he asked. "And why would the CEO of Proxy Nine need me to listen?"

"Rosemary."

It was a pleasure to see that the captain of industry could be rocked by just a word. He gazed at the letter in his hand, questioning its origins, and then looked up at me with the same query in mind.

"Where do you come from?"

I went into the story that had been going through my mind for the last twenty-four hours. I told him about Moving Day and Roger Frisk, about Tout Manning and being shot at in front of Benoit's Gym.

"Why would the police come to you?" Goldsmith asked.

"I'm a private detective. Not too many my shade of brown in L.A. The cops find that I can get work done where they cannot. Also I know things about the world outside my neighborhood."

"What kind of things?" he asked.

"Like that the man sitting outside your door wasn't you."

"Tom Crispin is so close to me that he could finish my sentences."

"Well," I said with a shrug, "I'm talking to you."

"And the police sent you here?"

"No, sir. The police told me not to contact you under any circumstances. But I'm suspicious by nature. I haven't read about the supposed kidnapping in the newspaper. And even though I'm aware of some of the crimes this Uhuru Nolicé is supposed to have committed, I haven't ever heard about him before either."

"So you don't believe the police?"

It was an odd interrogation. Goldsmith had no intention of sitting or of offering me a seat. I decided that this was some kind of superstition; that if he treated me in a civil manner he couldn't have me shot on the way out.

"Not necessarily," I said.

"And what do you want from me?" he asked.

"Like I said, somebody paid me six thousand dollars to start this investigation. I figure that was you. And if I'm working for you it's only right that we meet face-to-face."

Goldsmith's eyebrows creased slightly.

"And there's another thing," I added.

"What's that?"

"I have a daughter of my own and I wouldn't want somebody out looking for her that I hadn't met."

"I've never served in the armed forces, Mr. Rawlins, but I'm military just the same," Goldsmith said. "I live a Spartan life and work in armaments. I taught Rose how to make her bed when she was six years old. I told her that when a man or woman makes their own bed they sleep in it too."

His words were facts tinged with lament.

"So you're saying that you don't want me to find her?" I asked.

The gun-maker gave me a long hard look then. He was angry about something; maybe it was my question.

"Have you ever killed anyone, Mr. Rawlins?"

"Why? Have you?"

"Not by direct physical contact," he said as if he had been practicing a legal defense. "I have never shot, stabbed, bludgeoned, or asphyxiated another human being. There are people out there, however, who blame me for the deaths of thousands. They think because I make bombs that I am responsible for how those bombs are used. If a child is shot in the DMZ or Johannesburg with one of my guns they lay the crime at my feet. What about you?"

"Are you asking me if I blame you for people killed with your weapons?"

"I'm asking you if you have ever killed anyone."

"Why?"

"Like you said, I want to know what kind of man is out there looking for my daughter."

Less than two months had passed since I last killed a man. Keith Handel was a thug and a killer, a ruthless man who would, who *had* murdered his own confederates for money. I thought he was trying to kill me. If he got the upper hand he probably would have. But that night I was lucky. I strangled him while he was trying to do the same to me.

"In the war," I said.

"Is war your excuse?"

"Where I come from people don't have any use for excuses."

That got me another minute-long stare.

"Is there anything else I can do for you, Mr. Rawlins?"

"You could answer my question."

"Let me be very clear," he said. "I did not summon you or go to your house on Moving Day, as you call it. I didn't give you any money or suggest these things you say about my daughter are true. You are in the employ of the Los Angeles Police Department. So I suggest you address your questions and bring your findings to them."

Looking at Old Stony's hard facade, I wondered if stainless steel could rot.

He had, I believed, given me the answers to my questions, but I didn't understand their meaning.

The door behind me opened and I didn't have to look to know that Red and Mr. Push-up had somehow been summoned to see me out.

17

As we climbed out from Goldsmith's underground lair—Red, Mr. Push-up, Gregory Teeg, and I—I wondered about what crime had been committed. It could be that this was a simple kidnapping for ransom. It could be that Goldsmith's desk was actually a prehistoric boar trained to stand still and act the part of an inanimate piece of office furniture.

I was breathing pretty hard at the halfway mark of our ascent. This exertion made me crave a cigarette. When we were outside of the concrete bunker I pulled out a Pall Mall and a box of matches.

"No smoking on the property," copper-hued Teeg said.

"Why not?"

"Too many combustibles and flammables in the air."

I made it home by six forty-five. Feather was there in the bare living room, sitting in the chair and reading a book. She had rooted out our old brass lamp and a dark side table made from elm.

"What you readin'?"

"*La Condition Humaine*," she said. "*Man's Fate* by André Malraux."

"In French?"

"I don't really understand it but I can read the words pretty much. Bonnie gave it to me."

"You hungry?"

"There's chicken and dumplings on the stove," she said, putting the book down and standing up to kiss me.

————

She'd also made a green salad in the French style with a garlicky vinaigrette dressing. I sat at the rectangular table in the eight-sided room and my daughter served. Both my children had matured early. They were smart and focused from childhood, responsible and willing to help. These traits might have had something to do with my child-rearing but I couldn't explain it. I was a single parent who was often out in the world rather than at home. I had moved my kids around, kicked the woman we all loved out of the house, and was subject to sour moods. I had nearly killed myself and subjected Feather to a prolonged and spotty resurrection.

"How was it out at the Nishios'?" I asked when we were both seated.

"Nice. They have a big family and they all work together making clothes for Bryant's Department Store in Beverly Hills. They have aunts and girl cousins and wives all there working. Mr. Nishio is the only man, he answers the phone and cuts fabric. Me and Peggy sewed yellow trim into the hems of black cloth dresses. I even learned a few things to say in Japanese."

"That sounds nice," I said.

"Oh," she said. "What happened to your face?"

"Something hit the windshield of the Barracuda and it shattered."

"That's terrible."

"Blessing in disguise," I said. "I turned it in and got a new car doesn't hit you like a neon sign."

"Oh well," Feather said, putting the old car from her mind.

The house seemed empty, not only because of the sparse furnishings; it was also a new space that felt unlived in. This brought about a certain quality of intimacy that we'd never experienced in the home we knew so well.

"Daddy?"

I knew from her tone that something serious was up.

"Yeah?"

"You said that you were going to tell me about my real parents."

I think it was her making dinner that defeated me. She was a young woman asking a man she trusted to tell her the truth.

The story of Feather's parents' lives, and deaths, was X-rated. She shouldn't have heard it until she'd reached her twenty-first year, not her twelfth, but I knew I couldn't avoid it for a decade more.

"It's a sad story," I said.

"Are they dead?"

We sat there in the dinette for more than two hours. I told her about Vernor Garnett, her maternal grandfather, who killed her mother and her father. I said that it was because he was an important man and was embarrassed by his daughter Robin's wild lifestyle. I didn't say it was because Robin had had a Negro daughter and tried to extort money out of Vernor to hide that fact.

"I was on another case," I told her truthfully, "and came across those killings. After it was all over I found you with a friend of your mother's. Vernor was going to prison and your grandmother and her son Milo had left for the East Coast. I didn't want you with the county so me and Juice took you in."

"Is my grandfather still in prison?" Feather asked.

"He died."

"And my grandmother?"

"She knew about the crimes but the law couldn't, or wouldn't, prosecute her. She moved back east, like I said, I don't know where."

Feather got up from her chair and sat on my lap—there were tears in her eyes. I held her and she held me; both of us orphans on a dark street at night.

After some time I carried her up to her bedroom. She changed into her nightgown in the bathroom, crawled into her bed weeping, and I sat there beside her bed until an hour after she'd fallen asleep.

The phone rang at seven minutes after midnight. So much had happened that I forgot about the possible appointment.

"Hello?"

"Ease," Mouse said. "What's happenin'?"

"It's all fucked up, Raymond," I said to my oldest and deadliest friend.

I went on to tell him about Frisk and Manning, Mantle and Rosemary Goldsmith—who I had begun to think of as Rose Gold. I mentioned Uhuru Nolicé and almost getting killed on Crenshaw.

"Who is this Uhuru whatever?" Mouse asked.

"It's an alias that Mantle's using." I went on to tell him about the shootout with the police, the so-called assassination, and the armored car job Manning had mentioned.

"That's some bullshit right there," Mouse said.

"What you mean, Ray? I read about all those crimes in the papers. You sayin' they didn't happen? Men shot at me in my car."

"Did they hit you?"

"No."

"Then they weren't real killers, now were they?"

"They might have meant to kill me and missed."

"Look, Easy, I don't know about this Bob Mantle dude. I mean I seen him fight before but I don't know about his politics or whatever. I do know that those three cops got shot was killed by Art Sugar and his crew. Art was runnin' drugs and there was a shootout over on Slauson. I know that 'cause Art's right hand in Chinatown, Lem Leung, wanted me to help him get on a slow boat to Hong Kong."

I didn't ask if Mouse had helped the middleman on his journey; nobody was paying me for that.

"I guess he could'a shot that vice principal," Mouse continued, "but the armored car job couldn't have been your boy because I know the people did it. They offered me a piece but you know I don't shit where I eat."

Raymond Alexander had his finger on the pulse of crime in L.A., and elsewhere. He wouldn't have lied or passed on possibly faulty information, not to me. But if Bob Mantle couldn't have committed at least two of those crimes, then why was the LAPD so sure of it? Why didn't Stony Goldsmith show any real concern for his daughter?

"Easy," Mouse was saying with an edge to his voice.

"What?"

"Do you?"

"Do I what?"

"I asked if you needed me to come back there."

I was lost in the tangle of the case, or the possible case.

"No, Ray. No. I just have to muddle through this shit."

"I don't know about Mantle," he said, "but if you get mixed up with Art Sugar your ass be in a sling."

"I'll tell Etta if I get in over my head."

"Okay."

"I have another question, though."

"Shoot."

"You ever hear of a woman named Mary Donovan?"

"Not that I remember. What she do?"

"Makes her nut movin' boodle. At least she used to."

"What denomination?" Mouse knew the right words when need be.

"C-notes. Not very good ones, I think."

"Talk to this dude named Lambert, Light Lambert." He gave me the address. "Light's got his thumb all the way up in the counterfeit pie."

"Thanks, Ray."

"Try and stay alive till I get home, Easy. I found this new soul food restaurant make you think you was in Lake Charles."

Feather was asleep but I could tell she was having nightmares; the blankets and top sheet were on the floor. I covered her up and kissed her forehead, wondering if I should have lied to her about her mother and father.

I had just lain down on my bed when I realized that a streetlamp was shining in my eyes. There was no shade or curtain to block it, so I accepted the glare and turned on my side. In the morning I would fix everything—or die trying.

18

Coffee brewing in the morning brought me closer to feeling at home in the new house. Sunlight danced on the white walls and played interesting patterns through the mild prism of glass in my shadeless windows. I put on my tan linen suit, a milk-chocolate-colored turtle-neck shirt, and finally, after deep consideration, decided on dark green shoes.

My brown leather jewelry box was on the dresser. Feather had put it there, no doubt. I opened it to see if there was anything that caught my fancy for the day and the job at hand. There was in the upper corner of the second level of the box a thick platinum ring festooned with a three-carat emerald. That ring once belonged to Mouse. When I saw it on his hand I told him how much I admired it.

"Take it, Easy," he sang, tugging the bauble from his middle finger. "It don't fit me too good anyway."

It was too small even for my pinky but I took it. Mouse got sour when people turned down his gifts.

Something about the jewel seemed to resonate with the Rose Gold case and so I put the ring in my pocket.

I liked to think that I was a modern child of the twentieth century but the superstitions of Louisiana were snagged in the crevices of my brain. It felt like I needed a good luck charm from a powerful deity, and Mouse's juju was some of the strongest I knew.

Feather was in the kitchen making bacon and eggs, and Bisquick waf-fles on a machine that had been packed away for years. She was wear-ing blue jeans and a checkered blue and white shirt shot through with black lines that complicated, or maybe exhilarated, the design. The shirt had once belonged to her brother.

"That coffee I'm smellin'?"

"I'm using the percolator that Bonnie brought back from Marseille. But I got the French press out if you want that kind."

"That's okay," I said. "You goin' to work with your friend again today?"

"I thought I could use the money to buy a new bike."

I took a seat in the dinette, wondering if I should get a round or an octangular table for that room.

"Are you in trouble, Daddy?" my daughter asked, putting the breakfast plate and thick white coffee mug down in front of me.

Her question told me many things. First and foremost, she was saying to me that she'd accepted my story about her parents and my part in that tale. She would take her time and consider the details and one day she'd come back to me with more questions—and requests. But she could also see that the job I had undertaken had gotten under my skin and into my unconscious mind. I looked like I was in trouble because trouble had colored my mood.

"No," I said. "Why?"

"You always get that serious look on your face and stare out into space when there's trouble."

"How'd you come up with that theory?"

"Juice used to tell me when I was a kid."

"You're still a kid."

"Are you okay?"

"You remember those men that came over the house while we were moving?"

"Yeah."

"They were the police. They're looking for some guy and want me to find him."

"What do they want him for?"

"He knows a woman who's the daughter of a rich man. She's missing and they want to ask him if he's seen her anywhere."

Frenchie sauntered into the room then. Feather picked him up and sat down across from me with the dog in her lap.

"Aren't you eating?" I asked.

"I already did."

Somewhere in the world I had a blood daughter: Edna, whom I sired with Regina. Regina had left me for an old friend of mine from Houston. I wondered if Edna was as wonderful a child as the one keeping me company before she got on with the business of her life.

"Bye, Daddy," Feather said at the curb before crossing the street to Peggy Nishio's house.

"Look both ways."

She laughed at my trying to make her stay a child.

Peggy was outside waiting for her, smiling and waving.

Walking back to my front door, I glanced to the right and saw two white men in suits and ties coming toward the house. They were both the same height and hue, they had virtually identical haircuts, and probably tipped the scales within two pounds of each other. They reached the path of hand-cut granite brick, paused a moment, and then headed for me.

I considered backing into the house, slamming the door, and making it out the back. I had already placed a pistol on the high shelf of the kitchen cabinet. I could grab that on the way.

The idea of the gun called up the image of Stony Goldsmith sitting in a hole in the ground and stockpiling weapons. This thought arrested me. I turned my head to catch a last glimpse of Feather but she and Peggy had already gone into the Nishio home.

"Mr. Rawlins?" one of the men, who wore a dark gray suit, said.

"Yes?" I answered, addressing both the fraternal twins.

"I'm Agent Sorkin and this is my associate Agent Bruce. We're from the FBI."

"Do tell." I took a step backward so that I was standing inside the front doorway.

"We have been informed that you are looking for Rosemary Goldsmith."

"By whom?"

"That's not important," Agent Bruce, who wore a suit of dark blue, said.

"It is to me."

"May we come in?" Sorkin asked.

Neither man, at any point in our conversation, smiled.

"No you may not."

"We have to talk to you about this case, Mr. Rawlins," Bruce told me.

"That's your problem. You need to talk to me but I don't need to talk to you."

"You are getting involved in an ongoing federal investigation," Sorkin replied. "If you don't tell us what you're doing we can have you arrested for interfering."

"Okay. If you got a warrant or I committed some kinda crime, you got to do your duty. But I'm a citizen and I will not be bullied by the loose talk of strangers."

"This case involves kidnapping and national security," Bruce said because it was his turn. "You have a duty here."

"How did you find me?" I asked.

"We got your address from the LAPD."

"Really?" I was sure that neither Frisk nor Manning had given them my address.

"May we come in?" Sorkin asked.

"No."

"Have you been in contact with a man named Robert Mantle?"

Robert.

"I have not."

"Who hired you to look for Miss Goldsmith?" Bruce asked.

"I didn't say that I'm looking for her, and even if I was I have no idea of any supposed client's name. I don't even know if you're really FBI agents."

"You don't want to run afoul of the government, Mr. Rawlins," Agent Sorkin told me.

I figure that he and his partner were in their early thirties, college graduates who had a taste for law enforcement but didn't like doughnuts. Sorkin's flat pronunciation marked him as coming from the nation's heartland, and his consternation told of a deeply held belief that his culture was the true America whereas mine was that of Other.

He, and Agent Bruce, would never understand how I might rightfully refuse their superiority, their official status, or their birthright.

"Is there anything else?" I asked.

"Are you going to answer my questions?"

"I am not."

The FBI agents, who never showed me their ID, turned their heads to regard each other. Should they arrest me? Should they push me into the house and force me to answer their questions? I had no doubt that they might utilize such tactics. And if I was another kind of man in a different profession I might have tried to placate them.

But I was who I was and what I was by choice and inclination—and then there was history. Maybe if they had shown me their identification, asked for help, or at least smiled, I might have been persuaded to accommodate them. But the freedom I had to refuse had its own story. Millions of people had died, and there were those who were still dying for my freedom to say no.

Maybe one day Agents Bruce and Sorkin would understand that simple fact.

"This isn't some kind of game, Mr. Rawlins," Agent Bruce said. "We have to ask you to stop any activity you're involved in that has to do with Rosemary Goldsmith or Robert Mantle."

I gave him a wan smile and a crooked nod, then closed the door in his face.

19

There was a quarter cup of cold coffee left in the white diner mug. I took my time drinking the strong, bitter dregs, making plans as well as I could. I was almost completely in the dark about what case I was working on and exactly what crime had been committed. I'd been paid and paid well for this confusion.

The involvement of the FBI was a sign that I had strayed into some kind of minefield. I closed my eyes and tried to imagine Rosemary Goldsmith. Was she dead, tied up in a closet and scared to death, or laughing with her friends?

Because I couldn't answer any one of those questions I decided to take a walk.

There was no evidence of a surveillance team keeping watch on my new home, not that I would be able to tell if Uncle Sam really wanted to keep tabs on me. I didn't think that I was that big or that expensive a threat. Every pair of eyes used to watch a suspect had an hourly rate that went into time and a half before you knew it.

I couldn't imagine that I was being watched, but the world I lived in was quite a bit larger than my imagination.

So I grabbed a handful of change from a jar that survived the move, then sauntered up to Pico, took a left turn, and stopped at a phone booth outside of a Winchell's Donuts store near La Cienega.

"Hello," he said, answering the phone on the twelfth ring.

"Hungover again, Melvin?"

"What do you want?"

"I thought we had an agreement."

Suggs groaned.

"I asked about your guy and the girl too," he said. "Nobody knew anything more than what I already told you. For whatever reason the top brass seems to be holdin' this one close to the vest."

"That's not a surprise. Them comin' to my home on Sunday says that. But I was thinkin' . . . maybe I could be a little proactive."

"Pro-what?"

"Preemptive."

"Say again?"

Melvin knew what the words meant. He just liked to fuck with me sometimes.

"I'd like you to call your contact and find out if there's anything in the files about Bob's closest relatives," I said. "Maybe one of them knows something. Somebody said that he lives with his mother, at least he did until recently."

"I could do that."

"If you called 'em now then you could get back to me at this pay phone." I rattled off the number printed on the pay phone's dial. "My phone at home just might be bugged."

"Now?"

"Why not? The sun is up and the FBI just told me that the sands are already runnin' out."

"FBI?"

"Uh-huh."

"I haven't finished vomiting yet this morning, Easy."

"And here I am sober, out on the street looking for your wayward girlfriend."

Suggs paused then. He didn't like me calling him at home and giving orders, but the chain of command was wrapped around his desire to find Mary Donovan.

"Gimme that number again," he said.

I did.

"Okay, Easy. You sit tight and I'll see what I can see."

I stood there inside the modern, three-walled phone booth feeling as if I was at least in the game. I had always been a man of actions. I liked reading and thinking and making plans, but it was when I was on the move that I felt most balanced.

"Excuse me, mistah," a woman said. She was young and black-skinned, five-two in flat shoes, and lovely in the hard way that poverty imparts to its denizens.

"Yes?"

"I need to make a collect call to my auntie down Galveston."

"What she gonna say when the operator tells her that?"

"She gone be mad at me," the young woman said with emphasis. "But I need to talk to her father 'cause I lost my job an' been th'owed out my room."

I reached in my pocket and came out with a handful of quarters, nickels, and dimes. These I held out, offering them to the young woman. She must have been about nineteen.

"I need this telephone," I said. "I'm waiting for an important call. But take this money and call your aunt direct. There's a whole bank of phones in the parking lot of the five-and-dime across the street."

The woman looked at the money before taking it, and then she eyeballed the store and its parking lot. She turned back to me, peering deeply to perceive any catch to my actions or advice.

"Thank you," she said when she could find no defect. "Thanks a lot."

I was thinking that I should find out the name of Suggs's contact and go straight to the police with Roger Frisk's name, telling them that I'm on the case but a little confused.

"Pardon me," another woman said. This one was older than I, white, and tall—maybe five-eight. She wore red and had coiffed brown hair that was streaked with gray.

"Yes?"

Instead of saying anything she moved her head in a somewhat intricate fashion, communicating quite clearly that I should move away from the phone.

"I am waiting for a call," I said in Standard English.

"I need to use this phone."

"*This* phone?"

She stared.

I shrugged and leaned back.

"You aren't using it," she reasoned.

"If you saw a man sitting down in front of a plate of pork chops," I replied in the same condescending tone, "but he wasn't eating right then, would you just take his dish away?"

"Move," she ordered.

"There's a phone in the parking lot across the street."

"I'm standing right here."

"I know that," I said. "And I'm standing in your way."

The lady's neck quivered. She was, I believe, considering pulling me out of that booth bodily when suddenly she turned on her high heel and stormed off.

"Hey, pal," someone said as I watched the woman head east at a fast clip. "Let me get in there and make a quick call."

This phone patron was also white, in his thirties, and dressed in a sky blue suit that would melt, not burn, if exposed to an open flame. He was wearing a straw hat that was rigid and well formed. One lock of blond hair had escaped the band and hung down next to his left ear. I remember thinking that he might have been a hippie in disguise.

"I'm waitin' for a call."

"I'll just be a second and if they call while I'm on they'll just call back."

He was right, of course.

"I'm waiting," I said anyway.

"But this is a public phone," he argued. "You have to let anyone who wants use it."

It struck me that if I was lonely all I had to do was go to a pay phone and wait for people to come up and engage me.

"I'm waiting," I said again.

"I'll only be a minute," he said.

And then the phone rang.

"Easy?" Melvin Suggs said.

"Yeah, Mel."

"You got a pencil and paper?"

"Right here."

I took the small notepad and Bic pen from my breast pocket and wrote down an address on Hoover.

"That's for Belle Mantle," Suggs said, "his mother. She's the only blood relative currently residing in Los Angeles, at least that the department has on file. He has a cousin that lives in L.A. sometimes but right now he's overseas in the military."

"Thanks, Mel," I said. "You mind if I ask you to run a partial license plate past your friend?"

"Sure. But it might take some time."

"California plates. A-X-I were the first three characters," I said. "Then there was a two. I didn't get the last two digits. But it was a gold Ford Fairlane."

"Got it," he said, and then he hung up; going off to continue with his morning vomit, no doubt.

"Excuse me," a man said.

It was a policeman. He stood there with a partner and the angry white woman. The man in the straw hat was gone. I wondered, while taking in my latest visitors, if the young black woman had gotten in touch with her aunt.

"Yes, Officer?"

"This woman said you threatened her."

"She did?"

"Yes."

I produced my detective's photo ID from the outside breast pocket of my jacket.

"Easy Rawlins," I said. "I'm on the job for the LAPD. Call a man named Tout Manning in Roger Frisk's office. He'll vouch for me."

"This call had to do with that job?" the freckle-faced and beefy policeman asked, pointing at the pay phone.

"Yes, sir."

"Dwight," the one cop said to the other.

"Yeah?"

"Call it in."

"Okay."

"What are you talking about?" the white woman said in a very stern, almost loud voice.

"We're checking out his story, ma'am."

"There's no story. He assaulted me."

"He hit you?"

"With words," she said. "He assaulted me with words. He threatened me. He blocked my passage. I want you to arrest him."

"Make the call, Dwight."

"I want your name and ID number," the woman demanded of the policeman not named Dwight.

"Can I see your identification, ma'am?" he replied.

"My, my . . ." She turned away again and stomped off.

The officer watched her for a moment and then handed me my PI's license.

"I'm sorry about that, Mr. Rawlins," he said. "When a civilian comes to us with a complaint we have to ask some questions."

"That's okay by me," I said. "I got plenty of answers."

20

"Excuse me, mistah," a familiar voice said.

I was walking toward Point View.

The young woman who had to call her aunt wore a short, dark blue, one-piece dress. The tones of the dress and her dark brown skin were almost equal, suggesting the image of what she might look like naked. She carried a pink plastic purse and wore a thin silver band on the index finger of her left hand.

"Yes?" I said.

We had stopped there at the southwest corner of Crescent Heights and Pico.

"I wanted to thank you for givin' me the money to call my Auntie Lee."

"You already thanked me. Was she home?"

"She always home. Auntie Lee got arthritis in her legs an' she hardly go nowhere."

"Was it a good talk?" I had a soft spot for people from down home. Los Angeles was like the New World for Southern black immigrants as much as New York must have been for the Italians, Irishmen, and Jews at the turn of the century and before.

"Her father, Granddaddy Arnold, is in the hospital. I called her to ask him for help and she ended up askin' me to go help him."

Tears that refused to fall flooded her eyes. She was angry, sad, and lost all at once. For some reason I thought of the door labeled COMBUSTIBLES in Stony Goldsmith's underground weapons research fortress.

"What's your name?" I asked the young woman.

"Natalie," she said. "Natalie Crocker."

"My name's Easy Rawlins," I said.

We shook hands.

"Do you know how to clean houses, Natalie?"

"Of course."

I took out my little wire-bound notepad and scribbled a number and a name. I tore out the page and handed it to her.

"Julie?" she said in an attempt at phonetically sounding out the word J-e-w-e-l-l-e.

"No," I said. "Jewel like a diamond."

"Who is she?"

"She owns an apartment building up in Beverly Hills where they let out the place by the week to businessmen and people in the movie business. After they move out she has people come in and clean up. Tell her that Easy Rawlins told you to call. And here," I said, handing her two ten-dollar bills. "Use this to keep yourself together until you get the job."

"Why?" she asked. The question didn't need elaboration.

"It's nice to find a little bit of down home in a new place."

Her nostrils flared and once again she became wary.

"Call her," I said. "If you don't trust what you hear, buy a newspaper. There's a thousand jobs listed every day in Southern California."

I turned and headed for my new house.

Belle Mantle lived on South Hoover near Gage, down the block from the Good Shepherd Baptist Church. It was a single-story flat-topped bungalow, dirty pink in hue. It looked more like an incinerator building for some large manufacturing company than it did a residence. This industrial cottage consisted of two apartments; I could tell that by the two mailboxes standing on weathered posts at the outer edge of the barren lawn, that and the two front doors set side by side at the middle of the building—Belle was the door on the left.

I knocked and waited, knocked again.

"Yes?"

"Ms. Mantle?"

"Yes?"

"My name is Easy Rawlins and I've come to ask you some questions about your son."

"I don't know anything," she said. Her words could have been the first sentence in a French-existentialist monograph. I smiled at that.

"Please, ma'am, it's just a few questions."

"Who are you?"

"Easy Rawlins," I said. "I'm a private detective."

"What do you want?"

"Do you attend Good Shepherd?"

"Yes," she said. There was reluctance in her tone because with those words I was insinuating myself into her life.

"Is Wanda Bateman still Reverend Atkins's aide?"

"You know Wanda?"

"Why don't you call her and ask about Easy Rawlins. I know Wanda *and* Francis Atkins too."

"You wait here," she said through the closed door.

"Yes, ma'am."

"Wanda says that she didn't send you," the woman's voice said a few minutes later.

"She didn't," I agreed, "but I bet she also told you that I'm a good man who doesn't try to hurt my black brothers and sisters."

"What do you want?"

"I want to talk to you about your son."

A few moments more passed and then the chain rattled and more than one latch clicked. The brown door in the dirty pink wall pulled inward. In the shadowy room stood a buttery brown woman in a full-length gray-green dress that had big yellow buttons down the front. She was barefoot and wore white-rimmed glasses.

"Do you know my son, Mr. Rawlins?"

"I only ever saw him box, Ms. Mantle."

She couldn't help but smile.

"His father should have never given him them boxin' gloves," she said. "He wasn't meant to be no boxer but he sure did love it when he put them gloves on."

"May I come in?"

The small sitting room was almost a perfect cube. It had only one small and heavily curtained window. Three padded turquoise chairs were set in a semicircle around a low walnut coffee table. There was a partially completed twelve-hundred-piece jigsaw puzzle of the Golden Gate Bridge in the middle of the broad table. The box was on the floor.

"I don't have nuthin' to offer," she said after we were seated.

"That's okay. I'm only here to ask about your son."

"I already talked to them other policemen, Detective," she said. "I told them that I don't know nuthin' about where Bobby is but he didn't do nuthin' wrong."

"LAPD has already been here?" I asked.

"They was policemen in suits like you. They had badges and cards with pictures on 'em but I didn't have my readin' glasses."

"Do you remember their names?"

"No, sir. How do you know Minister Atkins?"

I knew Atkins because, a dozen years before, the married minister had had an affair with a young woman named Doris Mayhew. Doris had become pregnant by Francis and was blackmailing him. The congregation would have splintered if they knew about the liaison and so going to the police was out of the question.

After a day and a half of nosing around I learned from Doris's half sister, Maxine, that their mother, Lainie Mayhew, was devout in her beliefs in God and the right of a black man to make it in this world. I called down to Arkansas to the Hartwells, neighbors of Lainie Mayhew, and had them bring her to the phone. I told the pious Lainie about her daughter and sent her a Greyhound bus ticket to ride back to L.A. and confront Doris.

It worked out well enough. Francis agreed on child support and Doris moved back to Texarkana.

That was how I knew Francis Atkins but I couldn't share that story with Belle Mantle.

"He hired me to help a young mother whose wayward daughter was lost in the big city of Los Angeles. I was able to get her to go back home and start a family."

"That's strange," Belle said.

"What is?"

"You don't evah think about a detective doin' the Lord's work."

"Mysterious ways," I replied.

"Are you here doin' the Lord's work for Bobby?" she asked.

"I need to find him before I can tell you that."

"What you want with him?"

"The police say that he's been involved with robbery, murder, and kidnapping," I said. "I've asked around and there's some people who don't think that he's done a thing."

"He haven't," Belle Mantle said with a mother's conviction.

"How do you know that, ma'am?"

"They say he was the one in that shootout where the police got killed, right?"

"Yes."

"Three days after that shootin', that was Thursday, Bob was here with me in this room doin' a fifteen-hunnert-piece jigsaw puzzle of the Eiffel Tower."

"So?"

"He was wearin' a white T-shirt and brown pants."

"And that means he didn't kill anybody?"

"Bob has played dress-up since he was a child, Detective Rawlins. If he put on a fireman's hat he was a fireman until that hat came off. Whenevah I wanted him to water the backyard I just put that hat on 'im and told him the fire hose was out back. His daddy give him boxin' gloves and he was a boxer until the day they banned him from the ring. If he had done that killin' I would'a seen it by what he was wearin'. He wouldn't have been able to even put on those jigsaw puzzle clothes if he had kilt anybody. He likes to pretend and once he starts he cain't stop till whatever story he's dreamin' is ovah."

"He became a real boxer," I suggested.

"An' once he did he carried his trunks and his gloves everywhere he went. When he came ovah here to help me with my puzzle he didn't have no guns or weapons. He was just glad to sit on the flo' an' look for the right piece."

"Where does he live?"

"Here since he quit boxin'. He goin' to Metro College, though. He wants to be a actor but first he gonna learn how to be a bookkeeper. I told him that he had to have a way to pay the rent because I nevah see more than two Negro actors on the TV in a week's time."

"So he lives here with you?"

"Yes, sir," she said with almost no hesitation.

"Has he been here for the past two weeks?"

She twisted her face away, avoiding my scrutiny by concentrating on the puzzle.

"I can't help him if I don't know the truth, ma'am."

"He been runnin' with this new friend'a his."

"Who's that?"

"A white boy name of Youri, sumpin' like that. I don't like him much. I told Bobby that. But he still spend most the time with him, except that one night we did the puzzle. Other than that night he done slept out. I don't know what he been doin' but I swear he ain't killed or kidnapped nobody. If he had why haven't Jerry Dunphy said so on the news?"

"Will you let me look in his room?"

"So you can arrest him?"

"Listen, Belle, I'm a private detective. I'm workin' with the police but I'm not part of them. If Bob committed a crime I can't lie about that but you and I both know that if the cops find Bob they will shoot first. They will kill your son. If he's innocent I'll try and prove it. If he's guilty I'll make sure that he doesn't get gunned down like a dog."

The words I spoke fully encompassed the world we lived in; she knew that.

21

Belle stood in the hallway while I went through her son's things. The room wasn't large enough for the both of us. It was the size of a janitor's hopper room. There were box springs under a single mattress for a bed, with a drab green army-surplus trunk next to it. The trunk worked as both his night table and his closet. The window that looked out on the backyard wasn't wide enough for a man to squeeze through, giving his bedroom the feel of a jail cell.

Nailed to the wall over the bed was a cork bulletin board, four feet wide and three high. Upon the board were tacked pictures cut from magazines, newspapers, books, and comic books; photographs and drawings of men in all kinds of uniform. There were soldiers of differing rank from private to general, a policeman, a football player, Green Lantern, a head chef, an Eskimo, a Catholic priest, a rodeo rider, and many others.

The bed was made and the oak floor swept.

"You clean up in here, ma'am?" I asked.

"Not really, Detective. Bob has always been very neat and orderly. I only made up his bed again after the police pulled it apart."

"Interesting bulletin board."

"He don't have no girls up there but he likes girls. It's just that he looks at clothes and thinks that's what it takes to be somethin'. He always told me that clothes make the man."

"Can I look in his chest?"

"I guess you can. The other police already looked in there and didn't find nuthin'. My son don't have nuthin' to hide."

The balled-up socks and T-shirts were jumbled. I figured this was because of the police, or maybe it was an FBI search.

There was a black photo album with Kodak snapshots and, more recently, Polaroid shots of Mantle in various costumes going all the way back to when he was a child. Some of those costumes were in the chest.

His bookkeeping workbook was there. When I opened it a pink slip of paper fell out. It was a property receipt from the Beverly Hills Police Department issued to a Beaumont Lewis. The date stamped on it was the morning of August fifth.

"Who's Beaumont Lewis?" I asked.

"That's Bobby's cousin," she said, "my sister's son. She live in Houston and he's in the navy."

"He been here recently?"

"No, sir. He's over off the coast of Vietnam."

I looked a little further and took a few notes but there was nothing incriminating in the room.

"Did the other policemen take anything from this trunk?" I asked the fretful mother.

"Not that I noticed, sir. They didn't even write nuthin' down."

"Did you tell them anything that you haven't told me?"

"They just aksed me where he was at. They aksed that six times and I always answered the same: I don't know."

"Did you tell them about Youri?"

"They didn't ask."

"Do you know Youri's last name?"

"No, sir."

At the front door of the dark home Belle asked, "Can you help my son, Detective Rawlins?"

"I can try to keep him from getting killed," I said. "Maybe he hasn't done anything wrong. If he hasn't I'll try to get the police to understand that."

It wasn't much, but people like Belle and I had learned long ago to live with not quite enough and then to make do with somewhat less than that.

———

"Mr. Rawlins," a man said.

I was standing at the door of my nearly nondescript Dodge. The white man who called my name and the white man he was with walked toward me from a dark sedan parked two cars up ahead.

They were alike inasmuch as they both wore light-colored suits and out-of-style broad-rimmed fedoras. But that's where the similarities ended. The man who called me was pink-skinned and fat, not over five foot six. He was the elder, maybe fifty. His partner was tall and string-bean thin. He was a thirty-something white man with olive skin, dark eyes, and the thinnest lips I had ever seen on a human being.

"Yes?" I said.

"Andrew Hastings," the elder said. He didn't hold out a hand. "This is Ted Brown. We're with the State Department."

"Don't tell me. You're looking for Rosemary Goldsmith and Robert Mantle."

Hastings was breathing hard after the short walk from his black sedan to my maroon one. He wasn't happy with my tone.

"There is a national security aspect to the Goldsmith case, Mr. Rawlins," the fat man said as the thin one stared.

"I had no idea. Neither the police nor the FBI informed me of that fact."

"Neither the local police or the Bureau has any authority in this situation. Certainly no ordinary citizen, no"—he paused a moment for dramatic effect—"no Negro in white man's clothes has any authority whatsoever."

I have always considered myself a reasonable and intelligent man, familiar with the ways of the world I lived in. I know enough to know that if three different governmental law enforcement agencies seek me out, I am being told to back down, back off, and back away from a line chiseled in stone.

"What is it that I can do for you, Mr. Hastings?" I could have asked him for identification but by then I was sure that every official agency operating in Southern California was on the trail of Rose Gold and Bob Mantle.

"Where is Bob Mantle?" His lips were fat, having the blubbery quality of the wattles on the rooster that stalked Mona Martin's picket fence.

"I have no idea. I asked his mother but she didn't know. I asked at the boxing gym he teaches at but they didn't say."

"What did Foster Goldsmith tell you?"

"I told him that the police told me that his daughter had been kidnapped, but he did not corroborate that claim." I ratcheted up my language in an attempt to keep my head above water with the government men.

"What did the police say?"

"That she had been."

"What did they want you to do?"

"The police?"

"Yes."

"Find Bob Mantle so that they could ask him if he knew where Rosemary was."

Hastings had robin's-egg-blue eyes. The predatory attitude of those pretty orbs was contradictory and made him seem all the more dangerous.

Ted Brown made his hands into two fists and stacked them one on top of the other as if he were holding a baseball bat.

"You are going to stop any inquiries into the Goldsmith case," Hastings informed me. He took a wallet from his back pocket and a white card from there. "This is my phone number. If any question you have asked so far yields an answer you are going to call me and give that information. You will only call me. Do you understand?"

It was, I believe, the last three words that obliterated my common sense. Sure, give me a gold-embossed card, tell me that you're the bossman, tell me not to earn the only living I know how to make, but don't call me stupid on top of all that. Don't steal my money and then take my woman out to dinner with it.

No.

"I understand completely, Mr. Hastings, Mr. Brown," I said. "I am a patriotic American. I served in the war and learned to respect the chain of command. I'm sorry if I caused any trouble. You know I believed that the police were trying to do what was right."

"That's understandable," Hastings said. He clapped my shoulder and even grinned, but the smile came too late.

22

My next stop was a dirty brown-brick office building on Wilshire Boulevard, downtown. It was one of the older structures, eight stories high and without any kind of architectural personality. The blueprints for the boxlike edifice had been used in the fabrication of ten thousand of its kind throughout the country between world wars.

There was no doorman or front desk, no security guard or concierge to show you which way to go. Next to the elevator, under a glass pane held in place by a corroded chrome frame was a typed list of the residents and their office numbers.

Suite 5C was once occupied by Nifty Notebooks and Office Supplies, but that name was crossed out with blue ink and the name *L Lambert and Associates* had been scribbled in in pencil. The use of ink and then lead told me that some time had elapsed between Nifty Notebooks' departure and L Lambert's arrival on the scene.

An Out of Service sign had been attached to the elevator doors many months before. The cellophane tape that held up the handwritten sign had yellowed in that time.

And so I went through a doorway to my right that had a stenciled sign above it announcing STAIRS.

On the way up I thought about Belle Mantle calling me Detective Rawlins. She knew that I wasn't a real officer of the law. The use of the title was her attempt to show me respect and deference in hopes that I would help her boy. She was well aware that Bob was in trouble. Ever since he was a child pretending to be every kind of hero, she had known that he was going to get into hot water. Mothers and fathers of our heritage nurtured hopes of our children fading into the background like that uninspired building and its brethren. If they went unnoticed they had a shot at living fruitful lives, unmolested by the predators that picked off our heroes, and villains, every time one of them reared their head.

The door to Suite 5C was the color of a blood orange. It was ajar. I pushed it open and came into a sun-drenched room that had yellow walls and a forest green tiled floor. The blond desk opposite the door was big and solid. The windows through which the sunlight poured were thick and laced with metal wire. The door beyond the ash desk was made from unpainted metal.

But it was the man behind the desk that dominated the room. He was apelike and white with a thatch of medium brown hair and the slumped shoulders of a blacksmith. He had one foot up on the blond desk.

"Who're you?" he said, peering over his own big toe. He wore tan pants, a grass green sports jacket, black T-shirt, and polka-dotted yellow and purple socks under shoes the same color as his hair.

"I'm looking for a man called Light Lambert," I said.

The ape took his foot down and stood. He was of medium height with a chest that was truly barrel-shaped. I fought down the urge to pull the pistol from my pocket.

"I asked you who you were," the brutal man said. Even the way he talked sounded like fighting.

"Rawlins is my name."

"Get the fuck outta here before I kick your ass."

"That," I advised, "would be an uphill climb."

"The fuck?" he said.

He came half the way around the desk. I knew my words would set him off. I knew it but I was angry. I had been accosted by three different branches of government, shot at, cursed out, and insulted over and over again—and it was only Tuesday. I wanted to strike back. I intended to strike. But before the sham of a receptionist could get to me the door behind him swung inward and a tall man walked out.

"Elvis," the man said.

My opponent pulled up short, almost as if someone had grabbed him by the scruff of his neck and yanked.

The tall man smiled. He was wearing a coal-colored three-button suit with a light blue dress shirt and a lime and cranberry tie. He was well built, on the slender side, and pale-skinned.

"This guy just busted in here, Light," Elvis the ape said.

"This is Mr. Rawlins," the elegant counterfeiter replied. "Mr. Rawlins is a guest."

Elvis cocked his head, adjusting to this new view of me. He nodded once and went back around to sit in his chair. There he waited a moment and then put his foot back up where it was before I entered.

"Come into my office, Mr. Rawlins," Light Lambert said to me. "I've been expecting you."

He stepped to the side and gestured for me to go through.

Lambert's fifth-floor office had a ceiling that went to the top of the sixth floor, maybe twenty-two feet high. I thought at the time that this must have been a storage room for the previous tenants. The clear windows went all the way up and looked down on Los Angeles with its asphalt streets and palm trees, its blue sky over a dingy brown, smoggy horizon. The floor was laid with square black and white tiles, giving it the feel of a fancy Creole restaurant down on Bourbon Street in New Orleans. The walls were painted enamel white like a high-school toilet.

The furnishings of this office were incongruous for a business. Under the window there sat a fancy cream-colored couch that had dark wood legs and a corrugated arching back like the collar of an Elizabethan noblewoman. There were matching chairs at either end of the divan and a low coffee table where sat three telephones—white, black, and red. This plethora of phones reminded me of Stony Goldsmith's subterranean lair. In the far corner to my left was a folding card table surrounded by four folding pine chairs. There were poker chips and cards on the fabric-covered tabletop.

I looked around like Belle Mantle looking for a puzzle piece.

"Something wrong?" Light Lambert asked.

"Where's your desk?"

"Don't need one," he said. "I never write anything down."

"Not even a letter?"

"Not even a phone number."

"But you have phones."

"Have a seat, Mr. Rawlins."

I took one of the chairs because it was set at such an angle that I could look southward at my adopted city.

Lambert sat on the sofa in a very erect posture.

"How do you know my name, Mr. Lambert? Do you have the front office bugged?"

"Raymond Alexander called and told me that you might be dropping by. And yes, I do have a microphone in the front room. Whenever somebody crosses the threshold it comes on for one hundred and eighty seconds."

"You know Mouse?"

"I know everybody that needs it."

I sat back, absorbing the strangely domestic office and the idea that Mouse had built a reputation that included apes and counterfeiters. I stayed quiet because, even though I had a simple question to ask, I got the impression that Light Lambert was a man of custom and ritual.

"I got a pocket full of nickels and dimes for my calls," he said. "And even with that I replace my phones every six weeks."

I was thinking that if I met Lambert at a party or on the street I would have guessed that he was an undertaker.

"Is Light your given name?" I asked.

That was the right question. He smiled broadly, sat back, and crossed his left leg over the right knee. I noticed that he wore black and white scaled snakeskin shoes and no socks.

"My old man was a drunk," he said happily. "At least he was before I was born. But when the backwoods Tennessee midwife put me in his hands he stopped drinking and got a regular job in the coal mine. My mother, Lucretia Lambert, said that when he looked at me there was a light shining in his eyes, that he had seen the light and so that's what she named me."

"Now that's a good story," I said. I meant it.

"Our mutual friend tells me that you're the most trustworthy man he's ever known," Light said, letting me know that he was ready to get down to business.

I nodded and smiled, still biding my time. Raymond meant that *he* could trust me. I wondered if Light was aware of that subtlety of language.

"If you were to take a Greyhound bus to twelve, thirteen cities around the Midwest, Easy, pick up a package from general delivery downtown and then make a series of deliveries, I could guarantee you a windfall of fifty thousand dollars. Six weeks tops." He straightened his legs and sat forward, clasping his hands.

That little speech stopped me. I hadn't come there looking for a job but I wasn't a fool either. It was a safe deal. Mouse was better than Lloyd's of London when it came to insurance. Add to that the fact that my experience with the law of late (and during the course of my entire life) had been that it was at least corrupt and often downright evil; I could be arrested for bank robbery or loitering and end up on the same damn chain gang.

"That might be the best job offer I've ever had, Mr. Lambert, Light, but I'm going to have to say no." I held myself to a higher standard than public officials, the police, and even the government.

"No? You don't want a job? Then why are you here?"

"I'm looking for a woman named Mary Donovan. Mouse told me that you might be able to point me in the right direction."

Light sat back and put his right arm up on the collar of the couch. If his eyes were a binocular microscope, they would have just shifted from eighth to the six-hundredth power. Many thoughts went on behind that magnified vision. I'm sure that my death was one of the considerations.

"Mary got herself arrested," he said after the long pause. "Then she got hooked up with the cop that busted her. She was on the bad list for a few weeks there. Then I had a talk with her and all was forgiven. Mary changed her name and moved out to Twentynine Palms . . . solo."

"Sounds a little foolish of her to let you know where she ran to."

"She has a best friend named Celia Wolf. Elvis and Wolf had a heart-to-heart. It was Celia who convinced us that Mary was out of the business but not out to get us."

"She using her real name?"

"Mary Donovan isn't her real name," Lambert said with a grin. "Neither is Clarissa Anthony. But that's what she goes by out in the desert."

"I guess she's a lucky girl," I said.

"Her and that cop too," Light agreed. "You know the people we work with don't take prisoners."

I nodded sagely and then said, "Thank you," indicating the end of our talk.

"What do you want with Mary?" he asked.

"I was hired by an insurance man who she ran with for a month or two. I guess he kinda fell for her."

"What insurance man?"

"Cedric Blain at Proxy Nine."

"What do you plan to tell this man?"

"I think I'll do him a favor and tell him I couldn't find her."

23

Light Lambert shook my hand and bade me good-bye at the blood orange outer door of his office suite; Elvis felt no compunction to stand. I didn't mind. I didn't give a damn about either of them, their business, or their senses of decorum. Going there was the way that a man like me transacts business.

I didn't care about them but the story Lambert told put Mary Donovan, aka Clarissa Anthony, in a new light and my temporary partner, Melvin Suggs, in possible danger.

I called Suggs, got his answering machine, and suggested a rendezvous. Then I drove home.

At least I intended to drive home. I actually got all the way to my old house on Genesee before remembering that I now lived at a new address. It was this mistake that told me I was now fully committed to the case Roger Frisk had tapped me for. I sat there looking at my previous home with no feeling of alienation or loss. I was there simply because my mind was elsewhere.

Home for migrants like me truly was where I hung my hat, and, since Jack Kennedy's bareheaded inauguration, I no longer wore hats.

Feather was curled up on the solitary chair in the echoey living room, reading the French edition of *Elle* magazine.

"Hi, Daddy."

I kissed her forehead and sat on the edge of the couch.

"How was work?"

"I had lots of fun," she said. "Peggy's mom taught me all these Japanese jokes and curses that the old folks say; that and the song about the sun maiden."

"Nice song?"

"I didn't understand the words but her mom told me that it's about a beautiful young woman whose husband was a fisherman that got lost in a storm. She was so heartbroken that the gods gave her a boat of light and every day she sails it across the sky looking for her lost husband. It's a way to make the day seem so beautiful but sad too."

I smiled and thanked whatever gods there were that brought me my lovely little girl.

"I'm having dinner with Bonnie tonight," I said.

"I know. She told me."

"You wanna come?"

"Peggy and her mom invited me over and you and Bonnie need to spend some time together."

Since the age of six, Jesus had seen it as his duty to watch over and protect me from myself. At some point he had passed the baton of responsibility on to his sister. She knew that Bonnie and I were having problems without anyone telling her.

It took me a while to get dressed. It was a date and I had to look good but I didn't want to be too formal. Even though Bonnie and I were back together again—there was some distance there. She'd broken off her engagement to the Ashanti prince Joguye Cham and we saw each other often, but the bedroom was sometimes like a court where judgment was considered but never passed.

I decided on a pair of caramel pants and an auburn sweater. Under the sweater I wore a red T-shirt—maybe as a sign of my obscured passions.

McGirt's Steak House was on Third Street a block west of La Cienega. It was an old establishment and its employees were unconcerned with the race of its patrons. I got there at six thirty. Bonnie was already there, seated at our favorite table. She stood up and kissed me.

Even with my unsettled heart I was in love with Bonnie. She was ten years younger than I with dark skin and the almond-shaped eyes of western Africa. She was beautiful to me and to the rest of the world but not necessarily for the same reasons. She had a nice figure on a strong frame. Her face was both beautiful and handsome. Her hair was straightened because her employer, Air France, looked down on the popular "natural" hairdos that many black women wore.

Any man or woman who saw Bonnie would be impressed with her beauty, but for me everything started with her smile. When Bonnie laughed she turned into an adolescent girl who loved life so much that the feeling infected the hearts of those around her. That happiness was like a private doorway to the woman I loved.

The fact that I'd almost lost her stalked me.

"The waiter is bringing two Virgin Marys," she said, "and two rib-eyes on the bone done medium rare."

Her voice contained the lilt of the English Caribbean. The tone was both soft and strong.

I kissed her again and she gave me a quizzical look.

"Sit," she said.

When we were installed side by side, she smiled and I looked down.

"Feather says that you're on a case," she said.

"Yeah. It's a beast."

I spent a while telling her the situations, lies, threats, and dangers that I had already experienced.

"Maybe you should let it drop," she said after asking a few questions about the players and my impressions.

"There's no maybe to it," I said. "But I'm gonna have to pay for those improvements to my properties sooner or later, and Feather has her heart set on Ivy Prep."

"I could help with her tuition."

It was the first time Bonnie had offered to combine her finances with mine.

"She's not your responsibility," I said.

"I love that child every bit as much as you do."

"Listen, Bonnie, I know that I haven't been a prize lately."

"You're my man, Easy."

"I haven't proved it."

"You're here."

"You know what I mean."

"You almost died," she said, "and I was engaged to another man. Getting back from changes like that takes a while."

She took my hand and the waiter brought our drinks.

When he was gone I said, "Melvin Suggs is going to drop by here sometime after eight."

"Something about the case?"

"Yeah."

I couldn't remember Bonnie ever losing her temper or getting angry with me. She must have done it at some point because I knew that she had the potential for rage, but all I could remember was her understanding and love.

Melvin got there a little before nine. He was dressed in a gold suit with a dark blue dress shirt. These were clothes that he bought after meeting the counterfeit distributer, Mary Donovan. But when he was with her he was neater. Now the shirt was loose and the jacket wrinkled. He'd been drinking; I could tell that by the dour look in his eyes.

"You remember Melvin, honey," I said as the brooding cop sat down in a chair that the waiter pulled out.

"Detective Suggs," she greeted him.

"Not for long," he said.

"Anything to drink?" the waiter asked.

"Triple shot. Sour mash," Suggs snapped.

The waiter left and we three were quiet for a moment.

"Goddamned rookie stopped me on the way here," Melvin said as if answering a question. "Gave me a fuckin' ticket even though I showed him my shield. Me! A fuckin' ticket."

"I should be going," Bonnie said.

She was leaving because she knew how uncomfortable I felt about men cursing around women, especially women I cared for. Melvin's language didn't bother her. She was used to drunks and unguarded language because she worked first class on international flights week in and week out.

I walked her to her car. She drove a dark red late-model Citroën.

I kissed her lips and she pulled me close.

"I love you, Ezekiel Rawlins. I love you and I won't let the past take you from me, not again."

"I won't either," I said, my voice betraying the uncertainty in my heart.

She kissed me again, showing no such doubt.

I watched her get in the car and drive off. I waited there, in that little pocket of peace, for a minute or two before returning to the war

24

"I need you to sober up, Melvin."

He'd ordered a second triple shot and was putting it away with grim determination.

"You're not my mother," he replied.

"Maybe not but I think I know how to find that girl of yours."

"Where?"

"I need to talk to some people first."

"Who are they? I'll go talk to 'em."

"No, Mel, not while you're in this condition. I got to know I'm talkin' to a responsible adult. Anyway, I need to do a little more investigation before I let an L.A. bull loose in the Mafia china shop."

"Don't you fuck with me, Rawlins."

"Let me take you home and sober you up, Detective. It's not just you got troubles. I need a partner firin' on all eight cylinders."

"Where's your new house?" he asked.

"I'll drive."

"I got my car right here."

"You're lucky that the cop who stopped you didn't take you in on drunk driving, Mel. Your car can wait till morning."

"Good evening, Detective Suggs," Feather said when we came in the front door.

She usually waited up for me if I hadn't called; just one of the duties passed on to her by her brother.

"Hey, Feather," he said. "You gettin' taller and more grown every day."

"I like your suit," she said.

At that moment Frenchie came in complaining loudly in canine parlance. He not only barked but yelled and snarled too. I also think I detected a bit of glee in the dog's expletives; he was glad to have somebody to hate.

"Take your dog in the kitchen, honey," I said, "and make Detective Suggs a pot of strong percolator coffee."

"Okay, Daddy." She lifted the twisting, protesting dog up in her arms and walked off. I took Melvin upstairs and showed him the master bathroom.

"There's the tub," I said. "Use it. I'll take your things downstairs and bring you a robe and some pajamas. They won't fit you right but they'll cover what needs covering."

"What you gonna do with my clothes?"

"Wash what I can and press the rest."

There's domesticity even in police work. Stains and smells, patches of blood from wounds and busted noses—all had to be cleaned and set and put away. The new house came with a washer and dryer in a back room that was somewhat like a walled-in porch. I threw Melvin's underwear in the washer and examined his suit and shirt for stains. They were pretty clean.

"I'll iron them in the morning before I go with Peggy," Feather said.

"Thanks, honey. I'll stay up and put his drawers in the dryer."

For some reason these words earned me a kiss.

"I love you, Daddy. You didn't have to take me in or anything. You didn't have to love me but you did."

"And I do."

Feather was up and out before I opened my eyes the next morning. Melvin's clothes were ironed, hanging from a hook intended for a painting, on an upstairs wall next to the stairs. It struck me that that suit of clothes might be considered art in some avant-garde circles: *Homicide Detective's Suit.*

I set the coffee brewing in the kitchen and then went to the living room to check on the suspended detective. Melvin was asleep on the couch. He was snoring at a volume that might challenge a mama tiger's purr. I sat down in the lone chair and watched him for a few minutes, thinking about the case. I needed an in with the police and I was unsure about Frisk and Manning. They could have been on the up-and-up. But even if they were sincere in their desire to save young Miss Goldsmith, that didn't mean that they had my welfare at heart. On the other hand, I didn't want to get Suggs deeper in trouble with the force; and, for that matter, I didn't want to put him in an unmarked grave next to Mary Donovan/Clarissa Anthony.

"How you doin', Easy?" I hadn't noticed his eyes opening.

"I need to catch you up on what's been goin' on."

"You gonna tell me where I can find Mary?"

"Just as soon as I know."

"When's that gonna be?"

"Three days tops."

I could see the thoughts moving furtively behind the grizzled policeman's beautiful doe eyes. He was too smart and too sensitive for the LAPD and probably had few friends among fellow cops. Policemen socialized only with one another and so he was a pariah even before the suspension. He didn't like me being in charge but I was one of the only friends he was likely to have.

"What's this shit with Bob Mantle?" he asked.

I told him everything that he needed to know.

"The FBI makes sense because it's a potentially high-profile kidnapping," he said. "And the State Department has to get a toe in the door because it's political radicals and a weapons manufacturer. The best thing you can do is fly down to Mexico City and jump on a cruise ship sailing south from there."

"If you had asked me about a cop hookin' up with a female mule for a counterfeiter I'd say the same."

Melvin squinted; maybe he would have gotten angry but then the doorbell rang.

I put my finger to my lips but it wasn't necessary. Melvin knew what side of the law we were on. Quietly I walked with him to the entrance hall and then pointed the way that led back to the laundry room.

I counted to three and opened the front door on Tout Manning. He was wearing a suit that looked to be stitched from the skin of a brown toad that wanted to be red.

"Mr. Manning."

"There was a shootout on a Hundred and Tenth near Central last night," he said. He rushed past me into the house as if he expected to see something I was trying to hide.

"And that has something to do with me?"

Still looking around, he said, "It was that Uhuru Nolicé. He had a gunfight with two cops and then escaped in a dark green 'fifty-seven Cadillac."

"You want some coffee?"

"Coffee? The world's goin' to hell in a handbasket and you're talkin' about coffee?"

"Calm down, Mr. Manning. I got a pot brewing in the kitchen. We can sit out there."

I got him situated in the many-sided dinette and unplugged the percolator from the wall next to the kitchen counter. I poured us both mugs and asked, "You take anything with it?"

"Milk and sugar."

Luckily for him my little girl had gone shopping.

The ritual of stirring the milk and sugar into his brew peeled away Manning's anger only to reveal his rage.

"What the fuck are you doing, Rawlins? I mean what the hell are we paying you for?"

"We? I thought it was Foster Goldsmith footing the bill."

"You know what I mean."

Not really, but I decided to let that slide for a moment.

"I don't know how I'm supposed to stop your own police from shooting it out with a man wanted for kidnapping and murder," I said.

"You're supposed to be finding Mantle before it gets in the papers."

"That's what you say."

"What the fuck is that supposed to mean?"

"The FBI came to my front door and threatened to put me in federal lockup if I so much as thought about Mantle. And the Secret Service was waiting for me outside his mother's door, telling me that Uncle Sam had a deep dark hole for darkies like me."

"What were these agents' names?"

I told him.

"What were they interested in?" he said. "I mean what kind of questions did they ask?"

Manning's heat subsided as he slipped into the role of tactician.

"They wanted to know the same things you did," I told him. "They asked about Mantle and where he might be. They didn't want me to talk to the LAPD anymore at all."

"How did the government find out about you?"

"I guess Foster Goldsmith must've told them?"

"You went to see Goldsmith?" Tout's rage started to rise again.

"Yes I did," I said while staring directly into his eyes.

That was the moment of truth. This was going to be my investigation or the LAPD brass was going to have to find another black man to be their eyes and ears.

The hinges of Tout Manning's jaw became more pronounced and his eyes tightened. Then he took in a deep breath through his nostrils and asked, "What else?"

I considered the question a moment, then two.

"Like I said, the State Department people knew that I had gone to see Stony Goldsmith. I don't believe that they followed me there, so he must have called them. He might have called the FBI too—either that or they got some L.A. cop in their pocket."

"You say the FBI came to your house?"

I nodded.

"You were expressly told to stay away from Goldsmith," Manning said in the false calm of many a commanding officer I had reported to during the war.

"I'm not your soldier, man. You come here and tell me a man's daughter is missin' but you don't want me to talk to him, well . . . shit. I know if my daughter was in trouble I'd like to know who was sniffin' after her."

"What did he say?"

"He didn't even admit that his daughter was missing."

Manning was quiet for a moment after that. He took it pretty well. J. Edgar Hoover and Lyndon Baines Johnson were not enemies that any man in public service wanted to court.

While he was brooding I saw my opening and took it.

"So did any cops get killed last night?" I asked.

"No."

"Was Bob solo?"

"He had a . . . a confederate."

"Who was that?"

"It's not clear."

"Huh. Either Bob or his confederate shot?"

"Maybe. That's not clear either."

"Was it anything like the first shootout?" I didn't know what I was after but there was something missing.

"The first night a call was sent in about a suspicious auto at Pluto's Junkyard on Slauson. The officers called in when they got there, and then nothing until backup came to investigate."

"But three cops got killed?" I said.

"Yes."

"Ain't that unusual? I mean I never see more than two cops in a cruiser unless they on riot duty."

"I don't know what happened there. Maybe they were giving a friend a ride. Maybe it was their lunch break."

"What were their names?"

"Why?"

"I don't know. Usually if a cop investigates a murder he tries to find out who the victim was and why he was killed."

"You're not a cop," Tout told me, "and you're not being paid to investigate any murder."

"How many men were involved on Bob's side of the first shootout?"

"No witnesses."

"But you did ballistics tests on the bullets. How many different weapons were used?"

"You're not being paid to ask me questions, Rawlins."

"I got to know what I'm up against and what I can use to find

Bob. If he got a gang then maybe I could get to him through one of them."

"We don't have any information on his confederates," Manning said in a cold voice. "But Mantle was identified as one of two people who robbed a liquor store on La Brea earlier last night. It was because of the getaway car that the officers fired to stop them."

"Did they try to arrest him? Did they say halt before they opened fire?"

"This man is armed and dangerous. There's a shoot-on-sight order out on him."

"But there are no witnesses to any crime except this liquor store robbery."

"There was the shootout last night."

"Your officers shot first."

"That is our prerogative if the man we're after is considered a threat."

"I tell you one thing, man, anybody shoot at me I'm gonna shoot back at him. That don't make me guilty of nuthin' except good sense."

"Is the job too much for you, Ezekiel?"

I had enough trouble with Suggs and his bent girlfriend. I should have bowed out, I should have. But the thought that there was a shoot-on-sight order on a man who might not have been a killer kept me from quitting.

"I need a letter from Frisk saying that he has put me on this case as a private agent."

"That's ridiculous."

"Then I quit."

Manning appreciated the bind I put him in. You could see that he'd like to put out a kill order on me too.

"You stay on the case and I'll call Frisk," he conceded. "If I don't have that letter by tomorrow night you can quit then."

"Thirty-six hours," I said.

"Hopefully it'll be all resolved by then."

"Resolved how?"

"The bad guys in jail and the innocent saved."

I knew I was in trouble because I was being told a fairy tale by a cop.

25

"He's probably right," Melvin Suggs was saying at the dinette table forty-five minutes after I watched Tout Manning drive away in his festive Volkswagen Bug. "I mean if he's giving radical speeches, making incriminating statements, and then he's seen robbing a liquor store, well . . . If it stinks like shit . . ."

I didn't like the way he put it but Mel made a good point. If a man has a gun in his hand and bloody money in his pocket he's probably not an innocent bystander; *probably* not.

"You said you still had your shield?" I asked.

"Yeah. They couldn't take it without definite charges. The union wouldn't allow that."

"So if you called your contact and he told you where this liquor store was, you could go there and ask a few questions."

"If anybody found me doin' that I'd lose my shield for sure."

"Be nice and the guy won't complain."

"I don't see what you can get out of that," Melvin said. His eyes were clear and his voice more or less steady—he had even shaved. "I mean the regular cops already questioned him."

"I'm looking for anything I can about the robbery and about Mantle. I'm not trying to solve a crime. What I'm tryin' to get is some insight into Bob."

"He's a thug. What else you need?"

"Look, Mel, I know you're not used to taking orders from me. And believe me when I say that I don't see myself as your boss-man. I'm just askin' you to do some things. I could be wrong. It might be stupid. But don't worry about any of that. Just know that you're going to make some money and that in the next few days I'm gonna sit you down with your girl."

Suggs didn't think I was looking down on him or trying to reverse roles in some perverse attempt at racial retribution. It was just that he was used to challenging people with the weight of the LAPD behind him. But he was no longer the big man in charge and he needed a humble reminder of that fact.

"What are you going to do?" he asked.

"I'm going to go out and act as if I'm gonna find this Uhuru-Bob and solve the case of the millionaire's missing daughter."

"How?"

"Magic."

Melvin glowered but he didn't complain.

"I got a name and address on that partial license plate you gave me," he said instead.

He handed me a folded-up piece of notepaper that was violet in hue. I wondered as I read the name and address if the stationery was a leftover from Mary Donovan's days in his home.

"If you get a chance will you call me at my office about four?" I asked as nicely as I could.

Melvin grunted. That was the best I could hope for.

After dropping the cop at his car I drove down to Thurman Avenue a few blocks south of Venice Boulevard.

The tiny white cottage was set between two behemoth plaster-slathered apartment complexes; one pink, the other dull emerald, and both shot through with glitter. The little house was maybe twelve feet wide with an extra three feet on either side for a patch of grass on the left and a path on the right. The front door was oak bound by steel straps, and the one window that faced the street had crisscrossed steel bars over it. The little house had no driveway, but instead of a lawn there was a concrete patio where there was parked a dark blue 1954 Studebaker. I went around the car to the solid front door and worked the metal knocker.

"Who's out there?" a raspy and aged but very masculine voice called.

"It's Mr. Rawlins, Mr. Walton."

"Easy?"

"Yes, sir."

I heard three separate locks being disengaged before the door opened inward.

The man revealed was six-four even though he was a little stooped-over. The color-of-sandstone Mr. Walton was long past sixty-five. He was wearing a blue and white cap that had a jutting sunshade. His right hand gripped a single-barrel twelve-gauge shotgun.

Like Goldsmith's bunker, the entrance to the house was reminiscent of the opening to a crypt. There were, I knew, three slender rooms one after another—a sitting room then a kitchen and then the bedroom, where Mrs. Davis Walton spent most of her time reading religious literature and listening to the radio.

"What can I do for you, Easy?" Davis Walton asked.

"I thought we might do some business."

The old man's eyes were watery brown but resolute. His left eye nearly closed, expressing a natural wariness. Coming from Oklahoma and the Depression, Walton was the kind of man who found it hard to put his trust in anything. My advantage was that I had once been his supervisor when he was a custodian in the public school system and I had never tried to shortchange, cheat, or diminish him.

"Well," he said hesitantly. "I was takin' a break anyway. Come on in."

The rooms of Davis's house were all exactly the same size: nine feet wide and eight deep. The sitting room had two cushioned chairs, each with its own TV tray, facing a Philco Predicta television set. Davis once told me that he bought the naked TV tube atop its tower console for eight dollars from a Holiday Inn that was going out of business outside Reno.

"I spent more on the gas than I did on the TV," he'd told me. "But she's a beauty."

The kitchen had a two-burner stove and a yellow table with two chrome and green vinyl chairs. There was a two-door pine-veneered balsa wood cabinet on one wall with a painting of long-haired white Jesus opposite.

"Easy Rawlins comin' in, Ruth," Davis called at the door to the bedroom. "You decent?"

"Come on in," a pleasant female voice called.

Davis was so light-skinned someone from Europe might have mistaken him for a white man, but Ruth was black, not brown. She was a small woman with thinning and completely white hair, sitting at an old-fashioned electric sewing machine. She was doing piecework for one of six dry cleaners that paid her low wage in cash.

The sporadic hum of the Singer was both industrial and comforting.

"Hello, Mr. Rawlins," she said. "It's so nice to see you."

"How are you, Mrs. Walton?"

"The doctor give me three months to live four years ago. Said my heart was held together by Scotch tape and spit. But I'm still here and Davis cain't look for no new wife yet."

"You know I don't want no other woman, Ruthie," rough-voiced Davis crooned. "It done took almost fifty years to teach you how to make a good cup'a coffee."

"How are you doin', Mr. Rawlins?" Ruth said, smiling about the love of her man.

"'Bout the same as you. They have predicted my death just about once a month. But I found that if I go out the back door now and then it messes with the odds."

Ruth had a long face and a beautiful smile.

"Come on out to my office, Easy," Davis said.

He unlatched the three locks on the back door, also oak and banded with steel, and led me out into the yard.

The backyard was eighteen by eighteen feet surrounded by a high pine fence, behind which loomed the apartment buildings on either side and a white one from the back. Like the front yard, there was no lawn, just concrete. In three half-barrel tubs Davis had small lemon, tangerine, and kumquat trees growing. There was also a round redwood table that was shielded by a huge aqua and white parasol.

"I got that umbrella so that people cain't spy on me from their windows up above. You know they always lookin' down tryin' to get some dirt. Some'a the younger ones have jumped ovah and tried to burglarize me but my doors and bars is too much for 'em. An' they lucky at that 'cause if they did get in I'd shoot first with my twelve-gauge and follow that up wit' my forty-four. You know just 'cause I'm seventy don't mean I cain't kill a man half my age."

Davis Walton wasn't seventy. He was more than eighty but had lied to keep his janitor's job past the required retirement age. He'd been lying about his age for so long, he might have believed that he was a younger man.

"Have a seat, Easy."

I sat on one redwood bench and Davis took the other. He was ready to do business—which in the eyes of a man from his generation was somewhat like dueling.

"You still own that cabin out in the desert?"

"Yes, sir. Ruthie been too sick to travel but I go out there now and then to hunt rabbit. You know I appreciate the quiet."

Davis and Ruth were poor people. They were too old to be members of the Social Security system and had spent most of their money raising three sons. She took in piecework and he supplemented that with a small retirement check from the city, and a bank account in which he had squirreled away every excess dime that he'd ever made.

"I need to use your place for a few weeks," I said. "I'll give you four hundred dollars."

"What you mean use it?"

"Five hundred."

"What if somethin' gets broken or damaged?"

"Six hundred and if you find anything less than it was before I stayed there, then just give me the bill."

That was the end of our little talk. Davis took a small brass key from a big ring of keys in his pocket and handed it to me.

"This is for the padlock on the door," he said. "It also work on the generator hut and the outhouse."

I handed him six Ben Franklins and he led me back through the rooms. Ruth was waiting at the front door to shake my hand. Her touch was akin to a blessing but I walked to my car knowing that I was still damned.

26

Detective work, police work, riot duty—these are all inexact practices. Sometimes you might bust the wrong head or arrest the victim instead of the perpetrator.

I know a man named Charles Banning who is in prison to this day for a crime he could not have committed. I know this because he and I were in San Francisco together at the time he was supposed to have raped, robbed, and beaten the young white woman who identified him. I was in the courtroom for the entire three-day trial. I said my piece but the jury, mostly white people, didn't believe me. I could hardly blame them. That girl detailed the crime, identified Chuck, and cried so piteously that I believe a jury of twelve black sharecroppers would have sent him off to jail; maybe even to the gallows.

I try to drive up and visit Charles every other month just so he'll know that I remember; so that he can see his reflection in my eyes and behold an innocent man.

No . . . detective work is not an exact science. Sometimes, even when you do everything right, you come up with the wrong answers.

I was remembering this dictum while walking beside a hedge of poinsettia bushes. It was summer and there were bees working around the blossoms, gathering raw pollen for the master alchemists back at the hive.

I was navigating through a mazelike court of twenty-seven tiny cottage apartments not far from Avalon Boulevard. It was late morning and so most of the residents were either out at work or looking for a job. When I neared unit 213 at the back of the complex I dropped my half-smoked cigarette on the concrete and crushed it underfoot. The light green door of 213 was flanked by trellises that supported hundreds of bright red snapdragon flowers.

I was wearing a dark blue sailor's cap pulled down over my forehead, and sunglasses so dark that the midday world looked like twilight.

Somewhere there was an answer about the intentions and the whereabouts of Uhuru Nolicé. Maybe it was at the liquor store. Maybe this apartment was filled with the light of truth.

Balled up in my right hand was a small leather sack filled with nickels. I knocked with my left and took in a deep breath.

The man who opened the door was four inches shorter, fifty pounds lighter, and at least twenty-five years younger than I. He looked at me wonderingly. Maybe there was something familiar about my jawline or stance from Benoit's Gym.

"Cedric Reed?" I asked.

"Yes?"

"Did you lose your wallet?"

In order to reach behind him to feel for the billfold Cedric had to turn and lower his head, just a little.

Getting as much torque as I could in my hips, I hit him in the left temple with the fistful of nickels. The first blow stunned him; the second sent him stumbling backward and to the floor. If I was Mouse I would have shot him in the knee. If I was Fearless Jones I would have taken my chances with fisticuffs even though Cedric was a professional welterweight boxer.

We all had different ways of dealing with the world. The men who made it were the ones who figured out what worked best for them.

While Cedric floundered on the floor I closed the door and found the pull-cord for the overhead light. I also took a pistol from my waistband. There was blood dripping from the boxer's head and his eyes were rolling around looking for the cause of his sudden inebriation.

"Stay down," I told him.

The loopy boxer turned his attention toward my words like a man grabbing for a rescue line. He looked in my direction but saw little.

"You made me wrong, man," he slurred.

The words might not have made sense in that situation but I knew what he meant.

"Why you shoot at me, brother?" I said, gesturing with my gun hand.

Instead of answering he tried to get up.

I kicked him in the forehead with the heel of my left shoe.

"Oh no!" he cried.

"Stay down and tell me why you shot at me."

"I didn't," he said. "I didn't. I didn't shoot no gun. I was drivin' the car. Bobo the one. Bobo the one that fired. An' he was just tryin' to scare you. . . ."

"Get up in that chair," I commanded.

The small room had four chairs in it. Every one of them was from a different breed of furniture. There was straight-back oak, partially padded walnut, full sofa, and the folding variety made from gray metal piping and dark brown leather. There was a TV tray like at Davis Walton's house but no television at all.

"Get up in the chair," I said again.

When he didn't move I kicked him in the pelvis with the hard toe of my shoe. He squealed from the pain but he got up into the sofa chair. The blood and cries of pain did not move me. Cedric drove the car that carried the gun that could have killed me.

"I need a doctor," he told me when I leveled the pistol at him.

"You gonna need a undertaker you don't answer me quick."

"What you want with me?"

"Why you and Bobo shootin' at me, man? Do I know you?"

"Uhuru Nolicé," Cedric said as if the name alone were a political manifesto.

"Bob Mantle?"

"That's right!" Cedric claimed, coming more than halfway to awareness. "Bob out there standin' up for us."

"Us?"

"Seventeen months, two weeks, and three days ago I was stopped by the cops when I was out in Compton drivin' wit' my girl. They pult me from the car, took out they guns, an' say, 'Niggah, get down on your knees!' Here I haven't done nuthin' an' these men want me to beg in front'a my girl. I couldn't do that. I couldn't get down on my knees. I wasn't even speedin'. I hadn't had one drink. I told them that I was okay standin' an' happy to put my hands ovah my head. An' you know them mothahfuckahs beat me so bad that the next time I saw Elda I was in a hospital bed in three casts. The only reason the judge didn't put me in jail for assault was because I had to be wheeled into the courtroom. So when I hear that Bob Mantle kilt three cops down around where them four pigs done beat me I went out and drank a toast. And if you workin' for them cops I wanna be brave too. I wanna say sumpin' too. We wasn't gonna to kill ya. I hit a bump an' Bobo's aim went off. We didn't even mean to hit your car."

"Who said I was workin' for the cops?"

"Tommy said you smelled bad."

I pulled back the hammer on my gun because Cedric was getting excited enough to make a mistake. That sat him back in his chair.

"Did Bob say that he killed those policemen?" I asked.

"Yeah."

"To you?"

"Not to me personally. He on the run. But Bobo heard it from Angela Dawson who got it from one'a her girlfriends that Bob was on the hunt for the man in blue."

That was how we made myths back then. Something happened and then somebody said something; that story passed from mouth to ear until a whole cloth was woven from smoke and wishes.

"Stand up, man," I said.

Cedric obeyed the cocked pistol.

"Turn around."

"Why?"

"Mothahfuckah, turn around or I will shoot you in the gut."

He obeyed and I fastened a handcuff to his left wrist.

"What the fuck!" He whirled around and I held the barrel of my pistol three inches from his left eye.

"Turn around or die, Cedric."

He hesitated but there was no girlfriend around to impress. I attached the other cuff to his right wrist so that his hands were held firmly behind his back.

"Bobo should'a kilt you, niggah," Cedric said.

"Yeah," I agreed, "and maybe I should kill you—but I won't. What I'm gonna do is leave the key to these cuffs on your front stairs. Wait a minute or two after I go and then you can go out there and figure out how to free your hands."

"You scared'a me?"

"You bettah believe it, C. You'd bettah believe it."

I uncocked the pistol and hit Cedric on the right temple pretty hard with the butt. He went down on his knees and groaned.

I walked out of his house dropping the small steel key on the top stair as I went. I kept half a dozen pairs of handcuffs to use when necessary. I didn't mind losing one pair for a little satisfaction.

27

By noon I had made it to the dead end of Tucker Street, in Compton. I parked on the unpaved patch of land that neighborhood kids used for a baseball diamond after school. Then I struggled through a dense stand of avocado trees, eucalyptus trees, and thorny bushes. After all that I arrived at a yellow door that was crusty with green lichen.

I was ready to knock but the door came open before I could manage that feat.

"Easy," she said.

Mama Jo was taller, blacker, and might have been stronger than I. She was wearing a brown robe that was homespun and heavy. Somewhere around twenty years my senior, Jo came from another era than most other citizens of the modern world. She lived in a realm where true knowledge passed between those that were a part of history, not subjects to it. She was a healer and a seer, a fortune-teller and a repository of tragedy and love. For years she had lived with a black raven, a small cat that looked and acted like it was a lynx, and two armadillos that wrestled day and night.

"Come on in an' take a load off, baby," she said.

The floor was packed dirt and the walls were made from woven straw, adobe, and other, less identifiable materials. I sat in a chair framed by tree branches and fitted with unshaven animal hide. There were no windows in Jo's house but there was always a slight breeze moving through.

Jo sat down on an ancient bench behind which stood her alchemist's table piled high with hand-blown bottles and earthen jugs, twigs, blossoms, powders, and various crystals. She had a fireplace, above which was nailed a mantel. There were thirteen thick round candles glowing on that ledge, giving off a good deal of the light in the shadowy room. Thirteen candles that had been skulls the last time I was there.

Jo saw what I was looking at and what I was thinking.

"Coco thought that it was too grisly havin' them armadilla heads an' Domaque's skull on display like that," she said. "So I had Martin Martins come out here and build me a little shed out back to hold D and his friends."

Domaque Sr. was Jo's husband, the love of her life, who had died young. She'd named her unspeakably powerful and deformed son Domaque Jr. Jo loved both men, dead and alive, more than the ground any prophet ever trod upon.

"That's why I came," I said.

"To see the vault?"

"Helen Ray," I said. That was Coco's given name.

"Coco, baby," Jo said, raising her voice ever so slightly.

From behind a heavy burlap curtain printed with indecipherable sigils she came. Coco was what the culture of America calls a white woman. In her early twenties she had thick peltlike brown hair and sunkissed skin. She was wearing a raw silk shift that barely came down to her knees. I had once seen her naked but that was only because she was a hippie and didn't mind what people saw. She was as beautiful and potent as Jo in her own way. That was why, I supposed, Jo had taken her on as an apprentice and a lover.

"Hello, Mr. Rawlins," she said in a remote tone. Like many young people who had suddenly changed direction in their lives, she saw the rest of the world as if it were at a distance.

"Coco."

She sat down on the table's workbench.

"What can we do for you, Easy?" Jo asked.

Coco shifted closer to her.

"I need to find out some information up in Santa Barbara and Coco here is just the one to ask my questions."

"I'm busy," Coco said, barely even glancing at me. "I have my work here with Jo and I'm studying for the SATs to get into UCLA. I'm going to do premed."

"Coco," Jo said in a tone that could have been the double beat of a steel hammer on a helpless iron nail.

Moving only her shoulders, Coco shied away from the witch.

"The only reason you here is because'a Easy. The only reason you know me is because'a him."

"He didn't bring me here for you," Coco argued. "He just wanted to help that boy. *I* was doing *him* a favor."

I could have been a fly on the wall or maybe on the other side of the wall, as far as their argument was concerned.

"You been in this house wit' me for six weeks, Coco, an' you still don't know that everything in the world depends on everything else. You ask me to teach you but then refuse to learn."

"That's not true."

"Easy Rawlins is my best friend in the world an' here you cut your eyes away from him an' say you ain't got the time."

Coco took in a breath as if she were about to say something, but there was nothing to say.

"When my friend come in here an' ask for sumpin' I give it," Jo added. "I give it because he have never refused me since he was younger than you are now."

For a moment I remembered the sweaty evening when Jo showed me that I really didn't know anything about physical love. She was the first woman since my mother who proved to me that I wasn't alone in the world.

"I'm sorry, Mr. Rawlins," Coco said softly. "What can I do for you?"

"I need you to talk to some people for me," I said, "college students up at UCSB. You need to look half-hippie and half student."

"Most of my clothes are in storage up at Terry's."

The first little while on our trip from Compton to the hills above the Sunset Strip, Coco was turned toward the window, looking out on the streets of L.A.

Her youthful, gorgeous body reminded me of something I had almost forgotten after my near-death experience some months earlier. But it was her staring out the window that grabbed my imagination.

Since I moved to L.A. in the late forties, the center of my life had moved from sitting rooms and street corners, booths in bars and cafés—to cars. I was always getting into or out of some automobile as a passenger or driver. A big part of my life was spent getting the keys for or driving my car. My constant friend was the radio, and most of my conversations were not face-to-face but side by side in the front seat or through the rearview mirror of some jalopy that I would drive until it gave out and I had to buy a new one.

I was like some kind of futuristic hermit crab being carried by my temporary husk from place to place rather than feeling the sun on my head or my feet on the ground.

"I didn't mean to be rude to you, Mr. Rawlins," Coco said when we were nearing our destination.

"Come on now, girl. I know when I'm bein' shined on. You wanted me gone."

"And I'm sorry for that."

"Then I accept your apology."

"So what is it you need me to do?" she asked, the past forgotten.

I told her about Rosemary Goldsmith, Bob Mantle, the LAPD, FBI, and State Department.

"The only reason I took the job was so I could send Feather to that school," I said at the end of the tale.

"So you want me to ask around and find out where she lived?" Coco asked.

"I'll be close at hand," I said. "Jo would string me up if I got you hurt."

"How long have you known Jo?"

"I met her in 'thirty-nine," I said, "twenty-eight years ago. She hasn't hardly changed a bit."

"I'm in love with her."

"Yeah."

"Do you think there's something wrong with that?"

"No."

"Then why did you say it like that?"

"Helen," I said. "I don't prejudge people and I don't judge 'em. You're a free woman in the free world. Whatever it is you want, that's just fine by me. And you know I wouldn't even think about criticizing Jo."

I was pulling up into a driveway cut through a huge hedge in front of a cockeyed mansion on Ozeta Terrace. Terry Aldrich's big house was built slowly and over time by a dozen or more architects. It was both round and square, with pieces missing and additions tacked on. Terry was a young man, seventeen and quite ugly. His rich father had moved back east and sent his son regular checks so that Terry could finish high school while they lived separate lives.

"I guess I'm just a little sensitive," Coco said. "I've never been with a woman before. I feel like everybody is looking down on me."

"I'll pick you up in the morning at eight?"

"What are we going to do up there?" she asked.

"I don't know. I guess we could start by you going to the registrar's office and telling them that Rosemary is your cousin or something. I have her picture. You could go to the student center and ask around if the administration turns us down."

"Why can't you go yourself?"

"Yeah," I said, "right. I'll pick you up at eight."

28

I got back to my office at twelve minutes past three. That gave me time to sit without watching out for some two-ton steel automobile ramming into me; time to sit in a chair that wasn't vibrating.

I read the newspaper for relaxation as much as anything else.

The Buddhists in Saigon couldn't winnow down civilian opposition to a single opponent against the military strongmen Thiệu and Kỳ. Two U.S. bombers had been shot down over China; the U.S. government claimed that they went off course after a bombing mission in Cambodia. In Santa Barbara, 782 people had signed a public petition against the war. The McCone Commission had reported to Governor Ronald Reagan that "the most serious and immediate problem facing the Negro . . . is the lack of employment." A young black man had been convicted for draft evasion but failed to show up for the decision. Another defendant failed to show up for prosecution in an anti-war march in Century City. Mace, the chemical paralyzer, was used for the first time to quell Negro disturbances in New Haven, Connecticut. Two Southland soldiers had died in action in Vietnam. And, finally, the Burbank Board of Education set the high-school miniskirt limit at two inches above the middle of the knee.

There was nothing about a liquor store robbery on La Brea.

When the phone rang I was thankful for the distraction.

"Easy," Melvin Suggs said before I could muster a hello.

"How's it goin', Mel?"

"Crazy as a motherfucker in a room full'a beauty queens."

"Um." What else could I say?

"Chinese clerk at the liquor store says he was robbed by a woman."

"Not Bob?"

"Oh, Bob was there. He stood at the door looking scared. She had a sawed-off shotgun and pushed it up under Mr. So's jaw."

"What did she look like?"

"Your girl."

Damn.

"And Bob didn't do anything at all?" I asked.

"Just stood with one foot out the door and one foot in. The girl hit Mr. So upside his head and cursed him for being a traitor to his people. Then she stole his wallet."

I was considering the ramifications of Melvin's discoveries more like a lawyer than a private detective. I thought that if Uhuru-Bob made it to court he might have a case against the rich white girl.

"Easy," Melvin said, to bring me back into the conversation.

At that moment the door to my office came open and five very dark-skinned men in bulky suits walked in. It was over ninety degrees outside but they were wearing wool. I recognized three of them.

"I gotta call you back, Mel. Somethin' just came up here."

I cradled the phone and got to my feet just as the leader approached the desk.

This elegantly dressed and handsome killer smiled at me. His skull was oblong, making me think of some evolved species of human. But I wasn't fooled—Art Sugar was as primitive as a man could be.

"Easy Rawlins."

All of the men were wearing dark suits and shiny black shoes. Two of them sat on my blue sofa; another, Jess Johnson, perched on the walnut visitor's chair to the right. Art took that chair's mate, and Whisk Hill stood sentry behind him.

I waited a moment and then reseated myself. I considered reaching for the pistol wired under my desk drawer but nixed the notion.

Art Sugar was the top thug in South Central that year. He and his four associates ran roughshod over the majority of small-time hoods and held the grudging respect of the tougher class of crook. Almost everybody gave Art and his men their due.

And if Mouse was right he was the man that had slaughtered three officers of the Los Angeles Police Department.

He smiled and waited.

"Art," I said.

"You an' me can be truthful with each other, right?"

"I don't know about that," I said. "Sometimes the truth hurts."

That put some teeth into Sugar's smile.

"I got a man in the po-lice department, Seventy-seventh Street precinct," he said. "He tells me that the Crenshaw precinct has reported that you were involved in a shootout ovah thataway."

"Not me."

"He's lyin'?"

"The term *shootout* implies at least two guns."

"In what?"

"There was just one gun and it was firing at me. In order for it to have been a shootout I would have had to shoot back."

"Uh-huh." Art didn't have a proper education and felt a little intimidated when people used language he didn't understand. You couldn't do it too much but a word dropped here and there might help give you the upper hand. "The thing is I don't care about who was shootin' and who wasn't. But I heard that you was in Benoit's Gym lookin' for Battlin' Bob Mantle."

I didn't say anything because there was nothing to say—yet.

"Listen here, Easy Rawlins, I need you to understand something: I'm not afraid of Raymond Alexander."

I tried to keep my look from imparting the deeply held conviction that nobody ever says that they're not afraid of somebody they're not afraid of.

Art sat back and gazed at me. His four men considered me too. All of those eyes were saying that if Sugar wanted me dead right then, or later on, then I'd be dead and that would be that.

"I see myself as a peacekeeper," Art said after our nonverbal roundtable. "I like to keep the peace."

"And me gettin' shot at is not according to your rules?"

"The cops is all ovah the streets lookin' for Mantle. They bustin' up poker games and takin' party girls to jail before the night even starts. They rousted old Jess here when he was just sittin' on his mother's front porch."

"That's right," Jess averred.

"I cain't have that," Art added.

"I don't understand, Mr. Sugar. I asked a question and somebody tried to shoot my head off. What's that got to do with the cops up in your business?"

"I know what's goin' down, Easy," he said. "I know that rich girl got kidnapped and that the police think it's got to do with them cops got slaughtered in that junkyard. My man at the Seventy-seventh told me that much. But let me tell you somethin', brothah: If you and Mouse think you can score on this shit while my business goes to hell you got another think comin'."

Art was like a wild horse seeing threats behind every bush, smelling it on the breeze. I had to think of something to say that would calm down the situation.

"Raymond's not even in town, man," I said. "He's gone for a few weeks and I was just lookin' for Bob because his mother wants to know where he's at."

In my opinion this was just the right balance of truth and prevarication.

"I don't budge, Easy," Art said.

Before Art took over the wrong side of the street, a rawboned Mississippian named Brown held that position. Brown made the mistake of telling Mouse that he had to pay a tithe on his various liquor hijacking gigs. This demand led to a true shootout that left three dead and one wounded. Brown was among the deceased.

That was when Raymond decided to make a full commitment to the national heist syndicate.

All of this was before Art Sugar came on the scene but he, Sugar, was still worried that one day he'd have to square off with my friend.

"I'm not pushin', brother, and neither is Raymond. I just asked a question and they got mad. They overreacted, that's all."

"You know where that white girl is?" the gangster asked.

"No, sir."

"What about Bob?"

"I hear he got in a firefight with the police down on a Hundred and Ten and Central last night. He's prob'ly bleedin' to death in some flophouse right now."

This was news to the cop-killer and that was a good thing.

"How you know that?"

"I got friends on the force too."

"They shot him?"

"Think so."

"So you not lookin' fo' him no more?"

"They asked me down at his mother's church, the Good Shepherd, to find her son. I will still try to do that but I'm just lookin', not stirrin' no pot."

"I won't budge, Easy."

"And I won't push."

"If you find Bob I want you to tell me before you tell his mother, the police, or the Lord," he added.

Our eyes were on each other. Sugar was waiting for the right answer and I was counting the seconds that he would think necessary to consider that answer.

"If I say okay does that mean I'm workin' for you now?"

"No, brothah," he said. "It means you workin' to keep yo'self healthy."

After a moment we both smiled. Then he got to his feet and sauntered out of my office. His cohorts followed suit and soon I was alone again.

I locked the door and went to sit on the blue sofa.

It struck me that I was very calm for a man who just had a brush with death. You would think that being in close proximity to a man like Art Sugar was enough for me to change my life so that I would be safer and live longer. And that would have been true if it wasn't for John Smith.

John was a shipbuilder, a churchgoing one-woman man, married with three beautiful children. He attended Regent's Baptist on Sunday mornings and Wednesday nights and never so much as stole a penny.

One day John was walking down the street with his wife, Jane, when his minister, Dorothy Saunders, called out hello from a passing automobile. John turned to wave, took a misstep, and fell to the curb, cracking his skull on the granite edge.

It was a fatal blow but poor John wasn't blessed with a quick death, no. His brain swelled up in its casing and he never slept, much less lost consciousness. He went mad in an isolated hospital ward, cursing and biting and spitting at anyone who came near. His last words were a curse for God and everything in His kingdom.

Fifteen minutes after the gang of thugs had left my office I was walking down the western staircase remembering John Smith; certain that Death stalked every man at its own pace.

29

"Mr. Rawlins?" a man said. There was an odd accent to his words. It wasn't Asian or European, New World Spanish or cop, certainly not Black American. The intonation was something like slanting sunshine or a stiff wind.

I turned to see a man with the skin coloring of a copper penny that had been a couple of years in circulation, and straight black hair that was too long for office work but nowhere near hippie. Somewhere in his thirties, the man had dark eyes that seemed to contain centuries. He was maybe five-ten and strong the way good rope is—slender and knotted.

"Yes?" I said as the aboriginal American approached me.

"My employer, Mrs. Foster Goldsmith, would like to have words with you."

"And you are?"

"Teh-ha, but people call me Redbird."

"Any particular species?"

That got the man named Redbird to smile. I could tell by the cast of his face that this was not a common occurrence.

"The words *spirit* and *species* have much in common," he said.

Teh-ha Redbird wore crinkled but shiny black leather shoes, well-laundered black cotton slacks that had been ironed that morning, and a long-sleeved white dress shirt that was buttoned at the wrists and up to the neck but sported no tie. He was, I could tell by looking at him, more deadly than Art Sugar and all his men put together.

"What does Mrs. Goldsmith want?"

With a slight gesture of his head he told me that he didn't know or, at least, wouldn't say.

"And when is this meeting supposed to happen?" I asked.

"I can drive you there now." It came to me that he spoke English like a language learned by some erudite foreign scholar.

He gestured down the street, where I saw parked the King of Cars: a late-model dark gray Rolls-Royce Silver Shadow. There were five or six gawkers already hanging around the automobile. I wondered if there had ever been such a fancy vehicle parked on that particular block.

"I got my Dodge," I said. "It's parked a few cars behind yours."

"Then you can follow me."

There didn't seem to be much room or reason for argument, so I went to my car and Redbird to his. When the small crowd saw him coming they parted without rancor or even the hope of getting a ride. Redbird's regal bearing demanded such obeisance.

We wended our way on surface streets from the black environs back to Wilshire Boulevard, downtown. We came to a comparatively small but elegant hotel called the Dumbarton. I could tell by the address that we were only eight blocks away from Light Lambert's anonymous office building.

Redbird pulled his fancy car up to the entrance, where a nylon red carpet connected the front doors of the hotel to the curb. I pulled up after him and got out.

"Yes, sir?" a good-looking, sandy-haired young white lad asked. He wore the gray pants, silky blue shirt, and red vest uniform of the Dumbarton's valets.

"I'm with him," I said, pointing at Teh-ha, who was waiting for me at the doors.

"Oh," the reedy young man said.

"The key is in the ignition," I told him.

When I strolled up to my guide he turned and walked into the sumptuous hotel.

I followed.

The ceilings were high and the colors all royal and drenched. The paintings looked to be original nineteenth-century oils done by artists who you could find in books but not, as a rule, in your larger museums. There were still lifes and portraits and landscapes. I remember one huge canvas that was mostly grays and blues rendering a large ocean-side port crowded with great galleons and sleek schooners. It made me momentarily homesick for Galveston.

Redbird and I were the subject of many stares from the white patrons and multiracial staff of the hotel but no one spoke to, much less molested, us. We made it to the gilded elevator doors and Redbird pressed the button.

"Mr. Redbird," a man said in such a way as to demand attention, not to greet or recognize.

The white man was thin except for a slight paunch. His dark blue suit cost more than most Americans made in a month and half (before taxes), and his mustache was thin enough to slice bread. His authoritative posture suggested to me that he was an ex-policeman but not a beat cop. I would have bet for most of his career he'd been an officer, maybe even a captain. He'd retired and now worked directly for the rich people that had bought special favors from him when he was in power.

"Just Redbird," my guide replied.

"Who's your friend?"

"Mrs. Goldsmith's guest."

"Her guest?"

A silvery bell chimed and the elevator doors opened, making a sound like the sigh of a satisfied lion.

"After you," Redbird said to me.

"Floor?" the elevator operator asked. But when he saw Redbird he said, "Oh, penthouse."

The elevator door opened on a small dais of a room—nine feet square. With the lift behind us, a closed door ahead, the only furnishing was a marble stand on which stood a vase packed with a few dozen long-stemmed yellow roses.

Redbird surprised me by knocking on the door to the penthouse suite. I had expected him to press some button or maybe use his key.

A moment later the fancy, carved mahogany door swung inward and a young Japanese woman wearing a little black dress and white gloves bowed as her ancestors had done for centuries, and backed away for us to enter.

The room we entered was huge. More than a thousand square feet, it abutted upon a glass wall beyond which was a patio half again the size of the room we were in. The ceilings were almost the height of Light Lambert's double-floor office and the furnishings were expensive beyond the imagination of the ordinary upper-middle-class citizen.

I don't have the most educated eye but I recognized the styles of furniture from seventeenth- and eighteenth-century paintings; mostly wood with royal blue and deep red fabric here and there.

In a large chair with its back turned to the window sat a medium-sized middle-aged white woman with black and gray hair that formed naturally into ringlets. Her beauty was accented by a careless indifference. She wore a one-piece cream-colored dress that would be unremarkable anywhere but in a room where only gowns and service uniforms belonged.

She stood as I approached her and I thought that she seemed like an aging Greek deity; the mother of Titans and grandmother to gods.

"Mr. Rawlins, ma'am," Redbird said dispassionately.

"So pleased to meet you." She held out a hand and so I shook it.

"Nice place," I said.

"Have a seat."

Redbird pulled up a chair that was nicely formed but certainly inferior to Mrs. Goldsmith's throne. They held us at the same height, though, and so I wasn't insulted.

"Mr. Hodge called," the lady said to the Indian.

He did not respond.

"He said that he asked you a question and you refused to answer," she continued.

"I answered everything he asked," Redbird said.

"I've told you before that I need you to be courteous to the staff."

"I give as I get, ma'am."

At that moment a man from south of the border, possibly Mexico, came up to my chair. He was wearing a tuxedo and a starched white shirt held together at the throat by a hand-knotted black bow tie.

"May I get you something to drink, sir?" he asked with no discernible accent.

I was wondering how old a cognac I could get in a room like that. But I knew better.

"No, thank you."

The butler looked to the lady. When she shook her head, ever so slightly, he nodded and left the room.

"You can go too, Teh-ha," she said.

Thirty seconds later we were alone in the makeshift throne room.

Neither of us spoke for a minute or two but the silence wasn't uncomfortable. It was a lovely room with a regal woman who surrounded herself with people of color. Maybe this was some kind of inverse racism but it didn't bother me—not at that moment anyway.

"My daughter is trouble, Mr. Rawlins," she said, ending our respite of bliss.

"It would seem so. Does she have any siblings?"

"An older brother, Clyde, who lives in Verona, and a younger sister, Angelique."

"Where's she?"

"Staying with my parents in Concord, Mass.," she said with faint distaste in her voice. "But it's only Rosemary who's troubled. She is my blood, however, and I will do what is necessary to keep her safe. I won't have her martyred for my husband's simplistic sense of patriotism or because the police want some kind of revenge." Virulent vituperation, even raw hatred, crept into her tone.

"How did I even get here, Mrs. Goldsmith?" I asked.

"Because you're looking for Rose and I want to make sure that you help her."

"Who told you that I'm looking for your daughter?"

"My husband runs the weapons manufacturing company. It is even named after him, but it is my family that owns the majority stock.

Even though Foster and I live apart, there are people who work for him that report to me."

"I see."

"What do you think about the accusations against my daughter and this Bob Mantle person?"

"They had nothing to do with the armored car robbery or the first shootout with the police, I'm pretty sure about that. The killing of the vice principal was probably somebody else but the liquor store robbery—"

"What robbery?"

I gave her the account I got from Melvin.

"Oh, no," she said whenever her daughter was mentioned.

I ended with, "I'm sorry to be the one to have to tell you these things, Mrs. Goldsmith."

"Call me Lenore, Mr. Rawlins."

"My name's Easy."

"Easy," she said with a sad smile. "Easy, tell me what else you have learned about Rosemary."

As a rule I don't tattle about my clients' business to others. But in this case I wasn't even sure who it was I was representing. Foster denied it and Frisk and Tout said that the money came from somewhere else. So I told Lenore about the various branches of government, Belle Mantle, her husband's denial about hiring me, and also the ambush that took out my windshield.

"Are you a brave man, Easy?" she asked after hearing about the failed bushwhacking.

"I'm scared of bee stings, back-alley beatings, and bullets too."

She smiled. "That's very sensible. I need a sensible man representing my daughter in this thing. Will you be that man?"

"Sure." I liked the idea of having a client that I could see. "But I can't promise the results you might like."

"I just need a wedge against anyone trying to harm Rose. She's trouble but not really bad. How much will you charge?"

"I think in a case like this I'll give a sliding rate."

"What does that mean exactly?"

"If I bring Rosemary home and the cops don't come after her I'll ask twenty-five thousand. If I bring her back in one piece and she has to go to court but gets off easy I'll ask fifteen. If the courts slam her then it's only ten."

"And if you can't save her?"

"Then you won't owe me a thing."

These last words seemed like a pronouncement; so much so that Lenore Goldsmith lowered her head for a moment. But when her face raised up it was clear and strong.

"What do you need from me?" she asked.

"Some basic information about where she lived in Santa Barbara and the names of any people who might have some knowledge of her whereabouts, habits, and the like."

"You will have it," she said by way of agreement. "Teh-ha will be my contact with you."

"Good. I like him."

30

After maybe forty-five minutes of questions and note-taking, Lenore called out, "Teh-ha."

A minute and a half later the rich woman's wrangler appeared.

"Make sure that Mr. Rawlins, Easy, can reach you at any time. Give him anything he needs."

"Yes, ma'am."

The man calling himself Redbird walked me to the front door of the penthouse suite and handed me a business card on which was printed four Los Angeles–area code phone numbers, one from the Bay Area, and another from Boston.

I was surprised that this man had a business card. This I realized was a kind of adopted chauvinism that had been inculcated in me by American TV, books, newspapers, and a deeply flawed education. I mean, why wouldn't Teh-ha Redbird have a business card?

I scribbled what numbers I had on the back of one of his cards.

"I'll be here in Los Angeles unless I get in touch," he said and then he hesitated. He looked at me for a moment, gauging something. Coming to an unspoken conclusion, he held out a hand for me to shake.

This gesture felt like the unasked-for absolution from a bishop in a religion I had never heard of.

There was a huge tentlike open-air marketplace on Florence at that time. They sold fresh vegetables, fruit, and fish. It was out of my way but I had standing plans for Wednesday nights, and so I went there and bought eighteen filleted sand dabs, a pound and a half of cranberries, and a bag of oranges.

I got home by six. Feather was there reading some magazine in the living room.

"Jackson call?" were my first words to her.

"Him and Jewelle will be here at seven thirty."

"And Bonnie?"

"She had to take a friend's place on an overnight flight."

"How about your brother?"

"He'll be early as usual unless Bennie has trouble with Essie."

"Okay."

I turned toward the kitchen of the house that was yet to be a home.

"Dad?"

"Yeah?"

"Can we find out where my mother's mother and her son are?"

"You mean your grandmother and uncle."

"Yeah, I guess."

"Just as soon as I'm through with this case, baby."

Carrying the load of thoughts both pedestrian and deep, I started cooking.

First I put the cranberries in a pot of boiling water with a cup filled with equal portions of white and brown sugar and the grated peel of two oranges. Then I took out a two-quart plastic container of cooked collard greens, garnished with salt pork, from the freezer. (I had moved the entire contents of the freezer from the old house to the new in a Styrofoam cooler.) I used a butter knife to wedge the greens out of the container and put them in a pot on a low heat. I put three cups of white rice in another pot, added five cups of water, a teaspoon of salt, and three tablespoons of sweet butter.

While the side dishes were cooking, I cracked six eggs into a Pyrex bowl, mixed them a bit, and threw in the fish. Then I dredged the dabs in seasoned cornmeal and melted a big dollop of lard in my largest cast-iron skillet.

After all that, I sat down in the dinette and breathed a sigh of relief. Cooking calmed me. I was waist-deep in murder and kidnapping, my daughter was asking for knowledge that might break her heart, more cops than I had ever dealt with were looking into my life, and that wasn't all of it. But making a simple dinner for my family and friends put it all at bay for the moment.

Poor men understood that a brief respite now and again was the best we could hope for. Modern-day, university-trained philosophers studied existentialism; we lived it.

I sat in the little eight-sided room and Feather stayed where she was, knowing instinctively when I needed to be alone. Now and then I tended my pots and pans, appreciating how the steam and scents were in their own way seasoning the house for me and my girl.

The doorbell rang after that long span of quiet.

"It's Juice," Feather called out as she opened the front door.

"Set the table in the dining room," I said to my daughter for the first time ever.

"Okay," she replied as if it were a request I had made every day of her life.

By the time Jackson Blue and Jewelle had arrived, the sand dabs had fried to a golden color. I served the plates in the kitchen and Jesus carried them into the first dining room that I ever had.

The long room was somewhat bare except for the twelve-foot cottonwood table and chairs that I had bought years before and stored in my garage. It was a good deal but my little house hadn't been big enough to accommodate the length.

Feather had poured Jackson a shot of whiskey from a bottle that he'd brought with him. There were two strawberry rhubarb pies that Benita brought from a bakery I liked down in Venice.

"How's it goin', Easy?" Jackson shouted when I came into the room.

"The wrong direction down a one-lane, one-way street," I replied.

He laughed so loudly that little Essie got scared and began to cry.

Jewelle and Feather were whispering to each other. Jesus was already eating.

"Damn this fish smell good," Jackson said. "You know only a Louisiana boy know how to fry fish like this."

I sat down to eat and Feather and Jewelle went out to the kitchen, where they prepared three pitchers of water with ice cubes and a slice of lemon dropped into each.

When she put a water jug down in front of me I glanced at Jewelle and saw something odd in her face; not quite a grimace or a smile, a thought maybe—maybe not quite.

The conversation, as usual on Wednesday nights, was dominated by Jackson regaling us with hilarious stories of the old days when we were struggling to make the rent. He didn't tell the worst tales but there were some adventures.

He was recounting the story of how a woman named Coretta got mad at her boyfriend for fooling around, but because he wasn't there and Jackson dropped by the house she pulled a pistol on him. There was more to the story than just that but it was enough even to make Jesus smile.

I was thinking about women and jealousy when it struck me.

"Jewelle, are you pregnant?"

The tiny real estate dynamo looked up in shock.

"How did you know, Easy?" Jackson asked for her.

"Something about the way she looks at things," I said. "I don't know."

Feather grabbed Jewelle and hugged her but Jewelle was still staring at me with something like fear in her eyes.

The conversation was mostly about babies after that. Benita had a lot to say and Essie started laughing as if she understood that the topic had turned to her and her kind. We finished the meal and then did damage to the pies. Jackson, Juice, and I cleared the table while the women talked about motherhood, marriage, and men.

I washed the dishes and Jesus rinsed and dried, as usual. Little Jackson jumped up to sit on the far end of the sink, where he kept us company.

"What you workin' on, Easy?" he asked me. "For real."

I told him, with very little editing, about Rosemary, Uhuru-Bob, and all the various players in the confounding case.

"You wouldn't happen to know Mantle, would you, Jackson?"

"Only to see him box. You know he was a man just wouldn't stop comin'. I never met 'im but I bet I know how you could find him."

"How?"

"It's a black man hooked up with a white girl, right?"

"Yeah."

"Then you bettah believe that there's a black girl somewhere mad as hell. She knows things about Bobby that nobody else do and she's willin' to talk about it too. You know I'm right."

And I did, too.

After the dishes were done, Jackson took a filtered Kent cigarette from the pack in his shirt pocket.

"Not in the house, Jackson," I said.

"Why not?"

"I decided I wouldn't smoke in a house where I was raising a child. I don't know. It just seems kinda dirty."

Jackson stared at me a moment and then sighed.

"Okay," he said, "but I need me a smoke, so I guess I'll go out in the street."

"Me too, Blue, me too. But let's go out in the backyard. You comin', Juice?"

"No, Pop. I'm going to take Essie from Bennie for a little while." He glanced at Jackson and then turned full to me and asked, "Are you all right?"

He asked because if I was in trouble he would do anything to help me; he was just that kind of man—had been since he was six or seven. His concern meant more to me than a loaded gun. It was knowing how close we were that had kept me alive through many a bad time.

"Yes I am, son," I said. "It's a tough case but after that shooting I'm workin' it from the sidelines."

"You sure?"

I clapped my son's shoulder and said, "Come on, Jackson, let's go fire up some cancer sticks."

31

There was a wide round white table cast from some kind of synthetic concrete on the lawn of the backyard. Jackson found an outside switch and flipped on the floodlight I hadn't known was there. Three curved white benches made from the same artificial material surrounded the table. I took the bench facing the house but Jackson sat on the tabletop. He lit our cigarettes with a single match and for a moment we both experienced the elation of that first drag after a few hours.

"Congratulations," I said to my brilliant, cowardly, endlessly funny friend.

"Yeah," he replied, as if I had asked if his condition was terminal.

"You don't sound too happy."

Jackson sighed again and swiveled around to look down at me.

He had never been a handsome man. Skinny and scared for most of his life, Jackson had had the look of some kind of abused animal whose survival was dependent on the creatures that tortured him. But as the years rolled by a certain something, a kind of character, had formed where before there was only abject fear.

I knew a man in Houston who used to tell me, *It's true when they tell ya a man don't change. But he do get older and sometimes he grow into who he is and becomes a man don't look nuthin' like he used to.*

"What's wrong, Jackson?"

He sighed and took a drag off his cigarette, exhaled the smoke like some minor demon, and groaned again.

"'Bout three months ago Jean-Paul aksed me to come out to the marina to talk business on his boat. He do that pretty often. We was out there drinkin' good wine and talkin' 'bout how satellites one day might be able to transfer computer data at high speeds an' he wanna get into that. Because you see, Easy, all computer information is in what they call a binary format and you could translate anything into that simple language. And so we was—"

"What about why you so sour, man?" I asked to cut him off. When Jackson started talking about the technical side of his job he could go on for hours.

"Yeah, yeah, yeah," he said. "You right. You right. Jewelle always say that she can tell when I'm bothered by somethin' 'cause I start talkin' physics and math."

"And so?"

"Pretty Smart and her girlfriend Tanya Anika come out to the boat in the afternoon. JP had give Pretty a free pass to get on his boat anytime she wanted and I guess she come out with her girlfriend to get a tan.

"JP likes good-lookin' women. You know what Pretty look like and Tanya even finer than her—figure like a maple brown *Playboy* model and face that old boy Adonis might get distracted by."

"And?" I said to keep the story going.

"We was up near the wheelhouse talkin' and drinkin' and the girls went down on the lower deck right below us. Nobody could see in, so they took off all they clothes to lie in the sun. You know I was sweatin' but I had made up my mind to be good. Then Pretty called up for JP to bring 'em some wine. He brought me down to the wine cellar he got on the boat—"

"There's a wine cellar on his boat?"

"It's a big boat, man, almost a ship. Anyway he had four choices and so aksed me to help him bring 'em to the girls. Shit. Before you know it JP and Pretty was down in his cabin and Tanya sidled up next to me. . . ."

"Nobody could hardly blame a man for that, Jackson," I said. "I mean, damn. On a yacht drinkin' wine and a beautiful naked girl come up on ya?"

"My uncle Reynard used to tell me," Jackson said, "that there wasn't nuthin' in life for free. He was right about that. I got together with Tanya a couple'a times but when it started to get serious I explained about Jewelle. I told her that I would not leave my woman. But you

know, Easy, when a black woman meet a brothah on a yacht and finds
out that he brings down a hunnert and fi'ty thousand dollars a year—"

"That's how much you told her you made or that's really how much
you make?"

"That's the base. I didn't even tell her about my bonuses."

Damn.

"And so she was mad about Jewelle?" I asked.

"She knows a woman who knows another girl that works for Jewelle.
Somehow through that pipeline they let JJ know what I been up to. I
tried to explain. I was halfway successful 'cause she didn't th'ow me
all the way out the house. It took me a week to move back in our bed,
though.

"But in the meantime she was so mad that she had a thing with that
Percy Bidwell. She don't know I know but when she got together with
him it was at a Hollywood hotel I know pretty good 'cause JP go there
sometimes. JP's driver was in there with a business client and he saw
'em."

"What you gonna do?" I asked.

"It ain't that, Easy. I get why she did it but now she's all upset and
Percy pushin' on her to get you to help him. I'm pretty sure he's threat-
enin' to tell me about them bein' together."

"But you already know."

"But she don't know that and I'm afraid that if I tell her she'll get all
crazy again just thinkin' 'bout what happened. An' this time she might
just leave my stupid ass."

I would have laughed but I could see how torn up my friend was.

"Jackson?" Jewelle called from the back door.

"Yeah, baby?"

"Easy out there with you?"

"Uh-huh."

Jewelle, when she was younger, was a plain Jane kind of girl: basic
brown and round-featured, she had a slight figure and no outstanding
attributes. But as she aged there got to be something alluring about her.

"Feather tells me that she's been workin' part-time for the Japanese
people across the street," she said to me.

"Yes."

"I told her that maybe she'd like to see what it was like workin' in an office. I invited her to spend the night and come to work with me in the morning. Is that okay?"

"Sure it is. And you could get some mothering practice in."

Jewelle kissed me on the cheek. There was a tender spot in our hearts for each other.

"Thanks, Easy," she said. "Jackson, we should go. I want to make sure that Feather gets to bed on time."

"I'll be right in, honey."

After Jewelle was back in the house I asked, "The baby?"

"I don't know, man. I don't care. Anything that comes from Jewelle is fine by me."

"You want me to do what Percy wants?"

"I cain't tell you what to do, Ease. I just want him off'a Jewelle and things to be back like they was."

32

Staying alone in the big house was yet another step toward me claiming the new place as my home. The little yellow dog scrabbled around my feet as I wandered the floors. I went through all the rooms, taking mental inventory of space and the things I'd need to make it work. I'd sit on beds and chairs, the stairs, and even on the floor now and then—trying to get different views of the spaces and their potentials.

At one point I sat on the living room couch, then reclined to take in the space from that point of view. I must have been more tired than I knew because I fell asleep there. It was a comfortable rest with only one brief dream of me driving over the side of the ocean cliff.

When I awoke I was sleeping on my side facing the backrest of the sofa. Frenchie had jumped up and over me to nestle between my chest and the cushion. When I got up the dog cracked his eyes at me and decided that the best course of action was to go back to sleep.

After my third cup of coffee and one trip to the backyard to smoke I walked up to the pay phone at Pico and Point View. There I dialed a number.

"Yes?" she said with a sweetness that was laced with fear.

"Belle?"

"Detective Rawlins."

"Have you heard from your son?"

"No, sir."

"I was wondering something."

"Yes?"

"Do you know who his last girlfriend was?"

"There's been a few but the one he always went back to was Sister Godfreys."

"Come again?"

"That's what her mother named her," Belle said, "Sister. She's a very nice girl. I hoped that Bob would marry her and get a job workin' with his hands. But you know he changes girlfriends like some women do shoes."

"Could you tell me how to get in touch with her?"

"I don't know her number, sir. But I'm sure that she's worried about Bob too."

"Hello?" Jackson Blue said on the fourth ring of my next call.

"Hey, Jackson."

"Easy. What can I do you for?"

"Could you and Jewelle keep Feather one more night? My day might get pretty long."

"Sure. Jewelle loves that girl. They sat up nearly all night talkin'."

"Is Feather up?"

"Naw. She still sleep. Jewelle is too. She don't usually go in to work till after nine."

"I'll make sure that Percy leaves you and Jewelle alone, Blue. Don't you worry 'bout that."

"Thanks, Ease. You always come through, man."

Behind the high hedge, in the circular driveway in front of Terry Aldrich's house, I was barely out of the car before Coco appeared carrying two flat seat cushions. She had the pads hugged to her chest and was wearing a one-piece tie-dyed dress that was red, yellow, and green—mostly. She was dressed perfectly for the job.

"Hi, Easy," she said in a friendly tone.

"Hi, Easy," a young male voice echoed.

Coming after Coco was the teenaged hippie who owned the mansion/commune. He was barefoot, wearing jeans and a torn white T-shirt. Terry was tall and thin and ugly. His stringy dirty blond hair came down a foot or so below the shoulder. His nose was bulbous and he'd been scarred by repeated attacks of acne. None of this seemed to bother him, though. He enjoyed his life and seemed somehow blessed with luck while instinctively managing not to be blinded by it.

"Terry," I said.

"I gave Coco my special seat cushions. It'll make your ride easier."

"Okay," I said. I had the manners not to insult a gift, no matter how insignificant.

For most of the drive Coco's palaver was about Jo and how wonderful and smart and transcendent she was.

"She has this paste that she can put on a cut and it heals in less than a day and a half," she said at one point.

"I know."

"You do?"

"Yes, I've known Jo longer than you've been breathing."

I tried not to take away all of her excitement, however. I appreciated new love and also I needed to keep Coco friendly for the task at hand.

The tenor of her talk changed when we neared Isla Vista and the UCSB campus.

"So what do you need to know about this girl, exactly?"

Before I could answer a siren began its wail. The Highway Patrol car was in my rearview mirror reminding me of who I was, whom I was with, and where I could end up if I wasn't careful. While I was pulling onto the shoulder at the side of the highway, Coco got up on her knees in the seat, looked out the back window, and said, "Oh, shit."

"You got any drugs on you?" I asked.

"No," she said in a tentative tone.

"ID?"

"Driver's license."

A few moments later the highway cops were at our respective doors, hands on their guns.

I rolled my window down and said, "Hello, Officer, I wasn't speeding, was I?"

"Get out of the car." I noted that he didn't say *sir* or *please*.

I complied. Coco tried to open her door but her personal policeman said, "Not you."

"Arms up at your side," my cop told me. He was tall and gaunt, white of course, and green-eyed.

He patted me down. I could have gotten him then. With my training I could have kneed him, taken his weapon, turned, and shot his partner before wheeling back to kill him. These thoughts were so real in my mind that they were just an inch away from becoming reality.

"ID," my thin antagonist demanded.

I took my driver's and PI's licenses from my tan jacket pocket. He read both quite closely.

By this time the other patrolman, who was paunchy and shorter, allowed Coco to get out. He was going through her purse and asking her questions that I couldn't make out over the sounds of passing cars on the highway and waves from the surf.

"What are you two doing here?" my cop asked.

"Terry," I said, "my friend from down in L.A., wanted me to give Helen a ride. She's going to stay with some friends of his on an organic farm up here."

Coco and I had decided on this story in between her long and rambling elegy of love to Jo. I was expecting the law to stop us. I'm always expecting that.

"What's the name of this farm?" the cop asked.

"Nugent Farm," I said. I knew from a previous encounter with the hippies that this was where they often got their eggs.

"That was two turnoffs back."

"I realize that now," I said. "We were going to go down to Isla Vista and get there through back roads."

I looked the man in the eye. He hated that. But if I had cast my gaze downward he would have suspected that I was guilty of something. This way all I got was his ire.

"You two go stand over next to the rocks," he said. "Henderson."

"Yeah, Harley?" the other cop answered.

"Watch them while I search the vehicle."

There was a sandstone mountain at the side of the highway. Coco and I waited there while the chubby cop called Henderson stood between us and the car.

Again I worked out a plan to incapacitate my warden, killing him and his partner. If it was nighttime and I was Raymond Alexander they would both most certainly be dead.

The patrolman named Harley searched the front and back seats, investigated the cushions that Coco and I had been sitting on, and every paper in my glove compartment.

"You suck black dick?" Henderson asked Coco.

Harley used my key on the trunk. I held my breath, standing as I was between a rock and a hard place.

The rock was Coco's temper. I'd seen her get angry before.

The hard place was a .32-caliber pistol I had put in the trunk, thinking that the cops, if they stopped me, probably wouldn't look back there.

"I went to this club once in Frisco," Henderson was saying, "where they had this girl younger'n you suck on three black dicks at the same time."

Harley pulled out the leather medical bag I used to carry my piece.

"They came all over her," Henderson continued. "You ever been there? It's called the Black Pussy but they should have called it the White Cunt."

I was beginning to think that a double murder was my only way out of that jam.

"What's this?" Harley said, holding up the leather bag.

"The license is right in there with it," I said, partly relieved that Henderson was distracted from his insults. "California license. Permit to carry but I like to be careful and so I keep it in the trunk."

"Whoa," Henderson said when his partner approached us and pulled the pistol from the bag.

"Has it been fired recently?" Harley asked.

"No."

"Smells like it."

"No, sir. I clean my pistols once a month. You know a dirty gun can blow up in your hand."

My words made Harley's eyes tighten. The fact that I shared some kind of point of view with him caused me to come more into focus than he would have liked.

"Why do you need a gun to give a girl a ride?" he asked. "What she need a detective for anyway?"

"Terry's a friend. And I have the gun because when I get back down to L.A. I'll be on the job for Roger Frisk, special assistant to Chief Parker. Call down there and they will confirm that."

"You have a number?"

"LAPD," I said. "Chief Parker's office."

"Go make the call, Sammy," Harley said to Henderson.

"But, Harl, I was talkin' to the girl. I think she likes me."

"Make the call, Sammy."

Fifteen minutes later we were on our cushions again.

Frisk, or maybe Tout, had told Henderson that he didn't know why I was up there but I was doing a job for him. They let us go but, as had always been the case, I could have spent the next five years incarcerated for real and imagined crimes.

"Did you hear what that fat bastard was saying to me?" Coco said as soon as we were on our way.

"Yes I did."

"I could have killed him."

"If I killed every man who had insulted me and mine I'd be shoulder-deep in corpses from here to Nugent Farm."

"How can you live with people treating you like that?"

"You know, Coco, some questions just don't have answers."

33

We parked in front of an Isla Vista branch of the Bank of America. There I consulted my atlas.

"So we're going to this girl's house?" Coco asked while I perused.

"Yeah."

"But she's missing, right?"

"The police think that she's been missing from her dorm for two weeks or more, but really she's been staying at this house in town. It's a house full'a students and other young people not in school. Her mother told me that she used to have a friend there name of Willa Muldoon. Willa's doing a year abroad. All you have to do is mention that you went to boarding school with Willa at Thurgood Academy for Young Women, and that should get your foot in the door."

"Uh-huh."

"Look, Coco, I don't think this is at all dangerous. I'd just like to find out what they know about Rose, her friends call her that, and maybe Bob Mantle if you can. He's a black man in his early thirties who used to be a boxer and now talks all radical. They might be calling him Uhuru Nolicé."

When I figured out how to get to the address on Rancho Terrace, I put the Dodge into drive and rolled on. We drove no more than a mile in the winding sub-suburban landscape.

I cruised down Rosemary's block, pointing out the house to Coco as we went by.

It was a boxy two-story place that had once been white with green trim. Now the colors were turning gray. The lawn was bare in some places and overgrown in others. There was a brown couch out on the porch, and the front door looked as if it might have always been open wide.

When we'd parked, a block away, Coco looked up and down the street to see if anyone was coming, and, when she was sure that we were alone, she pulled the cushion out from under her and put it in her lap.

"Give me yours," she said.

While I lifted up to get my flat pillow, Coco cut along the seam of hers with a very small, very sharp pocketknife and pulled out a tightly wadded plastic bag of dried, dark green leaves.

"Dope?" I said.

"Uh-huh."

"You said you didn't have any."

"You asked if I had any on me."

"What you need that for?"

"I told Terry that I was going to ask some college students questions for you. He likes you and so he gave me these cushions that he always uses to keep his private stash on trips and stuff. He said I'd make a lotta friends with this."

While she was talking she cut open my pad and pulled out two more packets. These she put into her purple cloth purse/shoulder bag.

"You got that phone number I gave you?" I asked.

"Memorized and written down."

"I might throw these things away now that they're sliced open," I said. "You know if I get stopped again they're bound to ask what was inside."

"Okay." She leaned over and kissed me on the lips.

I took this kiss as a thank-you from a woman who had problems with men. Maybe she saw how I noticed her figure and refrained from making a move.

I drove down to a deserted beach, parked my car in a lot that had a phone booth, took a small bag of change from the doctor's bag in the trunk, and walked halfway to the water, where I plunked down on the packed sand and started rereading, for the sixth or seventh time, *The Grapes of Wrath*.

"Readin' good books is like meetin' a girl you wanna get to know bettah," Jackson Blue once told me. "You don't just have one talk and think you know her. If that was true there wouldn't be no need to get to know more; it wouldn't be worf it. Naw, man, you wanna talk to that girl again and again. You remember her phone number and every time you talk you find out somethin' else. Same thing with a good book. You got to read that suckah again and again and still you findin' out sumpin' new every time."

I liked the way Steinbeck understood the plight of a man displaced by nature and society, men like my ancestors, their friends, and heirs. I enjoyed the preacher best of all because he took that whole struggle up to a metaphysical level. It was the same with my people.

Every hour or so I'd call down to an answering service I maintained in L.A.

"What name?" the female operator would answer.

"Rawlins, Ezekiel."

"Password?"

"Porterhouse." That was my middle name.

"No messages," she said at four, five, six, and seven o'clock.

I paid the premium price for the service so I could have called every five minutes if I wanted.

At five fifteen I got a chill and moved up to the car. I could have kept reading about the Joads and their familiar predicament but there was an unlikely soul station on the radio up there and so instead I listened to James Brown, Little Anthony, Aretha Franklin, and the Supremes while closing my eyes, trying to imagine making some kind of headway on the mostly unwanted case.

I felt like a Bum of the Month throwing his name in the hat for a showdown with the Brown Bomber; a black man in Mississippi hoping for a rendezvous with some crazy white girl; the father of a son called off to fight and die in Vietnam. . . .

At eight o'clock the operator said, "A Miss Helen Ray just called.

She said that you could pick her up where you dropped her off in half an hour."

"At eight thirty?" I asked.

"That's what she said."

"Thank you very much," I said, and then added out of civility, "You must be gettin' near to quittin' time."

"Don't I wish," she said. "Lana got laryngitis and I have to pull a double shift. But at least there's time and a half I can look forward to."

"Maybe you could take a day off," I suggested.

"Maybe I could pay the rent on time for once."

I parked at the very spot where I left Coco off. I sat there for fifteen minutes imagining all kinds of trouble. Maybe she wouldn't come and I'd have to get my pistol and go to the house to pry her loose. Maybe the cops would grab me for suspicious behavior and she'd have nowhere to go. Maybe, maybe she'd get to the car and the cops would find the dope in her purse.

When the knock came on my window I almost jumped; maybe I did a little.

There was Coco in her tie-dyed splendor smiling.

I motioned for her to go around and get in.

As soon as she was in the seat I asked, "You still got that dope?"

"I left it all with them. What about the cushions?"

"In a beachside trash can."

"You worry too much, Easy," she said.

"That's what all my white friends tell me."

"What about your black friends?"

"They say I don't worry nearly enough."

"They sound like the people in that house," Coco said. "They're all revolutionary and stuff. They even got a name—the Lathe of Justice. They say that they set fire to a trash can in front of a police station and are studying guerrilla warfare. There's a couple of Vietnam vets and some students and freeloaders. They talk pretty radical but I don't think they've done that much. Mostly they sit around gettin' high and talkin' about what they should do."

I started the car and pulled away from the curb, not wanting to be a sitting target for the police or the radicals.

"Did they know where Rosemary was?" I asked as we wended our way toward the main drag.

"Uh-uh. She left about a week ago."

"With who?"

"Ten days ago a dealer named Youri brought the black guy up here, the one you were looking for—that Uhuru Nolicé. He told them that Nolicé was being persecuted by the police. Youri left Uhuru with them and he would give speeches in their garage at night. After a day or two he got tight with your girl. Before that she was with this guy Petrie. He acted like he didn't care but you know he was mad.

"Then, just a day or two ago, Nolicé came back but he was wounded. Somebody had shot him."

"Was Rosemary with him?"

"For a minute but then she went back down to L.A. to plan for them to leave the country."

We had gotten to the brightly lit main drag, where there were stores, restaurants, and bars.

"Is he up there now?"

"Uh-uh. Somebody brought him to a place where he could hide but they didn't say who or where to, and I figured that if I asked they'd get all paranoid."

We stopped in front of a coffeehouse from which emanated loud, live folk music.

"So Bob's up here somewhere with a bullet in him," I said aloud.

"And I have a date with that dude Petrie."

"What?"

"I told them that they could have four lids but I had to deliver some more that I had hidden. That's why they let me use their phone. Petrie liked me and told me that if I hitched up to this lighthouse north of Santa Barbara, he knew a good place to go camping. When I told him that I didn't have a sleeping bag he said that we could use his."

"Damn, girl."

She smiled at me and I recognized a kindred spirit.

"I think he knows something about where your Uhuru Nolicé is."

"Can you hang out at this place until a little later?"

"I guess. Why can't I come with you?"

"Man stuff."

"You mean stupid."

"Most probably."

34

Sixteen miles north of Santa Barbara was a turnoff marked by a leaning sign that read FILO'S SANDY HOOK. The winding off-ramp led to another deserted beach. This seaside cove was more hard earth and weeds than sand and shell. Above the ocean was suspended a half-moon that shone brightly in a nearly cloudless sky. Close to the water stood a three-story ruin that had once been a stone and mortar lighthouse. Other than that, there was nothing and no one else around.

I parked behind some coastal shrubbery and made my way to the onetime tower of light that was ever so slowly turning to dust. There was a doorway with no door that led inside to a cracked stone floor and a rusted-out iron corkscrew-shaped stairway that wound upward.

When I entered, a large rodent or maybe a feral cat hustled out through a hole in the wall.

There was no roof and so the inside was illuminated under a steady stream of lunar light relieved here and there by soft shadows.

I lit a cigarette and perched against a ledge that jutted out from the seaward side. Smoking in the tapered stone building, feeling the night chill of the coast, I allowed my mind to go wandering as I waited.

First I thought about the hippie girl who had fallen in love with the backwoods witch. She had come reluctantly to help me but then threw her full energy into the task at hand. She believed in peace and love and helping all people everywhere, but Coco also knew how to seduce a man with sidelong glances and subtle movements.

And then there was our victim, the guy named Petrie possibly looking for a night of passion, or maybe he planned to rob the girl who he thought was a flush dope dealer. Hippies had their crooks too.

It felt as if I were in the middle of a play that I didn't want to be in.

The story was the search for a woman and a man who were not what they seemed. And even though I would have rather been home with my daughter, I was frustrated that I couldn't manage to make definite progress in locating my quarry.

I smiled and lit another cigarette. *Careful what you wish for*, people said every day for probably as long as there had existed *Homo sapiens*. Soon, maybe in an hour, I'd find what I was looking for and wish that I had never made it that far.

My hands were cold. The susurration of the waves filled the air. I didn't have a work a day job. I was paid for my labors but not really answerable to anyone. The path I was on might lead to my death, but I was consoled by the fact that this was true for every human being that had ever drawn a breath, felt a chill, or looked up at the moon.

"Coco?"

It was a hushed call, male and hopeful, coming from just outside the doorless doorway.

I stayed still.

A footfall on the gravel brought a soft-edged shadow into range.

I snubbed out my cigarette against the wall.

Another step and I could see the form of a man entering the husk of a lighthouse. He was somewhere around five-nine, skinny, beardless with long hair that was probably blond, dressed in jeans and a festive, floral-patterned shirt. It was the shirt that told me that he had come there for romance and not robbery.

"Petrie?" I said with an upbeat tone to my voice.

He could have run but instead he came into a pool of moonlight.

"Who's there?" he asked the shadows.

Coming out of the shade, I said, "Coco's friend—Warren Lull," picking a name out of the chilly air.

"Who? Where's Coco?"

I chose that moment to show him my pistol.

He jerked backward, bumping into a wall.

"I could just as well shoot you in the back as in the front," I said, cutting to the quick of our conversation.

"Wha, wha, wha, wha, what you want?"

"Uhuru-Bob Nolicé," I said.

"I don't know who you talkin' about, man," Petrie said, his eyes as big as the moon above our heads.

I leveled the barrel of the pistol so that it was pointing at him. How could he know that the safety was engaged?

"Hey, man!"

"Uhuru Nolicé," I insisted.

"We're pledged, brother. We not s'posed to tell."

"That will be your last pledge."

"I don't know nuthin'."

I raised my gun hand, now pointing at his crown.

He started to weep.

Then I took a calculated risk. I flipped off the safety with my thumb and fired a shot over his head out a window behind him.

It was stupid of me but I was tired of the runaround. I wanted to get somewhere.

"He's in a cabin, he's in a cabin, he's in a cabin we use sometimes for parties." Petrie fell to his knees, crying out loud as he begged.

I felt bad about breaking him down like that. I didn't see myself as a bully or a ruffian but there I was treating my fellowman like he was a dog.

"Get up!" I barked, even while feeling I wanted to console him. "Get the fuck on your feet!"

He was so scared that it took him a moment to find his feet, but then he did as he was told, sobbing.

"You gonna take me to that cabin or I will bury you under this floor."

He nodded and I took out a pair of handcuffs, handing them to him.

"Lock one'a these around one wrist."

He did as I said and asked, "What about the other one?"

"Let's go," I said.

We walked over to where my new-old car was hidden and I had him get into the passenger's side. I worked the free cuff around the chrome handle on the glove compartment, binding him to my Dodge.

"Okay," I said once I was behind the wheel, "which way?"

———

It was an extraordinarily beautiful drive. We turned up into the coastal mountains on a series of graded dirt roads, through a vibrant pine forest made even more exquisite by the light of the moon. On the way I saw an owl in flight and a group of six magnificent tule elk crossing our path.

For the whole ride Petrie rambled and farted.

"It's not my fault we put him up here," he said between directions. "I don't even like the motherfucker. He took my girl and danced around like some kinda faggot in that African dress talkin' all kinds'a shit. It was Theodore and Moondog wanted to help him. They said that he was fightin' the Man but I think it must'a just been some jealous boyfriend shootin' him when he jumped out a window.

"You know I'm from Chicago and we just do what we have to do to survive but I never meant to hurt nobody. And I was just comin' up to meet with that Coco. But I didn't know what she was up to or nuthin'. . . . You know I came out here three years ago because I didn't like the winter. I'm just here for the sun, that's all. . . ."

His blathering had no through-line but, for that matter, neither did his life. I had to open my window because of the flatulence. His cowering made me want to lash out and hit him with the pistol in my hand—I held back, however. I knew that it wasn't his fault. He was in fear for his life and wouldn't have been able to stop himself.

We had driven for forty minutes or so when he finally said, "It's down in that valley. You could pull off the road up ahead."

I drove into a natural recess between the trees and got out. Maybe two hundred feet away and down across a sloping lea sat a lopsided shack with a steady white plume coming out from a smokestack up top. There was light coming through a window. Another car was parked in the recess: a white Ford Falcon.

"He's down there?" I asked.

"Yes, sir."

"Is this his car?"

"No. It looks like Meredith Taylor's."

"Who's she?"

"She lives at the commune."

"What commune?"

"The house where I met Coco at."

I took another pair of handcuffs and attached Petrie's other wrist to a steel bar under his seat.

"If I hear one peep out of you I will come back and put a bullet in your head, do you understand me?"

Nodding, he let out a long, plaintive fart and I walked away, down toward the smoking shack.

35

As I approached the door of the cabin I began to discern a knocking sound: clackety-clack, then a beat of silence before the next clack. One, two, one, space, two—one, two, one, space, two. The rhythm sped up for a few moments then slowed, then sped up again. There came a low feminine moan and I understood what I was hearing.

The door had a rusty iron latch, not a knob, and there was no keyhole. Gun in hand, I slowly depressed the metal handle then let the door swing inward from its own weight. I took a step into the one-room structure, remembering Petrie coming into the lighthouse.

There were three kerosene lanterns placed around the disheveled room. In one corner there stood a big iron bed. Against a sidewall there was a cast-iron woodstove that had an exhaust pipe going into and up the fireplace. Opposite the front door there was a rough dark-wood table. Leaning back, spread-legged on the table, was a chubby white woman. Between her legs, moving at an off-tempo to the beat of the knocking sound, was the naked back of a powerful black man: a welterweight.

"Oh, oh, oh," she said.

"That's it, baby," he answered, "gimme all'a that shit."

The only thing he wore was a bandage around the middle of his left thigh. The dressing was a futile attempt to stanch the bleeding of his wound. It might have worked except for his heart thumping out of control and him doing the shimmy-shake between the girl's lifted thighs.

She sat up to embrace him and saw me over a shoulder.

"Bob!" she shouted.

"I'm right here, mama. I'm right here."

"No! Behind you!"

"Say what?"

"There's somebody behind you!"

The man turned around quickly, which was a mistake for two reasons. First, there was a good amount of blood at his bare feet. This made for a slippery surface. Second, that amount of blood meant that he was weakened, making him unable to control the abrupt momentum and slide of the turn.

So Uhuru-Bob Mantle-Nolicé spun around, skidded on his own blood, and crashed to the floor with a grunt and moan, leaving the young woman with her heels still up on the table ledge exposing the place that he had been literally dying to get at.

"What do you want?" she said, looking from my face to the gun in my hand.

"For you to put on some clothes and get whatever first-aid kit you got so we can bind this fool's wound."

She grabbed a billowy calico dress from a chair, donned it, and then picked up a box from a corner near the table. The box had a big red cross on it but I didn't want to take the chance that there was a pistol in there.

"Leave it closed and bring it over here, then sit down on that chair," I told her.

She did as I said.

"What do you want?" she asked me.

"Who are you?" Bob said on a heavy breath. Now that he was on the floor, the weakness from his exertions was overtaking him.

"Turn over on your side," I said, "on the leg that's not shot."

Bob also followed my commands.

I opened the first-aid box and checked out the contents.

"Come here," I said to the girl. "I want you to pour the alcohol on the gauze and press it against the wound. Wrap the bandage around it twelve times, then tape it. After that, tie another cut of bandage around the leg just above the wound so that it's loose."

They were both addled by the sex and shocked by my sudden appearance in the middle of nowhere, and so offered little resistance.

I looked around the cabin; under the table and in the corners. There were no weapons in sight.

"What now?" she asked when she was finished with the initial dressing.

There was a washbasin on a counter next to the fireplace. I went there and saw a big wooden salad spoon in the drying rack. I took it and returned to the patient and his reluctant nurse.

"Put this under the loose bandage and twist until it's real tight," I said.

On the fifth turn Uhuru-Bob groaned in pain.

"Is the bullet still in there?" I asked him.

"Where else it gonna go?"

"So you were gonna sit up in here fuckin' and bleedin' till you got gangrene and died?"

"My girlfriend went down to get help. She probably comin' right now."

"I don't think so," I told him.

"Why not?"

"Because I'm just not that lucky."

Some private detectives spend long nights in darkened rooms listening to and taking pictures of the people next door; they sit for days parked down the block from the homes of insurance cheats or adulterers, waiting to get just the right incriminating photograph. Some upscale gumshoes are little more than accountants who go through thousands of pages of financial transactions until they find the one entry that indicts the subject of their investigation.

That's not me.

I'm the guy who helps put the bloodstained white dress shirt on a naked man who has a bullet in his leg. I'm the guy who, with the help of a lusty hippie chick, drags that same man uphill through a field to a car that he had to buy because someone shot the windshield out of his last automobile.

When we got to the Dodge I had the girl named Meredith sit on the farting Petrie's lap. Then I made Bob lie down in the back and cuffed his wrists to a metal rod under the driver's seat.

That was how I worked. My puzzles had human pieces and no one resolution. I was like the guy with the sack of corn, the goose, and the fox trying get across the river in a boat that could only take two passengers at a time.

Half the way down to the highway, where there was no human structure in sight, I stopped the car. All the way, Petrie farted and Bob moaned. Meredith kept silent. I liked her for that reason.

"You two listen to me," I said to Petrie and Meredith. "Bob here is wanted for robbery, kidnapping, and murder. You guys are what the police call accomplices. If I tell them about you you'll spend at least five years in the penitentiary. A solid five with no parole, no time off for good behavior. I don't need the headache, however. I don't care what you did. So I'm gonna let you out and give each of you a hundred dollars. I suggest that you hike back up to Meredith's car and drive north or south, anywhere but back to that commune. Because the police will be coming and I won't lift a finger to help."

After freeing Petrie I gave them both money and left them on the dirt road in the middle of nowhere, in the middle of the night.

Now and again I wonder about Petrie and Meredith. Maybe the trauma of that night brought them closer together and they married and had kids. Maybe they fell asleep in the cabin and Meredith woke up early taking his hundred dollars. It doesn't matter but I like to speculate—there's no harm in that.

"You really a cop, man?" Uhuru-Bob asked from a prone position on the back floor of my Dodge.

We were headed for Isla Vista.

"Private," I said. "I'm working for a guy who thinks that you've been set up but he doesn't know how and he wants me to prove it."

"What guy?"

"He doesn't want to be identified, for obvious reasons."

I figured this was all true. Because, as far as Bob was concerned, I was working for myself.

"Well, he's right," Bob said. "I haven't done none'a that. I mean I was there when Rose robbed that liquor store but I didn't even know she was gonna do that."

"What about that vice principal you said that you killed?"

"I never said I killed nobody," he proclaimed. "I called the paper and told them that he deserved it. I went to a high school where he taught at. Mr. Emerson always had a high-school girlfriend. He was just a dog. Some father or boyfriend prob'ly shot him."

"What about the shootout with the police?"

"The only shootout I had was when they shot me in the leg."

36

The name of the coffeehouse where I left Coco was Dylan's Dawn.

Uhuru-Bob gave little resistance when I wrapped first-aid tape over his mouth and around his head.

There was a lovely young woman with natural red hair strumming a guitar and singing about ugly things on a small dais next to the coffee bar. There were probably eighty customers, not one of them over the age of twenty-five. They all, except for the singer, looked my way when I entered. They all, except for Coco, were suspicious of a suited man my age among them.

Coco was sitting at a table flanked by three young hippie men. They could probably feel the passion she had for Jo and were hoping to get a little of that precious commodity for themselves.

When I walked up to the table a hale, black-haired, black-bearded young suitor stood and said, "What do you want here, brother?"

"Not you," I replied easily.

"Then maybe you should go," he suggested.

He had big muscles under a loose blue shirt and held himself in a military bearing. A vet, I thought, but that didn't bother me. I was a wartime veteran too—and I had a gun in my pocket.

"Hi, Uncle Thad," Coco said as she jumped up and kissed my check. "I was getting worried about you."

"Uncle?" the standing hippie said.

"Is something wrong with that, Roger?" my newly minted niece asked.

"But . . ." he said.

"Thad is married to my mother's sister. He used to change my diapers when I was a baby."

"We gotta go," I said.

"It was nice meeting you guys," Coco said as she went to get the purple bag, which was hanging from the back of her chair. "Sorry I can't go to that Doors concert with you."

"How can I call you?" Roger asked.

"I'll be back," she lied.

I installed Coco in the backseat, where she could keep up the pressure on Bob's wound while I drove. It wasn't the first time she had sat in the backseat of my car tending to an injured black man.

She took the tape from his head.

"Do you mind if I let you off at Terry's?" I asked the girl. "I don't think I have time to go all the way out to Mama Jo's."

"That's okay. She had this shopping list for me anyway. I can get somebody to give me a ride."

"You got to help me, girl," Bob said. "This man's gonna kill me."

"No," Coco said in a surprisingly sympathetic tone. "He will help you. That's the kind of man he is."

Half an hour later we were on the Pacific Coast Highway cruising southward. Bob grunted now and then. Coco and I had nothing to say. She didn't ask about what had happened with Petrie. Her deep trust, I felt, came from that four- or five-sentence exchange with Mama Jo.

When we saw the five-mile sign for an all-night gas station I had Coco put tape over Bob's mouth again.

"Hold him down," I said as I sidled up to the self-service pump.

"How?"

"He's weak from loss of blood. Sit on his wounded leg if he moves."

I got fifteen-point-three gallons for just under seven-fifty. After filling up and then paying the attendant, who was locked in a booth at the center of the station, I drove to the edge of the lot, where there stood a solitary phone booth.

———

"Hello?" a woman answered sleepily.

"Mrs. Simpson," I said. "Is your husband in?"

"Do you know what time it is?"

"All too well, ma'am, all too well."

I believe that it was the gravity of my tone rather than the words that moved her.

"Who should I say is calling?"

"Easy Rawlins."

She went away and a minute or so later a man said, "Mr. Rawlins?"

"It's that time, Eddie."

"What do you need?"

"A little while from now, not more than a few hours, a man will come to your door. He's going to say that he's from me and that you should go with him. Bring your bag and whatever you might need to treat a wound."

"What kind of wound?"

"The kind with the bullet still inside."

There was a moment of silent hesitation but then he said, "I'll be ready."

"Who the hell is this?" Melvin Suggs said, answering his line.

"Me."

"Rawlins?"

"You sober, Melvin?"

"Pretty much."

"Enough to drive?"

"As long as it ain't the Indy Five Hundred."

I gave him instructions and directions. He asked three questions about routes and then said, "See ya in the morning."

"How's the bleeding?" I asked Coco when we were getting near Terry's mansion.

"Stopped. But he needs to see a doctor."

"He will."

I stopped the car and she got out the passenger's side. Coming around to my window, she kissed me, once again on the lips, and said, "Be careful, Easy."

"So, Bob," I called out when we were well on the way to the desert. "You awake?"

"Why you doin' this to me, man?"

"I know it's hard to believe, brother, but I'm tryin' to save your ass. The federal government wants you from two different sides and the LAPD will shoot first—but you already know that."

"Why you wanna help me?"

"There's the man I'm workin' for, like I said, and then there's Belle."

"Mama?"

"I kind of made a promise to her that I'd keep you alive—at least. I have also been hired, by parties unknown, to rescue Rosemary Goldsmith from you."

"From me?"

"They say that you kidnapped her and then demanded a ransom?"

"No, I didn't." He could have been an eight-year-old denying pulling his sister's hair.

"Did she have somebody else do it?"

"I, I don't think so. I mean I guess I don't know. Last time I talked to her she said that she was gonna go get help like I told you."

"Help from where?"

"She just told me that she was gonna get help to get us both out of the country."

"You didn't ask how or from who?"

"I was shot, man. I just told her to hurry up."

"How long ago?"

"Right after we got away from those cops shootin' at me. Maybe two days, maybe not even. She was supposed to be back by last night."

"And how did you," I said, "an L.A. student from Metro Junior College, meet a coed at UCSB?"

"It's like this, man," he said in such a way that I knew I was in for a story. "I got this thing about costumes, have ever since I was a kid.

Cowboys, clowns, cops, or criminals; if I dressed up like something it's like I became that person, that thing. When I was a kid I always knew in the back of my mind that I was really Bobby Mantle. When my father gave me my boxin' gloves I let it go so far that after a while I really was a boxer. But then when they banned me from the ring and I went to college I started gettin' high. At first it was only grass and hash. I'd get high and put on one'a my outfits and it was like I was changed for real.

"Then I met this white dude named Youri, Youri Kidd. He was like a dealer. Mostly he just sold grass to college kids. We would get high together and I'd play around with hats and such. Then one time him and me ate mushrooms and I found these tap-dancer shoes. The whole night I was a fool tap dancin' and you know I believed I was the real thing. Youri liked that shit and he would bring me mushrooms or mescaline or even LSD sometimes and we'd go out lookin' for some kinda costume. When he brought me them African robes it hit me like some kinda magic. In my mind that meant I was some kinda political revolutionary. I started givin' talks and eatin' mushrooms. I didn't go to class or nuthin'. I was Uhuru Nolicé. I was a leader of the revolution. I gave talks and people listened. And I guess I got a little lost.

"I called the papers about Mr. Emerson because I knew that he was a dog. But I never said nuthin' when them cops was killed. I swear I didn't."

"Maybe you don't remember," I suggested.

"It ain't like that, man. I *see* what I'm doin', I remember it but it's like I cain't help it. But I know I never said nuthin' 'bout those cops. I know it.

"Anyway, the police started comin' around lookin' for me and Youri said he had a friend that lived in this house up in Isla Vista. That was Rose. One time he helped her somehow."

"Helped her do what?" I asked, just to stay in the conversation.

"I don't know. But he said that she was real political like and you know in my mind I was Uhuru Nolicé runnin' from the Man. I went up there with a baggie full'a mushrooms and gave speeches and they loved me; especially Rose. We hit it off the second night. She said she was in love with me. One time when Meredith tried to get with me Rose beat that girl with a stick. Shit. After that we came back down to L.A. I had run outta mushrooms and had to take off the robes so nobody would recognize me.

"That's when Rose realized that I wasn't what I acted like, that I was just playin' a part. She didn't leave me but it was like she took over. We met up with Youri again. He got us hooked up with this guy I knew about from the old neighborhood. Then after Rose took out that sawed-off shotgun and robbed that store I made up my mind to get away. I was gonna go down Mississippi where my mama's people is from but then the cops started shootin' at us and I was wounded and Rose brought me back up to Isla Vista."

"Who was this man you knew?" I asked.

"What man?"

"The one from your old neighborhood."

"He used to be named Delbert but now he calls himself MG. He didn't know me but I knew him from when I was a kid. Rose knew about him from her political shit."

It was quiet for a while after that.

"So do you know where Rosemary is now?" I asked.

No answer.

We were way out in the desert by then; no cars in front or behind us.

I got out and checked on Bob. He wasn't bleeding and he wasn't dead. The ex-boxer had fallen asleep on the floor of my anonymous Dodge.

37

We got to the Waltons' desert cabin a little after six in the morning. It was even smaller than their city home. The outer walls were tar paper tacked down under a frame of pine timbers. The slanted roof was made from cascading sheets of aluminum and tin. The structure was raised two feet or more above the desert floor, standing on a dozen four-by-four stumpy timber legs.

First I took off the padlock from the front door using the key that Davis Walton gave me. Then I unhooked Uhuru-Bob from the backseat. He opened his eyes for a moment but didn't say anything.

He only moaned a little when I lifted him up in my arms and carried him into the shack.

I put him on a wide bed that doubled for a sofa, thinking that I'd have to get Davis's bedclothes laundered and bleached. I shackled Bob's left wrist to the steel bar at the head of the bed.

"Ow," my prisoner complained. "That shit hurts."

"It didn't hurt you when you were bangin' on that girl."

"I didn't know it was that bad."

"Go to sleep, Bob. You need the rest."

He closed his eyes and I believe that he actually went to sleep. I wondered if being chained and in tatters made the chameleon-man think that he was a convict or slave; bound to take orders from a reluctant overmaster like me.

Carrying a plain pine chair from the kitchen table, I went outside to sit and smoke.

Prehistoric-looking Joshua trees stood out in the desert morning like ancient sentries watching over me and my prisoner. It was flat out there, the air clear and silent. You could see for miles across the dun-colored rock and sand. Here and there stood great piles of pale crimson boulders that had resisted the erosion of millennia while the soil around them had washed away. There was a chill in the morning air but soon that would give way to hundred-degree heat.

In a little shed next to the small house, Walton had a gasoline-operated generator. With that he could run a small air conditioner. I'd fire that up later. But in the meantime I sat outside watching the dew dry and the world turn.

I was a soldier again, my mind empty as I waited for the next challenge.

I saw the car coming down the country road from five miles off; a small puff of dust on the horizon. It was pleasant to see something coming; it gave me the illusion that I was in control.

Eight or nine minutes later the pale green 1956 Pontiac rolled up next to my dark car. Melvin Suggs was the first man out. He was wearing khaki Bermuda shorts, a blue and white Hawaiian shirt, and a wide-brimmed rather floppy Panama hat. Carrying a small straw suitcase, he waved as the passenger's-side door came open.

Dr. Edwin Simpson was the opposite of his squat and powerful driver. Not yet forty, Edwin was tall and almost as dark-skinned as I. He was lean and wore horn-rimmed glasses, the lenses of which glinted in the sun. He had on a short-sleeved white dress shirt and dark slacks. His shoes were dark leather. And he carried a medical bag like the one I used to transport my pistol, various handcuffs, and bags of change.

"Mr. Rawlins," he said, walking up to me.

I stood and shook his hand.

"Your patient is inside, Doctor," I said.

"What patient is that?"

"Like I told you on the phone—a man that's been shot in the leg."

"I'm not a gangster's doctor."

"Good," I said, "because he's not a gangster."

"How did he get shot?"

"It was, I believe, a misunderstanding."

"Why not take him to the hospital?" Edwin asked. "Why not call the police?"

"As I remember it, Doctor, the last time you thought about calling the police you ended up coming to me."

Edwin had an identical twin brother, named Tamber for their maternal grandfather.

Since childhood Tamber Simpson liked to play games of skill and chance while Edwin enjoyed reading and math.

Edwin went to Howard University medical school.

His brother moved to Reno. When Reno got too small, Tamber settled in Las Vegas. That was all good and well but Tamber was something a black man should never be—lucky; not only with cards but with women too. It was bad enough that he won $17,568 from an Oklahoma oilman named Joseph Hardman, but that same night he bedded Joe's mistress. The betrayal of his girlfriend somehow convinced Hardman that Tamber was cheating at cards too and so he hired a man named Tiberius Adderly to kill the gambler.

Tamber got wind of Tiberius from the mistress and ran to Edwin. Edwin went to the police. The police told the good doctor that maybe Tamber could go to Africa, where he could see Tiberius coming from a mile away.

That's when Edwin talked to some of his patients and came up with my name.

I told the good doctor that I could probably save Tamber this time but that a man like his brother was destined to die—violently.

"The good thing about it," I added, "is that he'll live life to the fullest every minute up to the moment of his death."

But Edwin loved his brother and felt guilty, as only a sibling can, about his good life compared to Tamber's world of trouble.

I gathered some information that I typed out on a clean white sheet of typing paper. After that, through gambling friends of my own, I let it be known that Tamber Simpson was residing in a flophouse near Skid Row in downtown L.A.

I rented a room in Tamber's name and then took another room across the hall. I only had to wait thirty-seven hours.

The man who worked the front desk had fifty of my client's dollars in his pocket. He knew that if he called me when somebody asked for Tamber he'd receive fifty more.

The white man came to the door and knocked; I saw that through my peephole. When nobody answered he tried the knob. It was unlocked and so the man took out a pistol and, ever so slowly, pushed the door open.

That was my cue. I stepped out quickly and hit the hit man in the head with a long-barreled .41-caliber pistol. He fell headfirst into the room and I rushed in, hit him again, and then kicked his fallen pistol into a far corner. After closing the door I sat backward on a maple chair, aiming my gun barrel at the battered man's head.

He wasn't completely out of it, just stunned.

When he rolled his eyes in my direction I said, "Hello, Tiberius."

"What the fuck?" He moved as if he was going to rise and so I pushed the muzzle of the gun a little closer.

"I will kill you," I promised, and I meant it too. We were both killers. There was no wiggle room to that.

"You're not Simpson."

"No," I said, and then I handed him the sheet of paper that I had so neatly typed.

On the page was Tiberius's full name, the name and address of his ex-wife, the name of the Vegas casino in which he worked security, the license plate numbers on all three of his cars, and the address of his mother, who lived in Austin. Between my fellow detective Saul Lynx and myself, we gathered that information. Saul only charged three hundred for the phone calls. I knew some black gamblers here and there but Saul had connections in Vegas that I couldn't even dream of.

"What the fuck is this?"

"Did you know that the Roman emperor Tiberius was the stepson of the great Octavian and that Octavian was adopted by Julius Caesar himself?"

"Huh?"

"I'm just proving to you that I know you and you have no idea of who I am. The next time you get a lead on Tamber it might be him and it might be me or one of my friends waiting. If Tamber dies I will go looking for you and if I can't find you I will ask somebody on that list. And believe me, Tiberius, I have all kinds of help. I know white men and women and Chinese and Mexican too. You will never see the knife coming."

I knew I was having an impact because he didn't respond.

"It would be best if I killed you but that shit is messy so instead I'll make you an offer."

"What's that?"

"I can promise you that Tamber will never again go to Vegas and so you can tell Hardman that he's dead and buried. If he does go there it'll be open season."

"And if I don't take the offer?"

I smiled and let my head loll to the left.

"What if Hardman finds out?" Tiberius asked.

"Will he come up on you with a big gun like this here?"

"Why didn't you just shoot me then?"

"Because I'm tryin' to save Tamber's ass. If you tell Hardman that he's dead then the problem is solved. If I kill you he could just hire somebody else."

That was a tense moment. Maybe Tamber *would* have to move to Liberia. But after a long moment Tiberius nodded.

"But if you fuck with my family I'll kill you," he said.

"Man, you don't even know who I am."

Tamber was poisoned by a jealous woman two years later. He died under his brother's care. In spite of that, Edwin owed me a debt.

I told him and Suggs not to give their names to Bob.

We went in and tied and held down the ex-boxer while Dr. Simpson extracted the bullet. Bob screamed and struggled but the restraints were enough. Edwin got the bullet and shot him up with antibiotics, penicillin I think.

"You need to keep him stationary for at least a week," he told us. "I'll give you a week's supply of morphine if he experiences too much pain."

"Thank you, Doctor," I said. "Now if you'll wait here for a few minutes, I need to talk to my friend outside."

"That's the guy killed the cops?" Melvin asked when we were outside smoking next to his car.

"I'm ninety-nine percent sure he didn't do it, Mel."

"Then turn him in with your evidence."

"I do that and he'll die in his cell."

"You don't know that."

"Just give me a few days to get my ducks in a row," I said. "I can promise you twenty-five hundred at the end, whether he's guilty or not, and in less time than that I will be able to tell you where Mary went."

Melvin was a cop. And there was nothing that cops hated more than cop-killers. But on the other hand he would soon be banished, maybe tried for some crime himself—and then there was Mary.

"What do you want from me?" he asked.

"Babysit Bob for a few days. That's all. I'll come back out here then with proof one way or the other."

"It's a felony to shield a criminal," he said.

"I haven't heard about any warrant out on him. Have you?"

That caused the lawman to grimace. He knew what I was saying: There was something hinky about the LAPD's persecution of Uhuru-Bob.

"Three days," he said.

"It's always a pleasure doin' business with you, Mel."

38

I drove Edwin to a bus station in Palm Springs.

Before getting out of the car he asked, "Are you planning to hurt that man, Mr. Rawlins?"

"No, Eddie, I'm not. They say he's committed some terrible crimes but I don't believe it. So either I'm going to prove him innocent or I'll turn him in. Right now I'm just tryin' to keep him alive."

"Who's that man you left him with?"

"He's all right," I said.

Edwin stared hard at me. He was a doctor and consequently expected to be in charge of any space he occupied. But there I was, the last piece of uncontrollable heartache left him by his brother.

"Don't call me again," he said.

"What would you say if I told *you* that?" I replied.

From Palm Springs I made my way to 29 Palms, stopped at a phone booth in yet another gas station, and called the information operator.

"Information," the lady said.

"Terry Calhoun from Floral Express. I'm looking for the number of a Clarissa Anthony. She's on Cholla Terrace," I said, looking up at a street sign at the corner. "I went to her house to deliver these red roses but nobody's home and there's another name on the mailbox. I want to make sure she's there before leaving anything."

"I see your problem, Mr. Calhoun," the friendly local said. "It says here that Clarissa Anthony has a new listing on Jacaranda Drive. Number forty-two. It doesn't say anything about Cholla Terrace. She must have lived with a friend, then moved and your company was given the old address."

"Well, I'll be," I said. "Thank you so much, ma'am."

Forty-two Jacaranda Drive was a catchall address for a trailer park on the outer edge of the small town. I should have spent the time waiting for Mary/Clarissa to show, but time was the one thing I didn't have.

There were twenty or more mobile homes in the big arid lot. Most units had been there so long that the tenants had landscaped the desert soil around their doors, putting in little gardens and small statues; one had a fir tree growing in a large terra-cotta pot. The fir had gotten big enough that it actually provided some shade.

The manager pointed me to a double-wide trailer that was painted pink, interspersed by patches of rust. It had been there quite a while.

"That's it over there," Park Manager Madeline Thrusher said.

She was short and wide, looking older than her years, and she was at least sixty. Her eyes were so beady and small that I couldn't make out the color. But I could tell that she was no fan of men of my race.

"That one looks like it's been here quite a while," I said. "The woman I'm looking for moved out here recently."

"That one's a rental," Ms. Thrusher said. "Man named Arneaux lived in it for eight years before he died last spring. He didn't have a family so it just stayed there."

"Thank you," I said.

"What do you want with her?"

"Just a moment of her time," I said, thinking that this shortcut might get a little bumpy.

I knocked on the flimsy aluminum door and waited.

"Who is it?" a woman called from somewhere inside.

"Mr. Rawlins."

The ensuing silence wasn't long. The door swung inward revealing a fair young woman. She was wearing a peach-colored one-piece, short-pants suit. Her hair was now blond, permed, and shorter than it had been when the picture Melvin gave me was taken. On paper she was dark but out here in the desert sun she was light and even bright. It wasn't just the dye and hairstyle that was different, however. The photograph hadn't done justice to the thirty-something counterfeiter's leg-woman. She was beautiful, yes, but there was something else about her that set off a charge down inside a man's chest.

I think it might have been the way her brown eyes took you in. It was a complete experience, giving rise to the notion that she could know you through and through and never turn her nose up at a thing.

"Yes?" she said.

There was the shadow of a mouse under her left eye. This reminded me of the ex-boxer Bob Mantle half naked, chained, and languishing— under the watchful eye of the man I was there representing.

"Mary Donovan?"

The smile went away. I was sad to see it go.

"I'm out of it," she said, raising her hands in a halfhearted surrender.

"I'm sure you want to be and I'm not here for that anyway."

"Then what?"

"I'm here because Melvin Suggs doesn't have the common sense of an alley cat."

That got her to smile again. She even showed some teeth.

"What's your first name, Mr. Rawlins?" she asked.

"Easy." I could have lied but this was the kind of woman that you wanted to speak your name.

"Come on in, Easy."

The inside of the trailer was reminiscent of a dollhouse. The furniture was small but still too large for the one-room movable home.

"Sit," she said, and I perched on the violet-colored love seat.

She sat opposite me on a stuffed red chair, placing her right foot under a bare left thigh.

"Well?" she asked.

"Mel's been suspended."

"Oh." She seemed really upset. "Because of me?"

I nodded.

"Is there something I can do for him?"

"I don't know. Maybe you could but he doesn't seem to care about losin' his job. They're tryin' to send him to jail but he's not concerned about that either."

"Did he send you?"

"I'm a private detective. Mel agreed to help me on another case if I found you and told you that he wants you back."

She winced slightly and frowned a little harder.

"You know about us?" she asked.

"You were spending hundred-dollar bills where Ben Franklin had a runny nose. He busted you but . . ."

She nodded and said, "When he arrested me I pretended to be afraid, just an innocent girl in bad circumstances. I don't think he ever believed it. I was expecting him to ask for sex after he let me go but he didn't. I guess that kind of surprised me. I'm not used to men not making the effort. I guess that kept him on my mind. I called him at his precinct station. We got together three times before I could get him to take me home. We started seeing each other and I was thinking that maybe I could get off the grift but then the man I worked for—"

"Light Lambert," I interjected. I think I was trying to impress her.

"Yes," she said with a questioning smile. "Light. He called me and said that he didn't approve. He's got this guy looks like a gorilla who works for him. They kill people. Light would have destroyed both me and Melvin, so I left."

"I don't think Light and Elvis will be a problem."

"Why not?"

"Because Melvin all by himself is a dangerous man and he's got friends too."

"Friends like you?"

"And some worse than Elvis," I said.

She gave a short laugh, snorting prettily.

"Can we find you here most times?" I asked.

"Here or at my job."

"Where's that?"

"I have the morning and lunch shifts at Dino's Diner on Main."

"Melvin's a bit undernourished."

"Have him come by. I'll make the burgers myself."

Just then the aluminum door slammed open. A scruffy-looking little white guy with a baseball bat in hand rushed in. He was younger than Mary/Clarissa but desiccated like Madeline Thrusher, the person who had probably called him at whatever bar he was haunting.

I put a hand on the gun in my pocket. Mary/Clarissa noticed this and jumped to her feet.

"What's wrong, Sterling?" she asked with just the right amount of manufactured concern in her voice.

The desert rat looked confused. He expected to find us in the bed and naked but instead we were sitting across from each other like civilized human beings.

"What the fuck is he doin' in here?" Sterling shouted, spittle leaping from his sparsely whiskered maw.

I took that moment to stand up, dwarfing the little man. I would have taken him to task for giving Melvin's girlfriend a black eye, but I couldn't see where that would help the situation.

"Eddie Long," I said.

"What?"

"Eddie Long," I repeated. "He owes Clarissa some money. He knew I was on my way out to Palm Springs for a poker game and asked me if I could drop it off."

"I don't know no Eddie Long," Sterling assured me.

"Eddie's an old friend," Mary/Clarissa said. "I knew him in L.A."

"How much?" Sterling asked, sounding triumphant, as if this question would catch us in our lie.

Sterling wore faded blue jeans and a bright red T-shirt that was probably brand-new. The bold color made his sun-worn skin look all the worse.

"Three hundred dollars," I said.

The little man lowered his bat. His mouth came open.

I reached into my pocket and came out with the cash.

"You don't mind if I give this to your man, do you, Claire?"

"Of course not, Skip."

I had to concentrate to keep from smiling. I handed Sterling the cash.

He stared vacantly at the three hundred-dollar bills between his fingers. Maybe he had never seen denominations like this before.

I was hemorrhaging money but that didn't matter. My only goal was to get to the end of whatever road I was on without killing someone—or getting killed.

39

When I got to Bonnie's house the veil was already lifted.

I rang the bell and she opened the door. Not saying a word, I advanced on her. She leaned into me and we were kissing. I picked her up and then we were in the bed making love to each other's body with skill, wonder, and deep hunger. I remember that our orgasms were surprises, coming at odd times and not at all in sync. What might have been a disconnect for others only served to bring us closer. We could luxuriate in the other's loss of control and see how powerful our impact was.

We were both sated after the initial encounter but couldn't stop kissing and caressing. Soon we were at it again.

After some hours I rolled on my back and stared at her bedroom ceiling. I relished the cool feeling of the sweat evaporating from my chest.

"Easy." It was the first word between us.

"Yeah?"

"What happened?"

I knew that it was Mary/Clarissa who'd wrought the change in my libido. Her life was both feral and passionate. She lived from moment to moment like Tamber Simpson. The world around her was a fuzzy black-and-white while she was in Technicolor, the only live person in sight.

On Bonnie's bed I realized that I was grateful for the confusing case of Rosemary Goldsmith and Bob Mantle. Mary/Clarissa's unrepentant and vulnerable passion had been the final moment of the resurrection that had been growing in me ever since flying off that coastal mountain and living when I should have died.

"I was out in the desert," I said in answer to Bonnie's question. "I was thinking that life out there is noble because the elements are so harsh and still those plants and creatures survive."

"You survived," she said.

"And now I'm alive."

We were in her sunny sitting room, surrounded by African artifacts and shelves lined with books both in French and in English. Bonnie had prepared a platter of cheeses, dried meats, fresh fruit, and a baguette cut into sections. She had white wine with the afternoon meal and I had apple juice.

"Do you think you can take Feather for a few days?" I asked after updating her on the case.

"You're worried about your safety?" Reaching out to touch my face, she ran a finger along the scab over my cheekbone.

"No, not really, but I might have to be out of the house too long. I don't want her being alone that much. I would ask Jackson and Jewelle to take her but they got problems of their own right now."

"The airline called last night," she said. "They want me to take Simone's flight to Fiji. It's a seven-day junket with layovers in Jakarta, Sydney, and Tokyo."

"Oh."

"But she can come with me. She already has a passport and she loves languages."

"She's been learning a few words in Japanese."

"Oh."

"When would you be leaving?" I asked.

"Tonight."

"She'll worry about not having the right clothes."

"That's just a good excuse to go shopping."

I picked up Feather at Jewelle's office. She was elated at the prospect of the trip. I made her dinner while she ran across the street to the Nishios' to tell them that she couldn't work for them the next week.

While she was there Bonnie drove over in her car.

"It would be great if you could come, Daddy," Feather said as she packed in her bedroom upstairs.

"That would be nice but I got to work."

"But will you come one day? On a vacation, I mean."

"Yes he will," Bonnie said. She had come up to the door. "I'll make him."

Feather laughed. She could tell that whatever trouble there had been between us had been settled—or at least quenched and quelled.

It was a little after six when Bonnie and Feather left for the airport. I kissed them both good-bye and waved for a while after they were out of sight. Then I went to the garage and rooted around through the boxes until I found the one with the word *Hose* scrawled on its side.

One of the reasons I decided on the new house was because it didn't have a sprinkler system for the lawn. I liked connecting the long black garden hose to an outside spigot then turning the nozzle to get that jet-powered spray.

While watering, I began to feel the calm of purpose. Feather was safe, Uhuru-Bob was in my custody, and Suggs would probably be given a second chance to crash his life on the exquisite coral reef of Mary/Clarissa Donovan/Anthony.

I was looking for Rosemary Goldsmith but I wasn't really hired for that job. Roger Frisk and Tout Manning had engaged me to find Bob Mantle. They had said this was to help them find Rosemary but the police obviously had a *shoot on sight* order out on the ex-boxer. Maybe, I thought, maybe the only object was to find Bob.

I wondered if there was some purpose beyond revenge. Who would pay that much money unless more was in the balance?

As I was having this thought four cars converged on my home: a police cruiser, two dark sedans, and a cranberry-colored Volkswagen Bug—a caravan of police and various G-men.

The gangs of government, I thought as I twisted the nozzle of my garden hose, strangling the lawn's fountain of life.

They all got out of their cars quickly and headed in my direction. I wondered how my new neighbors would think of me after witnessing this debacle.

"Mr. Rawlins," the short, fat State Department man Andrew Hastings said.

"Mr. Hastings."

The cruiser held a low-rank patrolman and a captain in full-dress uniform.

The FBI fraternal twins Sorkin and Bruce were in different-colored suits but they were of the same cut.

Tout Manning stayed on the periphery as the others came in for the kill.

"Excuse me," the police captain said to Hastings, "but I'm in charge of this interrogation."

"This is a federal matter," thin-lipped Ted Brown countered.

"What interrogation?" I asked the men.

All the sour faces turned to me as if I were some kind of annoyance. As if I had no part in the drama they were enacting.

"I am Captain Ira Reynolds," the police boss told me. He was thick-set with skin naturally tan in hue. When he was younger that heft was probably indicative of strength but now it looked like a little too much pastrami at lunchtime. "Can we come in?"

I wanted to say no. Maybe if I hadn't had the lifetime experience of a black man in America I might have refused the request. If it were just Captain Reynolds it was possible that I might have turned my hose back on and told him that I'd drop by his office tomorrow. But I knew that I couldn't hold off so many self-important officers of the laws.

"Sure," I said. "I don't know if I have enough chairs in any one room but I guess your man here could help ferry some in from the dinette."

Ten minutes later everyone, except for the unnamed patrolman and Tout Manning, was seated in my nearly empty living room. Captain Reynolds and Andrew Hastings occupied the couch, I had the cushioned chair, and the rest sat in wooden seats from the dinette.

It was all very civilized, considering what interrogations were sometimes like.

Reynolds let his eye move among the players. He stopped to gaze at Manning the longest.

Finally the captain said to me, "Stony Goldsmith got a ransom note in the mail this morning. Special Delivery." He paused after sharing this intelligence. I suppose he was looking to see if I would somehow incriminate myself.

"And?" I said.

"It was a demand for one million dollars in cash and the public release of certain documents that the kidnapper says Stony has." Another pause.

"Yeah?"

"That doesn't surprise you?" the captain wanted to know.

"Somebody kidnaps a millionaire's daughter and then asks for a million dollars. Makes sense to me."

"This isn't a joke, Rawlins."

"What happened to *Mister* Rawlins?"

"You should show some respect," the uniformed patrolman warned.

He was tall and fit, white like the fruit of an unripened banana, and blue-eyed—not more than twenty-five.

"In my house, Officer," I replied, "people call me mister. Just like Sidney Poitier in that movie."

"The people that sent the note call themselves Scorched Earth," Captain Reynolds said. He was looking for something, anything, in my eyes.

"Okay," I said.

Everyone was staring at me then. I wondered if I was implicated somehow in intelligence gathered from the ransom request.

"There was a woman's baby finger wrapped in the note," Reynolds said.

"Rosemary's?"

"It's her fingerprint. Her father had all the members of his family fingerprinted in case they ever had to be identified."

"That's terrible, Captain," I said when he paused again. "I have a daughter myself but what do I have to do with it?"

"Manning tells me that Roger Frisk asked you to look for the Goldsmith girl. Is that true?"

"Not exactly."

"What do you mean, Rawlins?" Tout said, raising his voice. "It was right here in this room."

"You and your boss asked me to find Bob Mantle," I said in a modulated tone. "You said that the girl was missing and you suspected Mantle."

"Is that true?" Captain Reynolds asked Tout.

"Technically," Manning admitted. "But it goes without saying that if he found the girl then that would be our main priority. I told him about the kidnapping."

"I asked around about Mantle," I said to the captain. "Somebody shot at me and then the State Department and the FBI told me to mind my own business."

"The State Department is involved with some very delicate intelligence here," fat Hastings said.

"Something about the war?" Captain Reynolds asked.

"These are state secrets," Ted Brown answered.

The lanky diplomat said more but I didn't listen because just then I looked out of the window and saw, half a block down Point View, a Silver Shadow Rolls-Royce parked at the curb.

"What about you two?" the captain was asking the FBI brothers.

"Kidnapping is under federal jurisdiction," Agent Sorkin replied. "A white woman has been abducted and so it falls to us."

"What if she were a black woman?" I asked, turning my gaze from the window.

"But there's the armored car robbery and the killing of three policemen," Tout Manning said in answer to the FBI man.

I realized that my question, and its meaning, had no place in my own home.

"What is Roger Frisk's interest in this case?" Captain Reynolds asked Manning.

"The chief wants to be kept abreast of the investigation to make sure that we know what's what before giving it to the press."

There was something lame about Tout's reply. I knew it and Reynolds did too. But even he couldn't question Chief Parker's office.

For a while there they all argued. I had enough time to smoke two or three cigarettes, if I still smoked in the house. They argued about jurisdiction, state secrets, even the war. The blustering and posturing went around and around until Reynolds finally said, "The federal government is welcome to involve itself in this case. We certainly don't want to hamper the war effort or to embarrass anyone. But the LAPD is in charge of keeping the peace. We have had assassinations, robberies, and the murder of three of our police officers. The FBI and the State Department are here because we recognize your part but we will be the primary force in this investigation.

"Now, Mr. Rawlins," he said, turning to me. "What information do you have about Mantle and Rosemary Goldsmith?"

I told them everything they already knew. I talked about how Belle Mantle said her son was innocent and that the boxers at the gym didn't know anything but rumor.

"When I went to talk to Stony Goldsmith he didn't seem too concerned about his daughter," I said.

"What about the mother?" Agent Bruce asked.

He really shouldn't have let that card show. He had someone watching the mother. Maybe her husband was suspicious of his estranged wife.

"That's kind of embarrassing," I said, allowing a brief insincere grin to take form. "I was hoping to get a little more money out of the family for work I had already done. She was too smart for that, though."

"Did she know anything about the girl?" Ted Brown asked.

"Only that she's been trouble all her life and now she's in trouble for real."

"How did you know where to find her?" Manning asked.

"I know a guy at Proxy Nine. He's a vice president. I asked him for an introduction to Foster Goldsmith and, when I found out that they were separated, for the lady's phone number. I called and she sent her man Redbird to show me the way."

I fed them pabulum for another forty minutes or so. The fact that no one even responded to my question about a black woman getting kidnapped convinced me that I couldn't trust those men. I knew that this decision was unjustified. I knew that we weren't there to talk about the racial inequities of the justice system. But sometimes you just have to follow your heart—and its hatred.

In the middle of the interrogation the doorbell rang. The patrolman answered, letting in four of his uniformed brothers.

"These men are going to search your house," Reynolds told me.

I could have asked for a warrant.

The sun was completely gone from the sky by the time the search and the grilling were over. My visitors left, telling me, as a group and individually, that I was to stop investigating any part of the case and that I should turn any and all information that might come later to each and every one of them.

"Yes, sir," I said at least fifteen times.

40

I saw them off at the door and then watched through the living room window until they were all gone. I expected Tout Manning to drive around the block and return for a special briefing. I hadn't mentioned that he and Frisk had paid me on behalf of parties unknown to take the case.

Manning did not return, however.

After ten minutes or so I went back to the stuffed chair and sat down among the empty seats that the captain and international and national agents had so recently occupied. There was little consensus among the different tribes of government. Even Reynolds and Manning seemed to have different goals in the case.

And then there was the case itself.

I hadn't believed that Rosemary had been kidnapped.

Bob Mantle probably had not committed a crime.

And yet still there were dead bodies, stolen monies, and now a detached finger of a debutante armed robbery suspect.

It was only when the doorbell rang that I remembered the Silver Shadow.

"I turned off the hose," Redbird said when I opened the front door.

"Come on in. Can I get you anything to drink?"

"No, thank you."

I made my way back to the living room and the rich woman's representative followed.

I sat once again in the stuffed chair while Redbird settled on a straight-backed cherrywood number. We looked at each other a moment or two.

"Mrs. Goldsmith wanted me to come talk to you," he said at last.

"Talk."

"Who were those men?"

I told him, in detail. "They informed me that Foster got a million-dollar ransom note with one of Rosemary's fingers wrapped up in it."

"They're sure?"

"Seems that Stony keeps the fingerprints of all his family members."

Redbird nodded and scowled.

"Do they think she's dead?"

"No one knows."

"Was it the boxer?"

"Absolutely not. He was wounded and a hundred miles away."

"How do you know that?" If there was any stress or urgency behind the Indian's questions he didn't show it.

"I found him up in the mountains above Santa Barbara. He'd been shot in the leg a day or so earlier."

"You turn him over to the law?"

I shook my head. Maybe I shouldn't have trusted Redbird, but even if he took what I gave him to the cops there was no proof, no leads that would bring them to the cabin in the desert outside Indio.

"The FBI is watching Lenore," I said. "They knew that I had been to the hotel."

"I'd like to talk to the boxer," Redbird said.

"Maybe later. But I think it's more important to look for your girl."

I told Redbird about how Rosemary had brought Bob up to the mountain cabin and then left promising to find help in L.A.

"I think that she came down here looking for confederates," I said. "Bob told me about a man named Delbert and nicknamed MG. You ever hear of somebody like that?"

"No," Redbird said. "But she's been involved with radicals since she was fifteen. There's a long list."

"You want to look into it on your own?" I offered. I had enough to do.

"Mrs. Goldsmith told me to work with you."

"I won't tell her if you strike out on your own."

The younger man looked at me with intensity. After a long moment he smiled.

"Those men could have put you in jail," he said.

"Yes they could."

"But you aren't afraid. You didn't give them the boxer."

"No."

"So I'll stay with you awhile. I know most of the people and you know the rest."

Like Melvin Suggs before him, Redbird slept on my couch that night. All he wanted was a glass of tap water and a thin blanket.

In the morning he accepted English Breakfast, scrambled eggs, and sliced ham.

We moved his Rolls into my driveway, pulling it far enough up that it couldn't be seen from the street, and drove my Dodge to our first destination.

Dawn Purdy had been friends with Rosemary since the ninth grade. They lied to the Goldsmiths and joined the Venceremos Brigade summer program two years in a row, going down to Cuba to work with the socialist peasants on farms and in factories.

Dawn's parents had inherited wealth and were dyed-in-the-wool communists. Foster never really knew about them. It was Lenore that got in the way of the friendship.

"How long has it been since they talked to each other?" I asked.

"I don't know much about that since Rose went to college," Redbird said. "But they had regular phone conversations through high school."

The Purdys lived way up in Bel-Air. Up where there were no sidewalks and street signs were rare.

There was no foot traffic whatsoever.

The turnoff to the residence was more like a country road than a driveway.

The house was akin to a royal residence.

I pulled onto a cobblestone parking area in front of the house and went with my companion to the front door. I pressed a button and from very far off came the sound of chimes—real chimes, not an electronic recording.

A few minutes later the extra-wide door came open. I expected a butler in a tuxedo or at least a maid in classic black and white, but the woman standing before us wore faded blue jeans and a silk shirt the pink color of coral that had washed ashore and dried. Her shoulder-length hair was black with a goodly amount of gray strands, and her face was long and handsome; at one time she'd probably been the old-time American ideal of beauty.

"Redbird," she said in a tone that was not necessarily welcoming.

"Mrs. Purdy," my temporary partner replied.

That was when she turned her full attention to me.

At first it was just a glance, a taking-in of my features, gender, and, of course, color. I expected mild surprise and maybe a little of the antipathy she felt toward my partner. But instead there was a moment of wonder and then an actual smile.

"Rawlins?" she said.

"Yes?"

"Um, uh, don't tell me," she said. "Easy, yes, Easy Rawlins. Johnson! Johnson!"

A very tall man came up behind the woman. He was at least six-seven, with black hair, no mustache, and a salt and pepper goatee.

"What is it, Virginia?" he asked, looking at us.

"It's Lenore Goldsmith's man Redbird with Easy Rawlins."

"Easy Rawlins," he said with real pleasure. He held out a hand. "Welcome to our home."

When we shook he said, "Come in. Come in."

The Purdy house was simple and elegant. The rooms weren't over-crowded with possessions, useless furniture, or, as a rule, ostentatious works of art. The foyer was three times the size of my new living room with much higher ceilings. The floors were tiled with roughhewn cream-colored stone that might have been semiprecious. The walls were finished oak.

From this room we came into a library or maybe a sitting room with bookshelves. There was a huge ebony-wood table that dominated this space. As a centerpiece there was a big, maybe five-hundred-pound, dark stone festooned with dozens of blazing orange crystals.

The far wall of the room was a big window looking out on a lawn that ended at a cliff. In the distance I could see the Pacific Ocean. There were three white sofas formed into a three-sided square that was open to the window.

"Sit, sit," Johnson Purdy bade us. "Virginia, get our guests some fruit juice."

I sat on the left-side sofa, placed perpendicular to the window. Redbird decided to stand behind me as Art Sugar's man had done for him. Johnson Purdy sat across from us.

"I saw you looking at the big rock, Mr. Rawlins," Johnson noted.

"It's beautiful," I said. "What are the stones?"

"Fire opals from Brazil," he said. "It was a gift from a small village down there where we built a hospital and a school. Virginia polished the gems herself."

Mrs. Purdy returned carrying four frosted tumblers on a tarnished silver tray.

"Lemon, pomegranate, and blueberry juices combined," she said as she handed me a glass.

She served Redbird and then her husband, finally settling on the central sofa.

"The police have already been here," Johnson said to kick off the business of our conversation.

I sipped my juice. It was delicious.

"About what?" I asked.

"Rosemary, of course."

"They thought she was here?"

"They thought our daughter might know where she was. When they asked us how they could get in touch with Dawn we sent them to an old address in the Mission District of San Francisco."

"Your daughter's not there anymore?"

"We'd never put the pigs on our own, Mr. Rawlins," Virginia assured me.

"Excuse me," I said. "But did the police mention my name?"

"No," Virginia said.

"Then how do we know each other?"

"You don't know us but we know Athena Wharton. She showed us a photograph of you and her adopted son Fennell."

"Virginia never forgets a face," Johnson said proudly, "not even from a photograph."

41

Some years before, while attempting to live the straight life, I spent a short stint as Supervising Custodian at George Washington Carver Junior High School. Athena Wharton, a ninety-five-pound dynamo, was the principal. She was a wealthy white woman from an old-money family who felt that it was every person's job to roll up their sleeves and do what they could for the world they lived in. She once told me that her industrialist father did not believe in charity.

"If you need charity for your people," she told me he'd said, "then your society has failed."

She had taken a special interest in an orphaned boy named Fennell Bryson. Fennell had various problems in school, what they call learning disabilities today, but he was a superb artist. He spent every extra moment sketching portraits and landscapes in layers of penciled texture that made you actually feel something—like a vibration underlying the mundane life that most of us lived.

Athena used to tutor the boy after school, and then one day he didn't show at the appointed hour; the next morning his uncle came to her office and told her that Fennell had run away from home.

The principal and I had coffee once a week and she knew something about my past and future life.

"His uncle Suleiman believes that he's run off with his father, Oxell Prideworth," Athena told me behind the closed door of her office.

"Not 'Bryson'?" I asked.

"Oxell never married Suleiman's poor sister. When she died she left her son only the family name. I want you to find him."

"That'll be kind of hard, A," I said. "You know I work all day and I got kids at home."

"I'll give you an informal leave of absence. Mr. Reed can do your job. I'll pay him extra out of my own pocket and you can spend every day looking for the child."

"What do you know about this Oxell guy?"

Athena was a good principal, she did her homework. From Suleiman she'd gotten a photograph of the father, and she gave me her own picture of the thirteen-year-old boy. It seemed like a chore for the boy to manufacture a smile but he did the work for his beloved tutor.

"The father has been arrested for robbery and spent time in prison," she told me. "He gets into fights and drinks. I want you to find Fennell and make sure that he's all right. If his father really cares about him they should be together but I'm worried that this is not the case."

My old friend from Houston, John the Bartender, had his own bar at the time. I dropped by that very afternoon.

"That's Ox, all right," the broad-shouldered Texan said when I showed him the photograph. "I'll ask around."

Three days later I put on some of my old work clothes and checked into a men's shelter in L.A.'s Skid Row. That night Oxell and his boy came in. I stayed in the shadows and corners as much as I could because, even with my skullcap and shades, I worried that the boy might recognize me from school.

Oxell was ten years younger, two inches shorter, and thirty pounds heavier than I was. Not all of his extra weight was fat. He was a habitual drunk and naturally angry. He took out the brunt of his inner rage correcting and criticizing his son. But Fennell didn't seem to mind. He took it like a soldier proud that he could carry an eighty-pound backpack on a thirty-mile forced march.

I watched while the man bellowed and barked at his son.

"Nobody gives a fuck about you, boy," he said at one point at the long table in the communal dining room. "Not these bums and niggahs in here and not your uncle or that school. Mothahfuckahs wanna keep us down, keep us apart. They don't know the love a man's got for his son."

I was struck by the drunkard's words. I had loved my father when I was a boy. He went off on a logging job down in southern Louisiana and never came back. I was eight years old. When I looked under his bed I found an old coffee can filled with silver quarters. I cried over those coins, wishing that I could trade them for just five minutes to kiss my father good-bye.

Athena Wharton had paid me up front and well. So after Fennell had fallen asleep I offered his father a cigarette and a sip of wine on the fire escape out a back window.

"Where you from, Rawlins?" the drunk asked.

"Fifth Ward, Houston, Texas, is where I became a man."

He took a deep draught from the bottle and said, "Texans can fight." And then he took another drink.

"I know a rich woman named Athena," I said.

"That's a rich name."

"She wants to adopt your son."

"The fuck she does. That's my boy in there and I will keep him with me."

"I told her that," I said, pretending to take a sip from the bottle. "And you know what she said?"

"What?"

"She said to tell you that she would pay you a thousand dollars if you gave up your right to him."

"Shit," his mouth said, but his eyes told a whole other story.

The business was transacted the next day at a lawyer's office in Beverly Hills. I paid Oxell money out of my own pocket, half the sum I had received from Athena. He would have taken a hundred dollars but I wanted to give him enough rope. Six weeks later the money was gone and Oxell was headed for prison after trying to rob a bank with an empty gun.

I could have given him a hundred dollars but money never meant much to me after I inherited that can of silver quarters.

"We need to speak to your daughter," I said to the Purdys after pushing down the painful memories of childhood.

"What about you?" Johnson asked the man behind me.

"Rose is in trouble," Redbird said. "Her mother wants us to help her if we can."

"Is that true, Mr. Rawlins?" Virginia Purdy asked. I got the definite feeling that they didn't trust Teh-ha.

"As far as I can tell."

The couple looked at each other. The woman nodded and the husband did too.

"She's living in a house on the ocean seventeen miles north of San Diego," she said. "When she was a child she had a make-believe friend named Alexis Storyman. That's the name she's using down there."

They gave us the address.

"Can we have the phone number?" Redbird asked.

"She doesn't have a phone," Virginia said.

"Then I guess we better be going," I said.

"Would you like me to make you some sandwiches to take along?" the rich wife offered.

At the front door of the four-story estate I stopped and turned to my hosts. Redbird was already walking down to the car.

"Does anybody else live here with you?" I asked.

"What do you mean?" Virginia asked.

"Servants, gardeners, security."

"We are, each of us, wealthy by inheritance, Mr. Rawlins," Johnson said. "I do my own gardening and there's a maid that comes in three times a week to help my wife with the cleaning. A man must support his own weight, no matter how much money or power he has; that is the law of gravity."

42

"Pass me one'a those sandwiches, will ya, Redbird?" I said when we were on the highway going south.

"Cheese and salami?"

"Sure."

Taking a bite, I said, "This is good. Bread tastes homemade."

"Okay," the copper man said.

"Where you from?" I asked just to make conversation.

"I am the last of the Taaqtam. My people lived in what you call the San Bernardino Mountains. They were here for many thousands of years."

"You from a reservation?"

"My uncle raised me in the desert. I liked to read and count things so he sent me to school. I went to college so that I could learn about my people and tell my uncle what had happened to us . . . before he died." An entire biography in three sentences; I was impressed.

"They taught about your people in college?"

"They gave me the tools."

I had rarely met a man or woman who actually went to school for knowledge. Most people were preparing for a job or career, trying to get a leg up on their competitors.

"What about Lenore?"

"I work. She pays me."

"She seems to collect different races up in there."

"Yes."

"What's up with that?"

"I don't know. I think she's looking for something, trying to make something. It doesn't matter to me."

Looking up, I saw an exit sign that read HADLEY'S CROSS.

"There it is," I said, and the spoken history lesson was over.

The off-ramp turned into a two-lane road that wound around until it ran southward along a white shell-strewn beach. Now and then there was a house or trailer to the left. At that time in Southern California these beaches were pretty empty, the land around them sparsely populated.

We came upon a large pink house that stood on a bluff. It was a three-story rambling wood structure. There was a large gateway made from graying timbers but no fence. A multicolored painted sign hanging from the upper timber announced GENESIS FARM.

We drove through the portal up to the house, where there were nearly a dozen other vehicles parked. Three young white men were sitting on the big porch passing a joint between them. One wore blue and red overalls, another army camouflage, and the third went bare-chested in loose-fitting swimming trunks. They all had long hair that ran from brunette to blond. They had beards and mustaches too, though with two of them the facial hair was rather sparse.

"Hey, brothers," the blond-haired swimmer greeted.

"Hi," I said.

"What can we do for you?"

"We want to talk to Alexis."

"Why?"

"Just to ask a question."

"What question?"

Our inquisitor and his two friends got to their feet.

"I'm looking for a friend of mine named Robert Mantle, also called Uhuru Nolicé."

"What you want with him?"

"His mother is worried sick that he's in trouble and she asked me to find him."

"And how did you get here?" the brown-haired man in camouflage asked.

"Alexis's mother told us where she lived."

I was hoping that the Purdys paid the bills at Genesis Farm. That way the tenants might be beholden to them. I wanted to make our way as smooth as possible because I suspected that soft-spoken Redbird was not a very peaceful man.

"My mom?" a young woman said.

A naked girl, not three years out of adolescence, stood framed in the pink doorway. Her figure was youthful, defying if not actually denying the weight of the world. She walked out onto the porch and all three of the young men looked at her. I could tell by the way she moved, and the absence of tan lines, that she spent most of her days in this state of undress.

"Her and your father too," I said, concentrating on her face.

Her features were unremarkable but who cared about that?

"Why?"

"Look, Dawn, let's just say I'm from another planet. Back where I come from, on Mars, men go crazy around a naked woman. So could you please put something on? For me and my pal here."

"Hi, Bird," the girl said to my companion.

"Miss Purdy."

The woman ducked into the front door and came out again in less than a quarter minute. She was donning a long-sleeved, red-flannel man's shirt. I will, for the rest of my life, remember the last glimpse of her perfectly formed and weightless breast.

"Yes?" she said.

"Can we talk alone?"

"You don't have to go with them," Redhair in overalls said. His voice was higher than I would have suspected.

"It's okay, Akra," Alexis/Dawn said. "I know Bird. Come on, guys, we can go to my garden."

She led us around the right side of the house into a fenced-in flower garden. There was a slender path through the profusion of brightly colored blooms. Among the blossoms were dozens of types of flowers, including delphinium, poppies, miniature sunflowers, dandelions, and fuchsia.

The path led to a smallish redwood picnic table. Pulling Redbird by the arm, Dawn made him sit next to her. I settled across from them.

"We're looking for Rosemary," the Indian said.

Dawn smiled.

"We think she's in trouble," I added.

"Rose is always in trouble," the young woman assured me. "That's the way she likes it."

"Somebody cut off one of her fingers," I said, "and sent it to her father with a note demanding a million dollars."

"Really?" she asked Redbird.

He nodded and she frowned, dropping her light mood.

"Oh, no."

"Do you know where she is?" I asked again.

"No. We haven't talked since we left the ashram."

"What's an ashram?"

"It's a place where people meditate and pray. A guy who calls himself Vandal is the leader. It's up in Laurel Canyon."

"You think she's there?"

She shook her head and said, "We left together. Vandal wanted us to get money for him from our parents. He wanted to buy land in the desert where he could start a real commune. When we said that we wouldn't help him he locked us in the pool house but we got away."

"You think she'd go back to him?"

"No," Dawn said with certainty.

"Do you know anybody that she'd go to if she was in trouble?"

"You mean like getting her finger cut off?"

"The kind of trouble you couldn't tell the police about."

"There was this guy we called Minx. He broke us out of that pool house one night when everybody else was asleep. Minx was in love with Rose."

"They had a thing?" I asked.

"No. She didn't like him like that."

"Do you know where he is now?"

"No."

"Do you know his full name?" I asked.

She shook her head.

"This is serious, Miss Purdy," Redbird said.

"I really don't know. After leaving the ashram Rose and I split up.

My parents bought this place and put me here. I was afraid that Vandal would come after me."

"How did he plan to get money from you?"

"He just wanted me to ask my parents and there was this secret that Rose knew." She hesitated a bit then.

"What secret?"

"It was something about her father's business. She said that he did something illegal with some revolutionaries or something. Vandal wanted to blackmail him."

"And this Vandal's in Laurel Canyon still?"

"I guess. It's at the top of Buena Vista Court. A real big house that belongs to the Newmans."

"You know the address?"

"It's the big blue house with golden rosebushes on the pathway leading up to the door."

Walking back to our car we were watched by nine pairs of hippie eyes. Most of the commune had come out to protect their meal ticket. I couldn't blame them. It was an idyllic existence down there looking over the ocean. Their life, I remember thinking, was as delicate as the wildflowers in Dawn's garden. It didn't matter that it wouldn't last.

Beauty never did.

43

Most of the ride back to Los Angeles, Redbird and I were silent, but that's not to say we were uncommunicative.

When I lit a cigarette he opened his side vent window.

I turned on the soul station KGFJ. After listening for twenty minutes or so Redbird switched the channel until he found a station playing classical piano.

I stretched my hand over toward the picnic basket that Virginia Purdy had given us. It was just out of reach and so he took out a sandwich for me.

"I think we should get some help with this Vandal guy," I said upon reaching the southern border of L.A.

"Okay."

We stopped at a street corner and I made a call.

"Hey," someone answered. It sounded like a teenager, probably a boy.

"Terry there?"

"Sure," the kid said and the phone banged down.

"Hello?" a tenor male voice said a minute or two later.

"Hey, Terry, it's Easy Rawlins."

"I took Coco back to Compton this morning."

"Actually I wanted to talk to you."

"About what?"

"Do you know a guy named Vandal that lives in Laurel Canyon?"

"At the Newmans' ashram?"

"You know him?"

"I know the Newmans. They used to have feasts up there. But then Vandal came and the vibes got bad."

"Bad how?"

"The Newmans, Lev and Anna-Maria, are old people, you know like in their fifties. But they like the hippies and opened their house to people like I do. Vandal came as a kind of holy man or something. He ran the meditation sessions and then he kind of took over the house. He makes everybody do things his way. It's just not cool."

"Would you meet me up there and introduce me and my friend to the Newmans?"

"Sure, Easy. Give me an hour."

I always get lost driving around up in the canyons. The roads twist and turn up there like maggots on an overripe peach. But Redbird could follow a map out of hell. Without one false turn we made it to the top of Buena Vista Court.

Dawn was right. The blue mansion and golden roses were the only address we needed.

The lot was at the crest of the hill and we could see L.A., the Valley, and almost all the way to the ocean. It felt rich up there.

Terry was standing next to his cobalt Jaguar. He surprised me by wearing a blue blazer and dark, dark green slacks. He still had brown leather sandals on his feet and wore no shirt, but he seemed at least to be trying for some kind of professionalism.

"Easy," he said.

"This is my friend Redbird."

"Hello," Redbird greeted.

"Good to meet ya, man," Terry replied.

There was no plan to go over. We just walked up the rosy path to the front doorway. The door itself had been taken off its hinges, so we went through, finding ourselves in a large room furnished with various sofas, divans, and settees upon which sat and reclined eighteen or more hippies. The scent of patchouli oil permeated the room; it almost overwhelmed the smoke of the joints being passed around.

The hippies were mostly but not all young. There were a few men and women in their thirties, and two as old as forty-five.

"You an Indian?" a young fair-haired girl asked Redbird. She was wearing a full-length East Indian dress of blue and burgundy velvet with tiny mirrors stitched in here and there.

"Taaqtam," Redbird said, and we moved out of the room of dreamers.

We passed through a kitchen where six young women were cooking, baking, and prepping—all the while chattering about things that had nothing to do with food.

It struck me that though the hippies wanted to turn the world on its head, they kept pretty close to the expected roles of men and women.

Outside there was a broad lawn, an Olympic-sized swimming pool, and a large jury-rigged canopy constructed from thick bamboo stalks and palm fronds. In the center of this shelter was a big chair covered with plush purple cloth. In the chair sat a man wearing black pants and a black, long-sleeved pullover shirt. His wavy, shoulder-length hair was also black, as were his eyes, which were penetrating even from twenty feet away.

Around the man, sitting on the ground in lotus and half-lotus position, were a dozen or so acolytes. Their eyes were closed and their faces rapt.

"Terry," a man whispered.

"Hey, Lev," our hippie guide said. "This is my friend Easy."

The man was in his fifties with a big gut, wearing a blue and green tropical shirt. His shorts were tan.

"Shh," Lev said, putting a finger to his lips. "It's meditation hour."

"What is this interruption?" the man in black said.

People all around were opening their eyes.

"Sorry, Vandal," Lev said, holding his hands up in surrender. He had a mane of salt and pepper hair and the strong hands and biceps of a man who'd spent a lifetime doing physical labor. "They didn't know."

"I know you, Terry Aldrich," Vandal said. He got up from his throne, his movements fluid and feline.

Redbird took a step forward. I didn't try to stop him.

"This is a sacred place," Vandal said, luxuriating in his power and his words.

In an instant I hated him.

"It's okay, Vandal," Lev was saying. "I'll see them out."

"Why are you here?" Vandal asked, ignoring his landed vassal.

"Rosemary Goldsmith," I said, looking over Redbird's shoulder into Vandal's daunting gaze.

"She betrayed us."

"I don't care about that shit," I said. "I need to find her and so I'm here asking."

There was a slight waver in Vandal's arrogant stare that lasted maybe a second and a half.

"Leave," he said, holding up his left hand with all the fingers extended.

That's when Redbird pounced. In my many years of struggle, from street fights to military battles, I had never seen a man move faster. The Taaqtam warrior knocked the cult leader on his back and, from nowhere it seemed, produced a large, gleaming hunter's knife. This he held to Vandal's throat.

"Where is she?" I heard the Indian say.

His prey coughed and stuttered but couldn't manage to speak.

"Tell me or I'll cut your throat right here."

The penitents were awake and rising to their feet but none of them approached Redbird and Vandal, so I left the pistol in my pocket.

Redbird slapped Vandal.

"Please don't kill me!"

"Where is she?"

"I don't know! I don't know! I don't know!"

The ensuing silence was probably the closest thing to a religious revelation that had occurred in the Newman backyard. Vandal had turned two shades lighter and Redbird was hunched over him like a huntsman about to gut his not-quite-dead kill.

For his part Vandal had been reduced to pure fear; there was nothing else in him.

"Brother," I said. I don't know why I didn't use his name. I didn't touch him because that would have certainly ended in violence. "Let him go. You kill him and we won't ever find her."

Slowly, Redbird rose up from Vandal.

"How about a man named Minx?" I asked the dethroned religious leader.

"He left when Rosemary and Dawn did," he stammered. "That was more than eleven months ago."

Moving on his back, using his elbows and heels, Vandal scuttled away from Redbird, who turned quickly away, walking past me and into the house.

Terry and I followed as the hubbub started up among the devotees.

Outside, next to Terry's Jaguar, I shook the young hippie's hand.

"Sorry about that, man," I said. "I didn't expect a war."

"Some people only understand the misuse of power," he said. "In my civics class they talk about how despots and dictators are often overthrown and killed."

There I was, talking to a high-school senior. He wasn't yet eighteen but there was a man behind that ugly mug.

"Terry." It was Lev. He hurried up to us, looking over his shoulder now and then.

"Hey, Lev. Where's Anna-Maria?"

"She got out of here. Last month she went off shopping with one of Vandal's girls, DeeDee. Anna gave the girl a thousand-dollar watch and she let her go."

"He's keeping you prisoner?" I asked.

"He spent all our money on his people. We're deep in debt and he wants the sewing factory. Anna's parents own the deeds and he wants to get them signed over so he can build his commune."

"You should come with me, Lev," Terry said. "Come on down to my house. I'm sure Easy here can talk to some people and get those free-loaders out of there."

"Do you know a guy named Minx?" I asked.

"Yes."

"Is that his real name?"

Glancing over his shoulder toward the house, the fat man said, "Youri Kidd. His name is Youri Kidd."

"You know where I can find him?"

There were a few big guys standing out on the lawn of Lev's house.

"No," he said miserably.

The men started walking toward us.

That seemed like a good time to take out my pistol.

Noting my gun, they stopped and conferred. Then they headed back for the house.

"Terry, you better take Lev down to your place. Me and Redbird'll meet you there."

I don't know if Vandal's men were going in the house to get guns of their own, because sixty seconds later we were gone.

44

Driving down the curvy mountain roads, I gripped the wheel tightly because my heart was beating so fast I worried that I might lose control. It is in tense moments like these, after the threat has passed, that thoughts flit through my head of their own accord, like flying leaves in a strong wind.

Alana Atman, her missing son Alton, came to mind. Time was running out for that business.

Then I considered lecturing Redbird about pulling out his knife, but my angry heart wasn't in it.

We arrived at Terry's mansion on Ozeta Terrace maybe half an hour later. The young master and his paunchy middle-aged guest were sitting in the kitchen. Lev was drinking whiskey, Scotch by the smell of it, while Terry sucked on a joint.

I lit a cigarette and Redbird opened the garden door, placed a chrome and green vinyl chair half in and half out, and sat.

"I found it, Easy," Terry said, his voice constricted by the smoke.

"Found what?"

"I know a dude named Millman who's hooked in with some bikers down in Venice. Lev told me that Youri Kidd was a dealer and Millman knows something about all that. I called him and he told me that Youri lives less than a mile from here."

Terry handed me a slip of paper that had a San Vicente address scrawled on it.

"Can you help me?" Lev asked while I studied the note.

"I don't understand," I said.

"You don't understand what?" Lev asked.

"Meditation is like prayer, right?"

He nodded.

"Then why were they smoking dope in the living room?"

"Vandal says that the herb enhances perception, that it brings us to a higher revelation. Minx was his supplier for a while."

"And you believe that prayer and getting high go together?"

"Not anymore," he said, and then finished off the glass of whiskey.

Terry was taking a long hissing toke off of his joint.

"Is your friend safe here?" I asked the young hippie.

"I can lock the doors," Terry said after exhaling. "And my father gave me the number for some bouncer guys if I ever got in trouble. I guess I could call them if I had to."

"Okay," I said to Lev. He was pouring himself another drink from a crystal decanter. "I'll take care of it right after this business I'm in. But it'll cost you one thousand dollars."

"Anything you say."

It was a strange moment in time. The scared businessman that had worked his way up by physical labor and hard sweat, the member of an extinct North American tribe sitting inside and in the sun at the same time, and the hippie inhaling his drug—it felt to me even then like a special moment that might never be repeated.

Youri Kidd's address was two blocks north of 3rd Street. It was a side-by-side single-story two-family house. It once had been a modest home but somebody got old and decided that their property could supplement their income, and so split the dwelling down the middle to assure their later years.

I knocked on Youri's door. When he didn't answer I knocked again.

Then I tried the door next to his. The mailbox told me that this half-home belonged to Miss Phyllis Landers. No answer there either.

Now and then a car cruised down San Vicente but there was little to no pedestrian traffic. That was back when most people had jobs from nine to six or eight to five, or even seven to four. Leisure happened at night and on the weekends for most folks.

"Maybe I should go around back," Redbird said.

"Maybe you should."

While standing out front I smoked a cigarette and wondered about Jackson Blue and Percy Bidwell. I find that it's helpful to think about seemingly simple problems while waiting for the more complex jobs to gel.

The door to Youri's apartment came open. Redbird was standing there. I remembered a time when I was the one who went around the back and came in through some window.

While pushing the door closed Redbird said, "He's in the bedroom."

An air conditioner was on full blast in the bedroom; that cut down on the odor and swelling. Pale, wearing only striped boxer shorts, the young man was quite thin and dead. He had been beaten before his throat was cut. His left leg was on a single mattress that had no frame or box springs. His penis poked out through the opening in the shorts.

"He's cold," Redbird said.

I saw no reason to check this claim. I noticed that my partner was wearing cloth gloves. I always had a pair in my back pocket when I was working. I took them out and donned them before going through the apartment looking for any sign of Rosemary.

Redbird concentrated on the drawers and closets while I studied the floor and went through the trash.

After forty-five minutes I had come up empty. The only thing Redbird found was a tiny phone diary that contained a couple of dozen numbers, not one of which was connected to a full name.

"You want me to do it?" I asked my fellow burglar.

He nodded once.

In the living room of the six-hundred-square-foot apartment there was a tan couch that had its legs sawed off. Sitting down, you were right at the floor. I took the big black phone next to it and started making calls.

"Hello?" a man answered for a number with the name *Manny* next to it.

"Am I speaking to Youri Kidd?" I stated in an official tone.

"Hell, no."

"I'm Sergeant Chris with the LAPD."

"Good. I hope you arrest his ass and put him in jail," the man said, and then he hung up.

No answers came from Humps's or Beady's numbers.

"Hello?" a woman's voice said for Nelda's line.

"May I speak to Youri Kidd?"

"He's not here. Who's this?"

"Sergeant Chris of the LAPD."

"Oh. Is Youri in trouble?"

"He's dead." A real cop wouldn't have been so generous with information, but most civilians didn't know that and I needed to cause consternation in my less-than-sly interrogation.

"No. Oh, my God. What happened?"

"He was beaten and stabbed to death."

"Oh, God. Oh, no. Oh."

"I'm calling numbers from his phone book to try to find out if he had any enemies or if someone was after him."

"If it's anybody it's that Rosemary Goldsmith and MG."

"Rosemary? I don't see her name anywhere. There's an R. Goldsmith."

"That's her. That bitch. He saved her life and she just left him. You know he was really in love with her but she just used him. She moved up to Santa Barbara and then came back with some black guy and took up with Most Grand and his people. Youri had left all that behind him."

"There's no Most Grand here. Does he have another name?"

"He does but I never knew it."

"Why do you think that Rosemary and this guy Grand would hurt Mr. Kidd?"

"Most was always talking about armed revolution and killing the pigs and the traitors. He thought Youri was a traitor because they said that he sold drugs. But Youri was trying to get his life together. He was a good guy."

"What is your last name? All I have in the book is Nelda."

There was a click in my ear. Nelda had gotten suspicious and hung up.

Redbird was standing at the shaded window, looking out for anyone coming our way.

The phone began to ring. I was pretty sure that it was Nelda. I figured that the first thing she'd do was call Youri to see if maybe it was a prank call. I let the phone bleat eight times while thumbing through the little diary. At the very back there was an entry for an *MG*.

When the ringing stopped I picked up the receiver and dialed again.

"Yes?" a young woman answered.

"Hi, my name is Chris Johnson. I'm a driver for National Delivery Service."

"Uh-huh."

"I'm supposed to be delivering a package to a guy but I only have his initials, MG. The address I had is up on Buena Vista Court in Laurel Canyon. But they said he wasn't there and gave me this number."

"I don't know how you got that address. Most—I mean MG lives on Theodore in Studio City."

"Can I have that address?"

"I don't know."

"Okay, but this is a time-sensitive cashier's check."

"Can he call you?"

"No. I'm in my truck."

45

It was a short drive up Doheny, across Sunset, through the pass, and down into Studio City; barely enough time to prepare a meal or take a bath.

"You work for yourself," Redbird said once we were well on our way.

I wasn't sure if this was a question but I said, "Most of the time."

"You ever work for a white detective?"

"No. Never."

I could feel him staring at me.

"You don't need them?"

"They need me. It used to be in the old days that if a crime happened in the black community nobody really cared. Either they arrested somebody or they didn't and if they did that man might be guilty and he might not; either way he was likely to go to jail. But when there's somebody white involved or something that might affect white people, they might find that they have to get to the real truth. That's when they call on me."

"So you still work for them," he said, turning away.

"Not usually. Most'a the time it's black people looking for help come to me. I trade this for that and do what I can. You the one askin' about me and the Man."

"So I am," he said, looking away and into himself, as if I had imparted some intriguing bit of information.

Theodore Lane was a secluded street and Most Grand's address was on a brown and yellow placard in front of a huge hedge of oleander. You couldn't see the house but there was a driveway. I parked the car a block away and turned to my companion.

"What do you think?" I said.

"Nobody's on the street. We could go through the hedge and use it to see them."

"We could also call the police."

"Lenore wants us to find out how her daughter is involved before turning to the law."

"How she's involved? She got her fuckin' finger chopped off—that's how she's involved."

"They won't see us if we're careful."

There was a gardener's lane cut into the north side of the poisonous oleander hedgerow. The opening was only four feet high and half that in width, so the copper-colored man and I crouched down and made our way to a place that overlooked the house. From that vantage point we surveyed the lot through a thin scrim of bright green leaves.

It was a one-story ranch-style house, small for such an impressive hedge. There were no cars in the driveway or the open garage. There was no sign of life whatsoever.

"Give it an hour?" I suggested.

"Two," Redbird said with certainty.

"You got a gun on you?"

"No."

He squatted down and I remained standing. I wanted a cigarette but knew that we were too close to the house for that.

"Tell me something," I said after five minutes of silence.

He stood, turning his attention from the house to me.

"Why are two departments of the federal government involved here?"

He gauged me for ten very long seconds, then looked down, considering the question.

"Rosemary was working with an aid organization in South America year before last," he said. "Volunteer work."

"What country?"

"That's better not to say. She was working in a small village when the president of the country, a real dictator, sent a platoon of soldiers to bring her and her friends to the presidential palace. They thought they'd be put in prison but instead the president held a feast for them.

"Rosemary had worked all summer with people who suffered from poverty in the rural countryside and she hoped to convince the president to help them, to allow them a greater say in the government. He told her that if the peasants had their way that they would bring in a communist slate. She said that if people are allowed to choose, then that choice would always be the product of democracy.

"He was surprised that she thought this and told her so. When she asked him why he was confused by an American wanting democracy, he told her that Goldsmith Armaments International had their regional headquarters not two miles from his palace. When she wondered why this should affect her allegiance to the poor, he said that the Goldsmith compound was where America trained its anticommunist rebels. He said that the men that killed the previous, socialist-leaning president were technically in the employ of Goldsmith International."

"I guess she didn't like that," I surmised.

"She felt that she was the cause of the suffering and death of the people she'd been trying to help."

"That's what might have made her turn into a radical?"

"That and *el presidente*'s fortune-telling witch."

"What about her?"

"This woman had a leather bag of little bones that she threw and read. Through this method of divination she would give the leader advice."

"So?"

"These bones were taken from the fingers of leaders tried and executed for rebellion."

"Oh," I said, thinking about that detached finger in a whole new light.

———

Maybe an hour after that exchange I said, "Either there's nobody down there, they're asleep, or they're dead."

Hidden by the bushes, we circled around to one side of the house, then made our way down to the south side. The windows there were shaded, and so it was unlikely that anyone could see our approach.

The windows at the back were also shaded, with curtains drawn.

The back door led out onto a wooden platform maybe three feet above the lawn. The only thing on the deck was a big tin trash can.

"You get around the side," I said to the Taaqtam.

"Why?"

"I'm gonna knock."

Once again donning my gloves, I sidled up to the back porch and gently pushed against the side of the can—testing it. It was empty, or mostly so. I shoved it hard enough to knock it down the pine stairs, throwing off its tin top and making a loud clatter.

Before the can had stopped rolling I was with Redbird peering around the corner and glancing now and then at the other side and at the windows to see if someone was looking out.

Nothing. No thumping of fast footsteps, furtive movements of window dressing, no sound or cracked door—nothing.

Five minutes went by, ten. Then Redbird picked up a palm-sized stone and threw it through a closed window on the side of the house. The glass shattered. We waited.

Nothing.

"I guess we should try knocking again," I said.

Redbird gave one of his rare grins and walked toward the steps of the back porch.

As he mounted the stairs I moved off to the right about eight feet back, got down on one knee, and aimed my pistol at the phantom enemy in the doorframe.

Redbird crouched down, tried the knob, which failed to turn, and then used his bright knife to slip in behind the latch bolt. He pushed the door open and jumped to the side, off and away from the potentially dangerous portal.

Even while going through these motions I could see how deft and how stupid we were. We worked together so smoothly that we said hardly a thing. It was like we'd been soldiers together, relying on each other for months in enemy territory. But that address could have been a fake and the police now called to arrest the burglars. Or, worse, the house could have been full of armed radicals ready to shoot it out with the law.

I understood that my whole life had been like this; that I and many of my friends and comrades played fast and loose with our lives. It was something I had always known and yet had never taken to heart. My life up until that moment had been like an unremarkable poker chip that, by chance, stayed in some trickster god's stack through all of his wins and losses.

Luck held. It was the right address and there were no armed anarchists lying in wait. The house was empty of life. There were only mementos of the souls that had stopped there: ashtrays filled with cigarette butts, the kitchen sink and table cluttered with dirty dishes, paper plates, and glasses; the living room had bedding and sleeping bags across the floor. And then there was the master bedroom, where a half-naked woman hung by her neck from the light fixture set in a nine-foot ceiling.

She was young, brown-haired, and dressed only in a white T-shirt that rode up above her waist. Her hands were bound behind her back and there was a piece of notepaper pinned through her shirt and into her flesh that read *TRAITOR*. She was white except for her face, which had bloated and turned a dark blue. The brass fitting had come out from its mooring a bit and so the big toe of her left foot touched the floor. She had been trying to reduce the pressure on her neck by pushing against the floor with that toe.

"We should cut her down," I said to the man with the knife.

"She's dead," he told me. "Let's leave the scene as much as we can the way we found it. Maybe the police will get something from her."

I wanted to be objective about the corpse, as my partner was, but I couldn't shake the feeling that I was the cause of her death. The body was still warm to the touch. She was, I believed, the woman who had answered the phone and foolishly given their address. She told the leader, Most Grand, and he made an example out of her.

An hour later we had found almost nothing that might tell us where the killers and their captive had gone. On a wall of the back porch there was a calendar with every other Monday marked with an X.

We left through the hedge again and walked down to my car, hoping that no one saw us.

46

After agreeing that he would return in the early hours of the next morning, Redbird took the Silver Shadow from my driveway and went off to whatever place extinct tribesmen go.

I wandered the house thinking about forces beyond my control.

When I was a child, no more than six, when my mother and father were still alive and everything in the world was right, I asked my father on the front porch of our shanty shack who he thought were the bravest men in the world.

"Sailors," he said without hesitation. "The ones in those old ships that used the wind to blow their canvas sails."

"Why them, Daddy?" I asked. I was snuggled up next to him on the big soft chair because it was cold outside. It must have been winter.

"Because, Ezekiel, a sailor would set out on a voyage that lasted for months at a time. Him and his friends were on a ocean so big that nobody could even see 'em and they rode on waves taller than mountains, fought storms that was big as God. It was like the entire world was against them and they was no more than ants tryin' to make their way through the mud and dung of the elephants' playground.

"It's brave to shoot a gun when you fightin' against another man with a gun, or to hunt a bear with your buddies armed with some spears and such, but to go out over the blue sea on a boat like a leaf with nothing but the wind at your back and emptiness that go on forever in front'a you—that's more than brave, more than foolhardy; that's courage, son."

This was the gist of his answer, though over the years I've begun to doubt the exact wording. But I remember faithfully what I felt like: the chill in the Louisiana air and the rumble of my father's voice all around me like a vast ocean itself; the smell of smoke from the woodstove and burnt kerosene from lanterns.

It felt to me that night while I tromped back and forth, up and down through the new house, that my father's words were like prophecy over the forty years that separated me from him and my mother's love. I was little more than an ant up against the assembled forces of a world that could, that probably would crush me and never even notice the loss. I skipped the windmill completely and went wielding my sword against the wind itself.

I loved my father something fierce.

"Hello," he answered on the sixth ring. It was maybe three in the morning.

"Mr. Manning," I said.

"What do you want?"

"The truth might be good."

"You mean like when you told Captain Reynolds that you weren't hired to find the Goldsmith girl?"

"The only one you and Frisk ever been interested in was Bob," I said. "You sent me to that gym, only wanted to know about him."

"What do you want, Rawlins?"

"You got my letter?"

"You can forget that. The LAPD doesn't employ private detectives."

"No? Then where did the money you gave me come from?"

"All American dollars come from the U.S. mint."

"Did Foster Goldsmith give it to you?"

"The only Goldsmith I'm interested in is Rosemary. And the only thing I said about her was that she had disappeared and that her father is an important man."

"Bob did not kill those policemen."

"You couldn't possibly know that for a fact."

"The night those men were shot he was in police custody," I said. "I have proof of it."

"I don't believe you," he said.

"You know what I think, Mr. Manning?" He didn't reply and so I went on, "I think that you or maybe somebody else wants to prove that Bob did something wrong, probably that he killed those policemen. I think that they were happy sitting back and waiting for him to get shot down in the street but then he got mixed up with Rosemary and the game got taken to a whole nother level. That's why I got brought in so long after he was supposed to have committed the first crimes."

There passed maybe fifteen seconds of silence and then the phone on the other end of the line broke connection. I waited, listening to the vast emptiness of the phone's dimension and then there came another click. I cradled the receiver and went out on the front lawn to smoke.

Out there I went over the short, one-sided conversation a few times. For the little he said, Manning was talking like an actor in front of an audience. He suspected that the phone was bugged; maybe by me or by parties unknown. His knowledge and his guilt were one and the same.

47

I was outside smoking when the Silver Shadow pulled way up into the driveway of my new house. That was five twenty-nine a.m.

Redbird and I didn't speak, didn't even nod. We got into my car, which was parked on the street, and I headed east. I tuned to a classical music station that was playing a long succession of uninterrupted piano concertos. Redbird didn't ask me where we were going. He, like those sailors of old, was the kind of man that let the wind take him.

It was midmorning by the time we got there. Melvin must have seen us coming. He was waiting out in front of the Walton cabin. He wore the same shorts and shirt and sported thick facial hair after only a couple of days without shaving. It was the beginning of a black beard, graying around the jowls.

"Easy," he said.

"Melvin. This is Redbird. He works for Rosemary Goldsmith's mother."

The men nodded at each other.

"How's our prisoner?" I asked.

"He just sits there. Every now and then I walk him to the outhouse out back. I had to go into town for provisions. He didn't even try and break his cuffs."

Melvin led the way into the cabin. The bloodstains on Uhuru-Bob's white dress shirt had turned black and rust. He looked up with big fearful eyes when we came into the room.

"There's water and beer in the cooler," Melvin said, pointing at a big white Styrofoam box in a corner.

"Hey, Bob," I greeted.

He just stared.

"You okay?"

"Yeah," he said tentatively.

"You know why we got you out here right, brother?"

"I ain't done nuthin', man. Not a damn thing. I didn't even know Rose was gonna rob that liquor store."

"You knew she had a sawed-off shotgun," Melvin said.

"The pig was after us, man. He was gonna kill us and be done with it."

"Pig?" the cop said.

"Mel," I said, to short-circuit the possible confrontation.

"What?"

"I need you to wash up and shave."

"Why? So the kangaroo mice won't smell my stink?"

"We got to go meet somebody."

"Who?"

"Somebody that's kinda helpin' me."

"Where?"

"Down in Twentynine Palms."

Suggs stared at me a moment or two and then went out to the little tin shack designed for showering. Davis had a two-hundred-gallon water tank propped up on a red boulder that hovered behind the little hut. A water service from town filled the tank whenever he called them.

Redbird lifted the lid off the cooler and took out a glass pitcher full of water. He got a tin cup from a shelf, poured himself a draught, then sat at the table staring straight ahead at a blank wall as if it were a window onto the world—he was a man apart.

"So, Bob," I said, now that he and I were virtually alone.

"Yeah?"

"You said you knew a man calling himself MG?"

"I met him with Rose but I already knew who he was, if you know what I mean."

"How's that work?"

"You see," ex-Uhuru Bob Mantle said as the story took him over, "like I said, Rose knew my friend Youri Kidd. Youri helped save her from this cultlike thing up in Laurel Canyon last year. After that he started doin' robbery and burglary and stuff with these people called themselves Scorched Earth. That was like a commune run by the guy you talkin' 'bout. He called himself Most Grand, MG. Really his name was Delbert Underhill but nobody but me knew that."

"So you knew that Youri was hooked up with this Delbert?" I asked.

"Not before Youri took us out there. He had just told me about the group and called the leader Most Grand. I didn't know nobody by that name. But even after I saw him I pretended that he was new to me. Delbert had moved from the old neighborhood to a new part'a town, changed his name, and lived a whole other kind of life. When I saw him again I could tell by how crazy he was that if you even called him Del he'd probably kill you."

"You two weren't friends before?"

"No. We was kids in the same neighborhood. We went to the same schools sometimes but I didn't hang out with him. He was three years older and really bad."

"Rose knew him from before?"

"No. She had just heard about him, about how he was this revolutionary, but that was just a lie. He's a crook is all."

"And when she heard about him from Youri she wanted a meet?"

"That's right. I recognized Delbert but I didn't say nuthin' about it. And Youri brought us there but he didn't do robberies anymore. He just dealt dope and mushrooms mainly. He took me and Rose out to see Delbert in the Valley somewhere but he didn't get along with Delbert no more.

"When Del and Rose met it was like they was lookin' for each other they whole lives. She just forgot about me and they talked all night long."

"And what's Del's story?" I asked.

"The people in his political commune were scared'a him but they loved him too, really loved him. And so when he was with Rose, which was a lot, they let some things drop because he was all they thought about. MG this and MG that. That's how I found out that he was on parole. His PO think he's workin' as a plumber but really he got this girlfriend in the master plumber's office fakes his work papers. He still has to go in every other week to the parole office but that's all."

I remembered the *X*'s on the calendar in the house of the hanged woman.

"What was he in for?"

"They busted him for larceny but his main thing was pullin' cons and plannin' heists. At least that's what his people bragged about. They said that he graduated from bein' a criminal to a revolutionary. He dropped outta school in the ninth grade after they held him back the second time but he's smart, real smart.

"Rose knew who he was because Youri would talk about the Scorched Earth and how they planned to overthrow the whole government, but as far as I could see really it was just a gang robbin' places and talkin' all big."

"So you and Rose came down to L.A.," I said, trying to map out the series of events in my mind, "got in touch with Youri, and he brought you to Delbert."

"That's how it was, man. Rose kept sayin' that she knew how to make it so that Delbert and his people could bring down her father's whole weapons company and embarrass the government too."

"But if Youri had broken from them then why would he help?"

"He didn't want to be part of it but Youri had a hard-on for Rose too. He didn't wanna take us out there but when she aksed he just had to give in."

"And that's how the three of you hooked up?"

"Delbert wasn't too happy to see Youri. He said that he told him that he never wanted to see him again. He said that Youri had betrayed him by leavin' Scorched Earth. He kicked that boy's ass sumpin' terrible and threw him out the house. Rose didn't like that but she still wanted sumpin' from Del."

"I don't understand, Bob," I said. "How can you tell me that you already knew this Delbert Most Grand man but it's Youri takes you there?"

"Delbert was famous in my neighborhood, brother. He stole from the student store at junior high and kicked the shit outta the woodshop teacher, Mr. Melview. Everybody for miles around knew Del."

"Did he kill Youri Kidd?"

Bob looked at me and for a moment or two he was himself: Belle

Mantle's son in the small house concentrating on jigsaw puzzles and watching reruns of *Sgt. Bilko*.

"Him and this white dude named Rex went out for a drive one night. They said that they was on a mission. When they got back early in the morning MG woke Rose up in our sleepin' bag and told her that he had to talk with her in his room. That was the day after we got there. I was mad that Rose left and so I went to the kitchen. Rex was in there with this oriental chick. When I was walkin' in I heard him say, '. . . kicked his ass and cut his throat like you got to do to any traitor.'"

"Is Delbert the one killed those three cops?" I asked.

"Naw, man, he didn't have nuthin' to do with that."

"How do you know?"

"Because like I said his people was always braggin' 'bout all the things he did. That's how they made like they believed in him."

Like you putting on costumes, I thought.

"So why would Rose be with Delbert now?" I asked.

"I already told you, man. It was like they fell in love the minute they met. He wanted her but he was paranoid-like and told us both that he didn't know if he could trust us. He had heard about my speeches when I was Uhuru Nolicé but that wasn't enough for him. He told Rose that he had to test her. I didn't know it at the time but that's why she robbed that liquor store; to prove to Del that he could trust her. She even took the teller's wallet so that he could check her out in the newspaper."

"When did you find this out?" I asked.

"After I got shot and she was drivin' me up to Isla Vista."

"Why did she take you back up north and not to Delbert?"

"I begged her not to take me to him. I was scared after what he did to Youri. I tried to warn Rose but she just thought I was jealous. She wasn't mad though. She said that she knew how to get us enough money to leave the country."

"How?"

"Blackmail her father," Bob said. "Get his money and make him admit to payin' for terrorists and dictators and shit."

"You told me before that you never heard about any kidnapping."

"Yeah. I lied, man. I didn't even really believe it but I lied because I thought just knowin' it might get me in trouble."

"Are you lying to me now?" I asked.

"Brother, I don't even have no pants" was his answer. "What I got to lie about?"

His nonsense reply, somehow, went half the way to convincing me.

"Where's your wallet?" I asked.

"In my pants back at that cabin you drug me from."

"If I looked in it would I find an ID for a Beaumont Lewis?"

"How you know that?"

"What the Beverly Hills police arrest you for on August five?"

"Public urination."

"Say what?"

"I had gone up to this political rally in a park south of the Strip. You know, I was like Uhuru Nolicé. After I gave my talk I was gonna walk down to Pico and take a bus. But I had to go so I went back in these bushes and took a pee. When I came out the cops was waitin'."

"And they arrested you and took you to jail?"

"Two days."

"But they had you as Beaumont."

"I like to pretend I'm other people, man. That's all. And I figured if they put a warrant out on Beaumont then he could prove he was ten thousand miles away on a battleship."

"Did they take your picture when they booked you?"

"Yeah."

Sitting there in the desert with the half-naked man and the man soon to be made extinct by Manifest Destiny, the three of us in the middle of nowhere, both safe and in danger—I tried to think of how to move forward, how to believe in something, how to get back to the life I knew but at the same time to become a different man who played by new rules.

"What does Delbert look like?" I asked Bob.

"Real light-skinned and tall. He kinda skinny but don't let that fool ya. He's naturally strong."

"How light?"

"From a block away even a brother might think he was white."

"Listen, Bob," I said. "Everybody is after you. The cops, the feds, probably Delbert if he saw you. Rose is with Delbert now. I don't know if she wants to be with him or not but I can tell you for a fact that I'm the only friend you got. Me and my two partners have to go try and get you and Rose out of this hole you in. So I'm gonna take off those cuffs and leave you here. You can run if you want but you already know that if the cops see you they'll shoot first—and they'll keep on shootin' till you're dead. All I ask is that you wait here for three days. Three days and it'll be settled one way or another."

"What you mean by that?"

"Have you killed anybody?"

"No."

"Then that's what I'm gonna prove."

Bob wouldn't meet my gaze. In the costume of a prisoner he took on that browbeaten persona.

"Do we have a deal, Bob?" I asked.

"Yeah."

I unlocked his cuffs.

I noticed that Redbird was looking at him then. I was hoping that Bob didn't do anything stupid because I didn't think I could stop the native Californian if he attacked.

Bob went over to the cooler and looked inside.

"There's enough food and drink in here," he said. "So I guess I could stay. I will stay. You know them cops shot me and I didn't do a damn thing to them."

"How's the wound?" I asked.

"It hurts."

"Lie down on your stomach and let me see."

I'm no doctor but I'd been around bullet wounds most of my life. There was no serious infection and the bullet hole was knitting nicely. I put on a new dressing and the chameleon-man thanked me.

A while later Melvin came back. He was wearing a wheat-colored suit that was somewhat wrinkled. His light yellow shirt could have used an iron too, but that was the way he always looked before shacking up with Mary Donovan.

"You took off his cuffs?" were the first words Suggs uttered.

"We got to be places, man, and if we get stuck he's gonna have to get outta here on his own."

"We could tell somebody where he is."

"The cops?"

"Why not?"

"Because he's suspected of murder and worse," I said. "We don't want our names in that."

"He might be guilty," Suggs argued.

"What you talkin' 'bout, Mel? He couldn't even rob that liquor store."

Melvin knew I was right. He had spent time with Bob and he had a second sense about criminals.

"He might be a wanted man," the almost-ex-cop countered, rather halfheartedly.

"When I'm finished he won't be."

"Do you know where Rosemary and this Delbert man are?" Redbird was standing over Bob, who was sitting up on the bed.

"I just know that they were at this house out in the Valley somewhere," Bob said, "behind these high bushes."

"We went there," Redbird said. "They were gone."

"Del's people said that they had a place down in East L.A. somewhere but I don't know where it's at."

"He got any family at all down there?" I asked.

"Naw. He was raised in foster homes all ovah the place. He always said that he hated every family ever took him in."

"I could ask my contact to look up the foster care records," Melvin said.

"We got to go" was my answer.

"Could you leave me them tan shorts you was wearin', brother?" Bob asked Mel.

"Why? So you could run?"

"So I could walk around without my dick hangin' out."

Bob's honesty made Redbird laugh loud and long.

48

Melvin followed my Dodge in his Pontiac. With Redbird at my side I led the way to Dino's Diner on the main drag, such as it was, of 29 Palms. There were as many empty lots as there were buildings, and most of the buildings looked as if they might have been condemned sometime before the last administration. But Dino's had some life to it. We parked in the little lot next to the boxy turquoise restaurant.

There were two old guys standing out front conversing in a dialect of English that I only had hints at understanding. Coming out from the front door of the diner was a corpulent woman in a rayon orange pantsuit. Her hair was also orange, as were her shoes. I couldn't help wondering about her underwear.

"Jessop," she said to one of the men, I couldn't tell which.

"Me and tinker you, ma'am," I think he said.

I'd say that the speaker was the older white man in blue jeans and white T-shirt but that description fit both men.

"All right then," the woman in orange said and she stomped off, making the concrete sound like a hollow wood floor.

"What are we doin' here?" Melvin asked. I think he was in a hurry to get back to his solitary drinking.

"It's where we're meetin' my contact."

"Do you need me?" Redbird asked.

"You got someplace better to be?"

"We need gas and I should call Lenore."

"You want I should get you something to go?" I asked.

"There's still some fruit in the basket."

After taking my keys Redbird went to do his chores while Mel and I walked past the old codgers into the claustrophobically constricted diner. There was a counter with five stools and three tables along the opposite wall. All the chairs and four of the stools were occupied and the two waitresses were working hard. There was a rectangular window cut in the wall on the other side of the counter. Through that space we could see the grizzled face of the short-order cook working over steaming foods.

"Number sixteen!" the cook cried as he threw up a plate of eggs over hard, oiled and boiled potatoes, and three strips of bacon that had been fried until they were almost black.

"Got it!" a sixty-something, impossibly black-haired woman in a pink and blue and white uniform yelled back.

"Can I help you?" another woman said.

She was standing at the cash register, looking down, making change.

Hearing something he didn't quite understand, Melvin turned his head toward her.

She was blond with a delicate tan, wearing different makeup than she had in the picture he'd given me. And so for a moment Melvin was confused. The look on his face was like an old friend to Mary/Clarissa. Smiling at him, she began to untie her white apron.

"I was wondering how long it was going to take for you to come looking," she said.

"Mary."

"What's goin' on out there?" the cook's head said from its hole in the wall.

"I'm quitting, Nate," she said, folding the apron and handing it to the elder waitress.

"So this is the one," the older woman said.

"That's my Melvin."

"He looks kinda wrinkled."

"He cleans up just fine . . . when he's got a reason."

No longer able to hold himself back, Suggs took Mary in his arms and squeezed her till she made a not-unpleasant grunting sound.

"You break it you bought it," she said.

"Hey," Nate the short-order cook said. He had come into the room and had a twelve-inch iron skillet in his hand.

I took a step forward and said, "Lover boy's a cop and I'm just a badass. So call your sister or your girlfriend to take Claire's shift because we're outta here."

Nate was probably ex-military. He'd been in enough brawls to know that what he had in front of him was a losing proposition.

"Fuck you," he said.

I smiled and wandered out with Mary/Clarissa and her man.

"I got the car right here," Mel was saying to her.

"Gimme a minute, will ya, Mel?" I said.

"I got to go, Easy."

"Look, man, I'm the one brought you here. I just need a few words."

"What is it?" he said after seating Mary/Clarissa in his Pontiac.

"Don't tell her anything about this business with Bob and Rosemary Goldsmith. Especially not Rosemary."

"Why would I?"

"Just don't, okay?"

"Sure. Is that all?"

"I'm still gonna need a little help with this thing, Melvin. You owe me."

He was like a teenager and she was Helen of Troy. He moved his head to catch a look at her. She smiled nicely and he turned back.

"Yeah," he said, "I owe you. Just call whenever you need to. I'll be there."

As I watched them drive away I worried that I might not have helped him at all.

"Where are they going?" Redbird asked at my back.

"To scare the neighbors and raise the dead."

"Lenore wants to talk with you."

"On the phone?"

"In person."

———

We made the Dumbarton in about an hour and a quarter. People still stared but the security staff left us alone.

"Your news is rather distressing, Mr. Rawlins," Lenore Goldsmith said from the big chair with its back turned to the sky.

I was seated before her. Redbird stood behind her and to the left.

"I mean," she continued, "you're saying, you're both saying that my daughter might have been party to her own disfigurement. I can't believe that."

"It might not be true," I said. "But Bob says that she wanted to get in with this Delbert guy and Redbird told me the dictator story."

"She despised the fact that the general used those men's bones."

"As much as she despises her father?"

"I don't want this to be true," she said. She was a woman who had in her life reversed many truths, changed natural laws that seemed immutable.

"All we can do is try to find out," I said.

"What do you suggest we do next?"

"Not we," I said, "me."

"You'll bring Redbird of course."

"Maybe later," I said. "I need to work on this alone for a bit."

"But the time has been set for the ransom drop."

"It has?"

"In forty-eight hours."

"Where did you get that?"

"From Thomas Crispin, my husband's personal assistant."

"Do the police know this?"

"No one does. After Foster received— When they sent, they sent that, that . . ." She took a minute to gather her emotions and said, "There was a phone call."

"From who?"

"Thomas didn't know, but Foster gave the order to gather a million dollars in circulated bills and he did not want the authorities to find out."

"Why not?"

"Not because he loves our daughter, you can be sure of that. He wants to protect himself from being exposed as a provocateur. He wants to get Rose away from those men and then, later, he'll take care of them."

"Why would he care about anybody talking about what he does for the government? They know, don't they?"

"As I told you, Mr. Rawlins, my family owns the controlling interest in Goldsmith Armaments International. If it got into the papers that he was involved in foreign intrigue, they would lose face and the faith in his ability to lead."

"Then why wouldn't you or Rosemary just tell them about him?"

"It's not the fact of his actions," Lenore Goldsmith said, as if talking to a child, "but the public spectacle. Rose knows that."

"And what if your family found out that Rosemary was in it with the kidnappers?"

"That's different. That's a family issue. Rosemary is of our blood and therefore above business concerns."

I spent a few moments digesting this worldview.

"This man Crispin is loyal to you?" I asked.

"Completely. He's been with my family his entire life. Both his parents worked for us."

"Will he know what your husband is planning?"

"I believe so."

"Look, Mrs. Goldsmith, I like you, and Redbird here is top-notch. But the people I have to deal with are particular. When we get down to the line I'll bring Redbird in, I promise I will. Just give me one day to look into things on my own. In the meantime Redbird can coordinate with your inside man."

Lenore Goldsmith wasn't used to being put off or left out but she was also the kind of person who knew when she had to concede.

"This time tomorrow?" she said.

"If not earlier."

49

Driving south and east of L.A.'s downtown, I felt relieved to be alone. Redbird was a good partner and a solid man to have as a backup, and he didn't talk too much either but I needed more than silence; I had to have solitude to pull together the edges of the broad cloth that comprised the problems presented by the gulf between Rosemary Goldsmith and Bob Mantle.

I stopped at a phone booth on Slauson, looked up an address, and wrote it down.

I decided against calling Sister Godfreys. I didn't want to spook or warn her so I drove over to her address on Wadsworth Avenue off of Florence Boulevard. She lived in a white plaster box that had four apartments—two upper and two on the first floor.

I checked the outside mailbox, walked in the front door, up the stairs, and then knocked on the door to the left.

Without asking who it was, she pulled the door open. She was tall and meaty (not to say fat), wearing a red T-shirt, coral shorts, and an auburn wig that stood high on her head, making her look like a backup singer in an all-girl Motown soul band. She was a sensual woman with dark skin and prominent features. Her expression was careless and friendly—qualities I found very attractive in women. Just looking at her, I wished that Bonnie wasn't winging her way to Asia.

"Yes?" she said.

"Easy Rawlins, ma'am. I'm here representing Belle Mantle."

"Oh. How is Belle? You know I haven't seen her since me an' Bobby broke up. She was nice but I moved since then and I didn't even think she knew where I lived at."

She stacked the facts one on top of the other like red bricks but there was no mortar of suspicion.

"Bob's gone missing," I said, "and she asked me to help find him."

I handed her my PI's license.

Upon reading the little card she said, "I don't understand."

"I'm a private detective and Belle is my client. She thinks that Bob might be in trouble. She told me that you two broke up but I said you might know something."

"It's that Rosemary Goldsmith, idn't it?"

"May I come in, Miss Godfreys?"

"Um. I guess it's all right. I mean you really are working for Belle, aren't you?"

"I just came from her house over on Hoover. She showed me his room with all the pictures of the costumes Bob loved on the wall."

"Okay, Mr. Rawlins. Come on in. But I don't have nuthin' to offer you to drink or eat or nuthin'."

She had two folding pine chairs and an oak bench for furniture in the otherwise empty sitting room. It was like the living room in my new house but I suspected that she wasn't going out to buy new furniture anytime soon. I thought it was a shame that a woman as young and beautiful as Sister found herself in such stark circumstances.

"Take a chair, Mr. Rawlins," she said. "It's more comfortable."

When we were seated I looked around the bare chamber. There were no paintings or prints on the walls, no plants on the window ledges. The floor was pine and finished, swept and bare.

"I don't have nuthin' to drink but water," she said. "I could get you a glass if you want."

"No thanks, Miss Godfreys. I'm kind of in a hurry to find your ex. You said something about somebody—a woman?"

She crossed her legs and the room became softer, more inviting.

"White woman," Sister agreed. "She come up here just yesterday an' give me money for Cousin. Three hundred dollars. She said it was from Bobby but I know for a fact that he couldn't save up that much money 'fore spendin' it."

"She left money for his cousin? Who is that?"

"Not his cousin," she said, "our son, Cousin. Didn't Belle tell you about him?"

"No. All she said was that she hoped you two stayed together."

"Me an' Bobby lived together in a nice apartment when he was still boxin'," Sister said. "But when he got banned he lost heart and moved back home with Belle. Cousin an' me both really miss him."

She turned her head to the side, looking out of the window wistfully.

I followed her gaze, noticing that there were neither shades nor curtains installed.

"And this Rose Gold brought you money for his son?"

"She was talkin' all political and all," Sister said, turning her attention back to me. "She was callin' me *sister* like we was blood an' it wasn't my name. She told me that Uhuru was workin' for the revolution but that he wanted to take care of his son. That's all some shit. Bobby only ever cared about how to be somebody else."

"Uhuru?"

"He started wearin' this dress he called a royal African robe. When he had it on he talked funny and said things about the revolution but it was all just dress-up. That white girl was fooled but I took her money though. Cousin needs clothes and food and I hardly make enough to pay our rent."

"Mama!" a high voice yelled. Then there came the thumping of small bare feet.

He was short and solid, dark with a big ball of woolly hair. He ran right at Sister, leaped in the air, and landed on her like some kind of predator attacking a leaf eater five times its size.

Sister grunted and then folded him in her arms. Somehow she turned him around with this embrace and he found himself looking at me.

"This is Mr. Rawlins, baby. What do you say?"

Somewhere between three and four, the boy was fearless in his mother's arms.

"Hello, mister," he said.

"This is my son," she announced, "Cousin Mantle."

"Hello, Cousin."

He nodded and then squirmed until he was out of his mother's arms and standing between her and me.

"Mr. Rawlins is looking for your father," Sister said.

"My daddy send a white lady with some money to buy me red cowboy boots."

"How long ago?" I asked in the general direction of mother and son.

"I 'ont know," the boy said.

"It was yesterday," his mother amended.

"Was she alone?"

"I think that there was somebody in a car downstairs."

"Did she tell you how to get in touch with her?"

"No."

"She said that when I get my cowboy boots that there was a merry-go-round with yellow and brown and red horses on it right across the street from her friend's house," Cousin said in a quick stream of words. "She said that I could ride a red horse to go with my red boots when I got 'em."

"She did?" I said with real interest.

"Uh-huh. An', an', an' she said that there was a ice cream truck that came by every day and that all the kids runned down to get ice cream on'a stick. They went swimmin' too but you cain't swim right aftah eatin' or you'll get a cramp."

"That's true."

"Uh-huh," Cousin said with a great nod. "An' I could ride a red horse an' eat ice cream and maybe my daddy would be there too."

Cousin had been named by his mother's tradition but he looked just like his father. Gazing on him, I thought about Alton Post; his mother, Alana; and his dead father—Fred.

"I'm sorry I couldn't help you and Belle, Mr. Rawlins," Sister Godfreys said.

I looked up from Cousin into his mother's eyes.

"Can I use your phone, Miss Godfreys?" I asked.

"They disconnected the phone six weeks ago."

"Then I guess I'll be going," I said.

50

"Hello," he said in a voice at least an octave lower than was his norm.

I was standing at a phone booth on East Slauson.

"Get your ass up outta that bed, Melvin," I said.

"What do you want?"

"I told you I was gonna be callin'."

"I've only been home a couple of hours."

"And we both know what you've been doing. But what you got to remember, Mr. Suggs, is that the reason you got that bass in your voice is because I found your girlfriend and brought you to her."

A woman's voice sounded in the background.

Melvin muttered a reply.

She said something else and then the disgraced detective came back to me.

"What do you need, Easy?"

"You think you could get your contact to help us do a simple job?"

"He won't do anything like babysit a wanted felon. I wouldn't ask him to."

"What I have in mind is hardly even bending the rules."

I explained my needs and Melvin asked his questions.

"I guess I can't see anything wrong with that," he said when the cross-examination was through.

An hour and sixteen minutes later Melvin parked his Pontiac behind my car down the block from a house on East 47th Street. I'd found the address by looking up *A. Cox* in the phone book. Pulling up behind him was a classic baby blue 1964 Ford sedan. From this car there issued a giant in a light tan suit. He was six-six at least with the shoulders of an even taller man. His skin was almost true white and the red hair might have connected him directly with the Vikings that had raided his ancestors' shores.

The two men walked up to me—Mutt and Prince Valiant.

"Anatole McCourt," Melvin said, "I'd like to introduce you to Ezekiel Porterhouse Rawlins, a man that I am proud to call friend."

The giant's eyes knitted for a moment and then lifted, bringing with them that smile the Irish are so famous for.

"Pleased to meet you, Mr. Rawlins," he said.

When we shook hands I felt as if he was being careful not to hurt me.

"Likewise," I said, looking up. Then I turned to Melvin. "It's the house with the blue door halfway down the block on the right side."

"They there?"

"They were five minutes ago."

"You sure about this?" Officer McCourt asked. His eyes might have been blue or gray depending on his mood, or yours.

"Absolutely positive."

"If he says so then it's true," Melvin put in, according me greater respect than he ever did before or after that day.

Anatole nodded and both he and Melvin climbed into their cars.

They drove only half a block down the street, stopping in front of the house. A gray dog barked at them and then scuttled away with its tail between its legs. It ran across the street in a sideways gait and stood on the opposite sidewalk barking like an old man debilitated by hard living and disease.

As they mounted the three front stairs my heart quailed. I took out a cigarette and a book of matches.

I could hear Anatole's big fist knocking on the front door from where I stood.

There was a pause and then the front door opened. Angela's loud voice could be heard cursing them and then a man joined in. McCourt and Suggs kept their voices down but Angela Cox and her friend kept up the ruckus. It got so loud that people were coming out of nearby houses to bear witness.

I worried that by sending armed white men to do this job I might cause a shootout or even a riot. But I also knew that using the law to deal with the country criminals was the best way to stem any future retaliation.

Melvin Suggs's voice raised up high enough to be heard but not enough for me to make out the words. The woman stopped arguing and a moment later the white policemen went back to their cars. Anatole was accompanied by a small brown boy.

As soon as the police were headed down the block I got in my car.

EttaMae lived about two and half miles from Angela's blue door. I got there maybe four minutes before the police.

I knocked on the door and waited. It didn't surprise me that the handsome young white man Peter Rhone answered.

A year or so before, Peter Rhone had a crisis of faith after his black girlfriend was murdered. Etta took him in and he became something like a self-indentured manservant to her.

"Hello, Mr. Rawlins," he said.

"Peter. I'm lookin' for Alana Post."

"She's here," the makeshift retainer said. "She and EttaMae are in the backyard with LaMarque."

"The police are going to be coming by in a few minutes," I said. "When they get here ask them to wait a moment and come back to tell us."

"Yes, sir."

A huge walnut tree dominated the Harris-Alexander backyard. The blue grama lawn was rich and thick, having finally revived after the years of LaMarque's rough childhood play. EttaMae, LaMarque, and sad Alana Atman-Post were sitting at a round redwood table that I helped Raymond install over a decade before.

Upon seeing me, Alana got to her feet and staggered in my direction. EttaMae followed her. LaMarque remained seated.

"Did you?" the white woman asked.

I nodded and she took me in an embrace that pinned my arms to my sides. She cried out loud and I stood there in her vise of love.

"My baby!" she yelled. "Where is he?"

"Some friends will be here with him in just a few minutes," I said.

"Let the man go, Alana," Etta said, pulling at her friend's shoulders. "He told you that Alton is comin'. Easy don't lie."

"But where is he?" Alana moaned.

"He comin'," Etta said. "LaMarque."

"Yeah, Mama?"

"Come ovah heah an' brang Alana to a seat."

"Yes, Mama."

As LaMarque did his mother's bidding Peter Rhone was coming out the back door of the house.

"They're here, Mr. Rawlins."

"Who is?" Etta asked.

"The police and Alton."

Etta glanced at the picnic table where Alana cried and then she turned back to Peter.

"Count to fifteen and then bring 'em back here," she said.

Peter nodded and went to accomplish his task. Etta laid a hand on my arm.

"Raymond been callin' every day," she said. "He told me that I should tell you sumpin'."

"Why didn't you call me?"

"He said that it might could put us all in danger if I told you on the phone."

"What is it?"

"He told me to tell you that them cops got killed a while back was in business with the men that shot 'em. I would'a gone out to look for you if I wasn't afraid that Alana might kill herself."

If Satan played bingo in hell, I had just gotten my final winning/losing number.

There was nothing for me to say but even if there had been there was no time to say it because Melvin Suggs and Anatole McCourt came into the backyard with little Alton Post between them.

"Mama!"

Alana screamed something. She ran toward her son, tripped, and fell onto the thick lawn. She scrambled to her feet and grabbed up the boy like he was a rag doll. She was crying incoherently and he was steady talking.

"Don't get mad at the men, Mama," he was saying. "They just wanted to bring me home from Auntie Angela's house. I know you wanted me to stay with her because you was too sad to take care'a me but the men said that a boy had to be with his mama."

Anatole McCourt was watching the reunion closely, assuring himself that he was doing the right thing. Melvin was looking at his watch, counting the seconds it would take to be back in his lover's arms.

Etta ushered us all to the table and sent Peter to bring out a platter of her famous shortbread cookies.

A few minutes later Alton was sitting on his mother's lap eating cookies. The cops were seated, a little uncomfortably I thought, accepting the gratitude of the white woman's friend.

"I told Miss Cox and her boyfriend that this was a kidnapping charge and that I would let it slide if they desisted," Officer McCourt said. "But I'd suggest you move somewhere where they won't be able to find you. Miss Cox's auntie believes that a black child should stay with his own kind and she is very upset to see him with you."

It seemed to me from Anatole's tone that he might have agreed with that assessment.

"I gotta be goin', Easy," Melvin said. When he stood up, Officer McCourt followed suit.

"I'll walk you out," I offered.

Standing next to McCourt's blue Ford, I shook the man's hand and thanked him.

"This is Raymond Alexander's house, isn't it?" he said.

"When he's in town."

"There's a standing stop-and-search order on Alexander," Anatole said to Melvin.

"Can't do that if he's not here," the elder cop replied.

McCourt shrugged, frowned, then smiled and nodded. With nothing left to say, he climbed into his Ford and drove off.

Melvin was about to do the same thing when I put a hand on his shoulder.

"How much do you trust your friend?" I asked.

"A woman named Patricia Knapp worked the street for a rough pimp named Lucky. I busted her carrying drugs for him. She was too afraid to turn him in and she had this little boy named for her dead father. I pulled a few strings and had Lucky put away without her help and then I made sure that Anatole got brought up right. When he was of age I got him on the force."

"You know those cops got ambushed?"

"Yeah. Sure."

"I'd like it if your friend would look into them."

"What the hell for? I mean even if they had some infractions you can't hold it against them after they got murdered."

"You can if the infractions are what they were murdered for. You can if the men that killed them were in business with them."

51

Melvin agreed to ask his Irish ward to find out what he could about the dead policemen, and then he jumped into his own car and was off.

I stood on the street in front of my friends' home appreciating the hot sun on my face and hands. I had helped Etta, and in turn her husband, from thousands of miles away, had guided me. The street was empty and two cops had done my bidding because I did a favor for one of them.

Most of the inhabitants of that working-class block were at some job somewhere getting paid by the hour while they slowly, inexorably sank into debt.

It occurred to me that my debts had no dollar signs attached to them. This thought brought a grin to my lips.

Half an hour later I was sitting in my office chair, reviewing the harvest of my labors.

It was my self-imposed purpose to salvage as much of Uhuru-Bob's life as I could. I liked the young has-been boxer simply because I understood him. He was a fool and a genius in his own way. If he was born another color he might have been recognized as something special.

It might have been my purpose to protect Bob but my first priority was to help Rosemary Goldsmith. This wasn't because I was being paid to save her; money helped but I never worried too much about where it was coming from. No, money wasn't the reason that Rosemary's predicament took precedence in my work. If the white girl was to go down, then Bob would too—that's just the way things happened. Innocence was rarely a key factor for justice in the world Bob and I inhabited.

It was a mistake to be sitting alone and thinking about the unfairness that defined my world. The only thing that would come from that line of thought was unbidden rage. And anger at injustice was the last thing I needed in my heart.

But there I was—smoking and infuriated. Why couldn't I just walk into Chief Parker's office and tell him that there was a conspiracy, conscious or not, against a poor black man who liked to pretend? Why couldn't the truth be enough to keep a mostly innocent man from getting shot down in the street?

Try as I might, I couldn't get the burr of anger out of my heart. I had a job to do but I had to quell the rage inside me.

That's when Fate came knocking on my door.

I put my right hand on the pistol attached by wires underneath my desk and called out, "Door's open."

Percy Bidwell in all his coiffed glory came in wearing a gold iridescent two-piece suit. His shirt was a pale blue and the jacket had only one button.

I hated him on sight but that's not saying much; I would have hated Black Jesus if he crossed my path just then.

The young man walked right up to my desk and looked down on me.

"Mr. Bidwell," I hailed in false greeting.

"Call Jewelle."

I released the pistol, sat back, then stood and came around the desk to face him.

"Say what, young man?"

"I told you to call Jewelle."

"And why would I want to do that?" Every slight, every insult, every affront to me and all of my ancestors and his were roiling in my breast.

"Because I said so," Percy said.

Then there came a lull in my rage. This was a bad sign, I knew, but I was beyond instructive experience at that moment.

"She told me to tell you to call her," Percy said, somehow intuiting that his up-front approach had failed in its purpose.

"Now let me get this right," I said, almost feeling the calmness my voice exuded. "You gonna fuck my good friend's wife, bully her to try and bully me, then you gonna walk in my door and order me to call her. Not ask but command me."

"That baby—" he managed to say before I hit him with a medium-hard straight right hand.

His head bounced back but he wasn't hurt or even pushed off-balance.

He threw a left hook over my extended arm and so I lowered on my haunches and came up with both fists against his chin. This moved him half a step backward. I thought that I had hurt him but he was just bracing for his next attack, which was his right fist against my chest.

Who would have ever expected that a man named Percy Bidwell with a beauty shop hairdo would be made from stone? The punch knocked the wind from my lungs and I would have hit the floor if the wall hadn't been there to keep me from falling.

My eyes opened wide and a wolfish grin came to my lips. When Percy bum-rushed me I tilted to the side and slammed him in the left ear with my right hand. In response he threw a right hook that only managed to numb my shoulder. I lowered my head and butted him in the jaw, then stood up and hit him flush three times.

If he felt any of it you couldn't tell by his actions.

Arms out wide, he moved to put me in a bear hug but I pushed against his shoulders trying to shove him away. He was too powerful to be moved but I was thrown back and out of reach.

Unafraid that I might hurt him, I kicked Bidwell in the midsection. He buckled six inches, no more, so I hit him twice in the nose.

I felt something snap and blood gushed forth from the fop's nostrils.

Percy brought his hand to his nose and then looked at it—his fingers were dripping with blood. Rage and childish fear came over his face. He was a powerhouse but untrained in the ways of battle and the self-control needed to overcome pain. So I picked up my least favorite visitor's chair and hit him for all I was worth.

The chair shattered. Percy finally went down; not all the way but to one knee. I used the wooden leg left in my hand to hit him on the head, then I hit him again. He was sitting by then but still trying to rise.

That's when common sense took hold and I went around the desk to take the pistol from its nest.

When Percy saw the gun he put up his hands. There was blood coming from his nose and also from the two places I had hit his skull.

"You got a hard head, Percy Bidwell," I said. "I hope it's not dense too. Because I wanna tell you that the only way you gonna live to enjoy that college degree is to leave Jewelle and Jackson alone. If I evah hear that you did anything to make them unhappy I will kill you. And if I don't get to you I'll make sure my friend Raymond Alexander does."

"I just—" he said.

"Don't talk, man. Don't say a mothahfuckin' thing. Just get your ass up and outta here. Don't go back to Jewelle's office and don't talk to her. Change your phone number and forget you ever heard about any'a us."

I pulled back the hammer of the .45-caliber pistol.

Percy rose up on his feet weightlessly, as if a higher force had reached down and grabbed him by the shoulders. He stumbled out of the door trying to stanch the bleeding with his hands.

Three or four minutes after he was gone, still standing there with the cocked pistol in my hand, I exhaled and realized that the rage I'd felt had evaporated.

52

Sitting on a pine bench at the edge of Belvedere Park in East Los Angeles, I considered the unexpected blessing of Percy Bidwell. If he hadn't come to me when he did I might have gone off into the world blinded by anger at things I would never control.

I had picked a fight with a man who could have easily killed me with his bare hands. I fought that man and, impossibly, I won. As a youth I might have felt victorious, but nearing fifty I knew that it was just dumb luck that saved my life.

I had been sitting in the park for nearly two hours; long enough for the feeling to return to my left arm—that and the dull ache of wisdom.

The common was filled with brownish people, most of whom had hailed from Mexico or were born to parents that came from there. They spoke Spanish and English with deep accents. From little children to old men, the park was lively. There was the smell of chlorine in the air from the public pool. Young mothers and their babies, silent men and their hefty wives, meandered through the barrio common. They were every color from red to bronze to brown; Indian and Negro mixtures of ancestors who had been raped and plundered by Spanish conquistadors and then left to work the land; the legacy of ancient empires.

I was eating a novelty ice-cream sugar cone that was first dipped in chocolate and then in crushed peanuts. Across from me was a fancy merry-go-round with yellow and brown and red horses prancing in a circle to the upbeat tune of canned calliope music. It was the only carousel of its type in L.A. that I knew of.

I was armed but didn't need to be. After Percy, I had no intention of getting into another battle. It was late afternoon and I was happy watching the groups of pretty young girls and the boys who pretended not to be watching them.

The barrio was a good place for a crook to hide. Your color hardly mattered there and no one wanted to have undue contact with the authorities. Just pay your rent in cash, speak a few words in Spanish, and remember to keep your head down, and you could go unnoticed for years.

I saw her bandaged hand first. The dressing was white but there was a spot of red on the outside edge of the left palm. She wore a blue-gray shift that hid what little figure she had. Her shoes were yellow rubber flip-flops. Next to her was a tall sand-colored man wearing dark sunglasses and a sleek straw hat. His square-cut shirt was dark navy, his trousers black. There was a big straw purse hanging from her right shoulder and her blond hair was limp and greasy.

Rose had lost a few pounds since the photograph in my pocket was taken. But it was her. She was no longer smiling. Rose's somber gaze seemed to be turned inward while the man next to her kept looking from side to side.

When they were half the way across the two-block-wide green I got up and wandered in their general direction. They seemed to be alone but I wasn't taking any chances.

On the other side of the park they were accosted by a rotund honey-colored man carrying a fanciful box draped with Mexican flags and filled with pink and blue cotton candy in clear plastic pouches. He smiled and said something in Spanish. Rose suddenly came to life, chattering with the man and buying one of his flags.

I walked past the couple, considering for a moment a confrontation.

I had a gun and the element of surprise. I could have ended the whole problem with a few quick movements. I might have tried, if not for the blessing of Percy Bidwell. Delbert and Rose probably had guns too. And they were desperate, both of them dialed directly into survival mode.

I reached the pavement and turned right to walk down the crowded sidewalk. Seven steps away there was a man with a Polaroid camera offering to take photographs of babies and lovers for a dollar a shot. A smiling mustachioed man holding a crying infant was posing for the lay photographer. I stopped to watch the spectacle and saw through the corner of my eye Rose and Delbert walk across the street and up the stairs of a big wooden house that was flush up against the opposite sidewalk.

"Smile!" was the only English word the photographer spoke.

I looked up to set in my mind the house that the couple was entering.

At just that moment Most Grand took off his dark glasses and swiveled his gaze in my direction.

Our eyes met for only a moment but that was enough for him, maybe, to have marked me. I turned away and by the time I looked back the revolutionaries were walking through the door of the two-story house.

I went down to the end of the block. From there I could watch the front of the rebel hideout and make a call from a corner phone booth.

Because Delbert might have seen and suspected me I couldn't leave the scene. If they were paranoid they might pack up and leave. If that happened, either I would have to try to stop them or, more likely, search their place for clues to their next destination.

I thought about calling the police, the FBI, and the State Department in turns. But not one of them was worried about the outcome for Bob. And Bob, after all, was the only one I really cared about.

"Goldsmith residence," a young woman said after the Dumbarton operator connected me to the presidential suite.

"Redbird please."

"Mr. Rawlins?" he said, coming onto the line a minute or two later.

"You got a car don't stand out like a sore thumb?"

For the next hour or so I moved around the park and up and down 1st Street, keeping an eye on the hideout. In that time I marked eight people coming in and out, including Rose and Delbert. There were two black men, one Asian woman, and three white men all thirty years old or younger except for high-yellow Delbert. He was nearer forty but hale.

Only two, the Asian woman and one of the white guys, actually left the premises. The others sat out on the porch smoking and talking—there was no drinking that I saw.

Redbird and I had made our rendezvous point the corner phone booth at six. He wore faded jeans and a red and black shirt that was long-sleeved wool.

Walking through the park I pointed out the house and related the intelligence I'd gathered.

"We can't tell the police," Redbird said after I laid out the situation. "They'd probably just come in with guns blazing. Rosemary might get killed."

"And you care about her?" I asked.

"I owe her mother."

"Yeah," I said, thinking about Bob. "I guess we all owe somebody something."

"The ransom payoff is tonight."

"Where?"

"Crispin couldn't get the details," Redbird said. "Goldsmith is making the drop personally. This is our best bet right here."

"Eight armed and dangerous revolutionaries and us," I said.

Redbird's grin had no humor to it.

"Among my people," he said, "before the Spanish came, if a young man wanted to be a chief he had to hunt and kill a bear armed only with two stones and a flint knife."

"That ain't nuthin'. In my neighborhood we got to get through worse than that just walkin' down the street in the mornin'."

53

Redbird and I argued strategies on a park bench not far from the carousel. The sun had set but the sky was still light and there was a mariachi band playing somewhere close by. The park was even more alive and, if I closed my eyes, I had the feeling that I'd left white, European, and English America behind.

"We can take them by ourselves," Redbird said after ten minutes and no détente in sight.

"That's not the question, Teh-ha," I said.

"No? Then what?"

"The question is, can you take them by yourself?"

Redbird was a country unto himself; an independent nation that would fight to the death for the sanctity of its sovereignty. He would have let me walk away if he wasn't in a war to save the daughter of a woman, a vestige of his prior colonization, who had to be appeased for an obscure article in some ancient treaty, written in a dead language.

"Can you trust these friends of yours?" Redbird asked me, his necessary ally.

"Oh yeah."

"Two men could do this," he said, trying one last time to convert me.

"Not without some serious violence."

The aboriginal American hunched his shoulders maybe a quarter inch. The downturn of his lips could be measured only in millimeters.

"You got kids, man?" I asked him.

"Three."

"Where are they?"

"In Berkeley with their mother."

"My girl's on a plane right now but when she comes home she expects me to be there. It's only me that she's got."

Redbird made a small gesture with his left hand, conceding with a flick of fingers.

"What now, Easy?" Melvin Suggs said on the line.

Mary/Clarissa had answered the phone. When I told her who it was she was delighted to go and get her man.

I was calling from a pay phone in the tiny lobby of the Roosevelt Hotel, a four-story ramshackle inn, two buildings down from Scorched Earth's HQ. The Roosevelt was the kind of establishment that rented rooms by the week or the night, or by the hour if that's all you needed. Redbird was up on the roof watching the front door, side windows, and backyard of the hideout.

"Officer McCourt find anything yet?" I said into the phone.

The short span of Suggs's hesitation told me more than words.

"Melvin," I prompted.

"There was an investigation of Leonard Scores."

"Who's that?"

"The senior officer killed in the shootout. They thought that he was doin' work in the drug trade."

"Somebody actually told him this?"

"Score's precinct captain's secretary. Women like Anatole."

"You said, *there was an investigation.* They called it off after the killings?"

"Before."

"Why?"

"Because Roger Frisk, after delegating the investigation to Tout Manning, said that there was no foundation to the accusations."

"Oh."

A paunchy and middle-aged white man wearing a polyester green suit came in with his arm around the waist of a reed-slender, teenaged Mexican girl. Impossibly, she seemed to be holding him up. They went to the podium that stood for the front desk. A tall and slender woman appeared from behind a red curtain. She was a dark-skinned Hispanic woman with suspicious eyes and an incongruous smile on her lips.

The desk clerk and girl had a short conversation in rapid Spanish.

At the end of the exchange the girl turned to the man and said, "She wants fifteen dollars."

"That's too much," the man slurred.

"It's the honeymoon suite," the woman said through her false smile.

"Easy," Melvin Suggs said in my ear.

"Yeah?"

"Frisk must be putting a frame on Mantle to hide his involvement with Scores. If they can prove that he was part of the Goldsmith kidnapping nobody'll even question the shootout."

"And Art Sugar goes away smelling like a rose."

"Sugar killed them?"

"That's what I hear."

"From who?"

"Why don't you grab Officer McCourt and come down to the Roosevelt Hotel on East First?"

"I asked you a question, Easy."

"Ask me again when you're reinstated."

"And you'll tell me then?"

"Probably not."

The paunchy man paid the desk clerk from a crushed-up wad of one-dollar bills, then he, with the help of the girl, climbed the narrow and rickety staircase. I wondered, while watching them, if someone were looking at the way I conducted my life, would they see what I was seeing in the desultory climb of that man and that girl?

Melvin was muttering something.

I cut him off, saying, "I'll see ya when you get here. We'll probably be up on the roof."

Redbird was watching the extortionists' front and back doors from the top of the hotel.

"Are they coming?" he asked.

"Oh yeah."

"They won't act like fools?"

"They won't call in their brothers in blue until we're sure how to get done what we need."

I lit a cigarette. Redbird snorted once then left it alone.

The roof was layered with tar paper, and there was a ledge against a defunct brick chimney that we propped ourselves against.

Scorched Earth's backyard was completely paved in pale asphalt and surrounded by a tall chain-link fence. There was a long clothesline stretched from one corner of the fence to the other. At twilight a man came out and started hanging shirts and pants along the line.

"We might be able to get in through the back," Redbird suggested.

"We were lucky once, man. Why push it?"

Forty minutes later Melvin and Anatole joined us. They were dressed in black jeans and medium-colored shirts—McCourt in blue and Suggs in dark red.

After introducing McCourt and Redbird I told the cops what we were looking at.

"We should just get a riot squad and break down the doors," McCourt said.

"What if they're barricaded?" I asked. "And what about Frisk?"

"What about him?"

"He wants to hang this thing on Bob Mantle but in order to do that he needs to take out these guys too."

"Then we just won't tell Frisk."

"You can bet that he's told every precinct chief and desk sergeant to report any news about Mantle or Rosemary."

"We don't have to mention them either," Anatole argued.

"So we just point the riot squad at a house full of armed radicals and let the bullets fly," I said.

"How do you want to handle it, Easy?" Suggs said, intervening.

"Watch and wait. If anyone leaves we let them go but grab 'em before they come back."

"Why not pick 'em up as soon as they're out of sight of the house?"

"Tonight they're picking up the ransom."

"Then the law is already on it," Anatole put in.

"Mr. Goldsmith didn't tell the police," Redbird said. I was a little surprised that he said anything to the white men.

"That's against the law."

Teh-ha went to the edge of the roof and squatted down. With this movement he effectively turned his back on the younger cop's stupidity.

"They'll probably only send two or three of their people to pick up the money," I said to Suggs. "If so, I think I might have a plan."

"What kinda plan?"

"Cops got one'a them safe houses around here?" I asked.

"Not too far," Anatole said.

"Can we get it?"

"I'll see what I can do." I had the feeling that the Irish cop was good at working the system in ways that his mentor couldn't even imagine.

I laid out a far-reaching plan that included everything from stalking and abduction to health insurance and retirement benefits. By the time I was through I had converted all three men to my religion.

After that, things moved slowly for a while. Redbird and Suggs watched the clothes dry in the backyard while Anatole went off to secure the safe house. I went down to the room we'd rented, sat in a chair next to a window, and watched as the mostly Mexican population moved around on foot and in cars, on bikes and in baby carriages, even in wheelchairs and with the help of canes and crutches just like other people did in other parts of town and all over the world.

At a little after nine the door to the small room came open and Melvin Suggs rushed in.

"White guy and a Chinese chick just left the house," he said. "Your boy climbed down the fire escape and followed them."

"Alone?"

"He said that they wouldn't even see a brown man on the street around here."

"What's the plan?"

"Anatole is watching which way they go. He'll meet us downstairs and we can follow."

Moving down East First we'd made it about a block and a half before encountering Redbird, who was on his way back.

"They went to a locked one-car garage," Redbird told us right there on the street. "Then they came out in an old blue Buick."

"Let's go check it out," Melvin said.

It was a solidly built concrete bunker of a building, freestanding with a heavy oak door. There were four thick padlocks securing the entry port. On the right side there wasn't enough space for a dog to traverse but on the left there was a constricted concrete pathway that we managed to negotiate.

There was a door at the back of the building that was solid and also locked.

But a strong lock didn't mean much to Anatole McCourt's impressive shoulders. He slammed into the green door five times and it flew open.

I found myself wondering how many blows it would have taken Percy Bidwell to achieve the same end.

Redbird found the light and Melvin located a small armory in a large wooden locker on a sidewall. While Anatole looked around I stood in the center of the car-sized empty space imagining myself transforming into another kind of man with a slightly different life.

"Two of us should wait here for the man and woman to return, and one should keep watch on the house," I said.

"What about the fourth?" Melvin asked.

"You remember where the desert cabin was?" I asked Redbird.

He nodded.

"You go out there and bring back Bob."

"What you want with him?" Melvin wanted to know.

"Trust me, Mel," I said. "I got this shit covered."

54

It was decided that Anatole should head back to the Roosevelt because he was the only official lawman among us. We agreed that if the man and woman in the blue Buick came back to the hideout rather than the garage, and Delbert and his merry band decided to move, McCourt could call in the riot squad. Redbird didn't like that wrinkle but he finally agreed.

I wasn't worried, because there wasn't enough room for all of them in the one car, and even if they did try to leave, the cops could get the drop on them outside their fortress.

Melvin and I moved to the opposite corners next to the port door. That way, if the extortionists returned, we could come up behind them as they exited the automobile.

We turned out the lights and hunkered down. Anatole levered the back door into place from outside, and so the garage was in almost perfect darkness.

"You get much sleep lately?" I asked my unseen confederate.

"In the desert I did," he said. "You know when the sun goes down out there it's just like you got to close your eyes. But since Mary's been back I've hardly even blinked."

"You need me to goose you every now and then so you don't doze off?"

"I won't," he said. "And even if I did, a car driving in here would wake me."

"Okay," I said.

"But before we go silent tell me something."

"What's that?"

"How did you tumble to the hideout?"

I told him most of the story of the dead bodies and the clue innocently given up by Bob Mantle's son.

"Did you call Emergency when you found the bodies?" Melvin asked when I was through.

"They were already dead, Mel. There didn't seem to be any emergency."

After that we were quiet.

I sat in the darkness with no real thoughts in mind. I was a Neolithic hunter, maybe one of Redbird's ancestors, waiting by a watering hole for some big dumb creature to raise its woolly head.

I might have heard the engine idling on the other side of the garage door, or maybe it was the padlocks clacking open and banging against their brass hinges. Whatever it was, I was fully awake by the time the dark sedan with its headlights blazing pulled past me into the space. I wondered if Melvin had fallen asleep too.

I couldn't worry about that. My only choice was to scuttle forward toward the passenger's door and hope that Melvin was doing the same on his side.

My target door was only halfway open when I heard Melvin shout, "Hold it right there, sister—police!"

That meant the woman was driving and that the man was in a position to shoot through the window at my partner. I leaped toward the car door, swung it open, and slammed the side of my pistol into the back of the white man's head. He staggered in his seat and I hit him a second time, remembering again the blessing of Percy Bidwell.

"Easy!" Melvin shouted.

I stood up and he threw me a pair of official handcuffs. I then pulled the skinny white guy out of the car and he tumbled onto the concrete floor like a half-empty bag of laundry.

While I was securing his wrists behind his back the woman screamed—or, more accurately, she began a scream that was cut short by a hard slap.

I went to the garage door and pulled it down before anyone could come investigate. I was still a little disoriented by sleep but it seemed to be very late. The little I saw of the street was empty, even desolate. The car's headlights were still on but I flipped the switch for the overhead light anyway.

Melvin was putting the cuffs on the stunned woman. I never liked hitting women but in this case I understood. Melvin was acting on his own while under suspension. If we were caught the whole game would go south. But my indifference toward the extortionists had other origins also; first among these was the hanging corpse in the Studio City hideout, the woman who tried and failed to save herself from strangling with one big toe.

There was a tool cabinet at the back of the garage next to the cache of arms; in there Melvin found a roll of black electrical tape. He used this to cover the woman's mouth, then he threw the roll to me. I did the same to my captive.

"We should use the tape to bind their legs," I said. "And then we could put them in the backseat of the car and tape their hands and ankles to the handles on the doors."

"Why not put them in the trunk?"

When Melvin asked this the woman jumped and tried to run. Melvin caught her by the arm and pulled her back. She kicked him in the leg and he pushed her hard enough that she lost her balance and fell to the floor.

"Throw me that tape," he grunted.

I did as he requested.

My captive had his eyes open but I don't think he was seeing anything.

He was a featherweight with acne scars on his face. He, and the Asian woman, wore dark pants and shirts. It was like they were playing at crime. Just wearing those clothes at night could have gotten them arrested. At the very least their attire might have brought cops snooping around.

Melvin whistled and I looked up to see the tape flying at my head. I caught it and bound the man's ankles. Then I dragged him onto the floor of the backseat and bound him to the handles of both doors in the way I'd suggested. His hands were behind his back and so I twisted the tape, making it like a rope pulling his arms up so that movement was almost impossible.

Melvin had much more trouble with the woman on the backseat cushions. She wriggled and bucked, would have bitten and scratched if she could have. But he finally managed to bind her.

When they were lying facedown and bound, ankles and wrists, to the chrome door handles, Melvin and I turned our attention to other matters.

Suggs took the keys from the ignition and opened the trunk. Therein we found two dark green trunklike suitcases that were large enough to need wheels and handles on both the long and short sides.

We each pulled out a bag.

"You think Daddy might have laid a booby trap?" Melvin asked.

"No," I said. "I mean he could have. He's got the right tools at that research factory. But there would be no way for him to plan who was going to get killed."

"You really believe that?" Melvin asked.

I nodded.

"Then you open one," he said.

Both bags had three latches along the side. I snapped mine open and lifted the lid.

"Shit." That was Melvin but it could have just as well been me.

The traveling trunk was filled with cash—filled. Mostly tens and twenties that had been in circulation, in wrappers that had amounts scrawled upon them.

Melvin opened the other case. It was the same thing there.

"A goddamned million," Melvin whispered. "A goddamned million dollars."

The silence in that hangar was akin to the hush of a church.

We were both thinking the same thing: about Moving Day. This was a once-in-a-lifetime moment. We could take the money and leave the radicals to be found by Delbert later that day. I'd fly off to Liberia or Brazil. Later I'd call Bonnie and she could bring Feather.

It wasn't stolen money.

We were Tom Sawyer and Huck Finn falling into a cave and landing on a fortune. And in this story Becky was one of the bad guys and Injun Joe was on our side.

"You thinkin' what I'm thinkin'?" Melvin asked. He sounded like a child.

"Uh-huh" was all I could manage.

"We could just take this money right now."

"Too many loose ends, Melvin. Anyway, we got to leave *some* money for your brothers in blue to find."

We drove the car sixteen blocks to a brick house with an attached garage. This was the LAPD safe house for that neighborhood. It was where they secluded themselves when planning one of their larger operations or when a senior officer needed some private time with his mistress.

The keys were in a false brick on the right side of the stronghold.

We unlocked the door of the garage and parked inside. After that Melvin and I lugged the bags inside, leaving our squirming prisoners in the backseat.

Officer McCourt had paid off the right people to have the house for the night. He told the district supervisor that he was giving a bachelor party for some fellow officer and promised the requisite three hundred and fifty dollars.

The house's walls were thick and the few windows bulletproof. The front, back, and side doors were solid steel. There wasn't much wood and so fire wasn't a concern. It was a fortress and we were defending sentinels.

Sitting in the kitchen, Melvin was drinking a beer while I satisfied my thirst with a glass of tap water. I knew what was to come next.

"So, Easy," he said. "Which one?"

"Either you or me."

"We could both go."

"You wanna leave a million dollars and two murderers with no supervision. There ain't a bank vault outside'a Fort Knox that secure."

"You can trust me," he said.

When I hesitated he said, "We could flip a coin."

"Why not a simple math problem?" I suggested. "An equation."

"What kind of equation?"

"Which is greater," I said, "the possibility of me running off with a million dollars or the woman back home in your bed?"

Reminding Melvin of Mary/Clarissa was all I had to do. In a week or maybe two he would no longer feel indebted to me, but after long weeks of pining for his lost love he couldn't turn me down.

"You know I'm gonna be quick," he warned.

"Take the keys to our friends' car," I offered. "Take off the distributor cap and flatten all the tires. I will be right here when you get back."

Maybe ten minutes after he left I went out to the garage to check on our captives. They were secure but all the tires were flat. Mel didn't have time to let out the air. He came through with a knife and punctured each one.

55

Half an hour later I was sitting in the kitchen reading the only book I could find, *Atlas Shrugged*, a work I'd heard lots about but never read. I knew that Rand's philosophy, Objectivism, was the talisman of free thinkers and capitalists around the world but in the few pages I got through I couldn't make out her argument.

Of course I wasn't so much thinking about abstract ideas of laissez-faire capitalism with a million dollars in the hall closet.

By then it was early in the morning, a little after five. The reason I fell asleep was that the man and woman, Willy Buckingham and Sheila Yamagata, had taken five hours to retrieve the ransom. It was much later I found out that Sheila and Willy were secret lovers. Delbert considered all the women of Scorched Earth to be his private domain and so they took part of the time to satisfy their lust.

Who knows? Maybe Mel and I saved their lives by grabbing them, because if they had come in so late Delbert might have suspected their purpose and hung them both from the clothesline in the backyard.

On page twelve of *Atlas* the front door to the police house banged open. Melvin came in followed by the motley crew of Anatole, Redbird, and Bermuda shorts–wearing Uhuru-Bob Mantle. Bob walked with a pronounced limp and Redbird seemed like a nervous patriot, unhappy to be in the consulate of an enemy nation. Officer McCourt didn't like their company but was exercising toleration. Mel went right to the closet where we stashed the trunks. After a few minutes he came out again.

"What?" I said. "Don't you trust me, Mel?"

His wry grin was strong enough that I could almost smell it.

"So what's the plan?" Anatole McCourt asked.

"Are they still in the house?" was my answer.

"They were when we left."

"Then we need to call them if they have a phone."

"I got the number," Officer McCourt said.

"How?"

"I thought we might need it so I called a friend at the phone company and he looked it up."

"A friend?"

"What good is it being Irish if you can't be friendly?" he said.

This sounded like some kind of self-deprecation but I couldn't fathom it; and neither did I care.

"Is it connected?" I asked.

"Only one way to find out."

"Bob," I said to my actual client.

"Yeah?"

"I need you to do something for me."

"What's that?"

"Do you know who Raymond Alexander is?"

"Sure I do. That's Mouse you talkin' 'bout right there. Everybody know Mouse. He the man give bad a good name."

"I want you to pretend to be Mouse and to call Delbert."

"But Delbert knows me."

"Yeah, yeah, yeah, I know. But what I want is for you to feel like Mouse in your heart and then tell him that you got his money and if he wants it he has to give you back your woman."

He gave me a questioning scowl and I said, "Rose."

"Uh, um," he mumbled. "I don't know, Mr. Rawlins. I mean I could call him and say that but maybe not the way you want. I mean I don't know how to do anything like that. . . . I mean not on purpose."

That moment was the only true experience of revelation that I had on the Rose Gold case, outside of the Blessing of Percy Bidwell. Bob didn't know what he was capable of; he just did things and only believed in what he was doing while he was doing it.

I took the totem ring from my pocket and handed it to him.

"This here is a present I got from Ray some years ago. I told him that I liked it and he just gave it to me."

Bob took the ring gingerly, cradling it in his left palm and stroking it lightly with the fingers of his right hand.

"It's beautiful," he said.

"I want you to have it."

"I couldn't."

"If you just try and talk to Delbert you will have earned it."

The chameleon-man looked up at me, his eyes filled with surprise and wonder. He slipped the ring on the pinky of his left hand and said, "What is it exactly that you want me to say?"

I went over what we needed a few times with Bob. He fiddled with the ring on his finger and looked everywhere but in my eyes.

His attention seemed to be wandering and so I asked, "Do you need me to write it down?"

"Naw, man," a different Bob said. "I'ont need that. I *know* what I'm gonna say."

We set him up at the phone in the kitchen. I hurried upstairs and lifted the receiver on an extension line while keeping my hand on the button. At a prearranged moment Anatole handed Bob the number. After he dialed the seven digits, Anatole motioned to Melvin at the foot of the stairs, Melvin signed to Redbird, who was stationed outside my room, and Redbird waved at me. When I let go of the button there was a phone ringing in my ear.

After six rings someone answered, "Yes?"

"Delbert there?" new Bob said.

"Wrong number."

"I call him Delbert but you say Most Grand."

"Who is this?"

"Get Delbert, man. That is unless you wanna lose all yo' money."

"Hello?" another voice said.

"Hey, Del, I need you to do sumpin' for me, man."

"How you know my name?"

"Delbert Underhill, right?"

"Is that you, Uhuru?"

"Who is Uhuru? Some kinda punk? You know who I am, Del, at

least you should. For a few years there you lived just a couple'a blocks from my mama's house."

"I'on't know you, niggah."

"Maybe not but I'm ovah here sittin' on two trunks full'a money, mothahfuckah, and you ovah there messin' wit' my woman. I want Rose and you want yo' money. That's grounds for a trade right there."

"Fuck you, man! You ain't got shit."

"I got yo' numbah. I got Willy and Sheila. I got a million dollars in two big bags. What the fuck you got, niggah?"

"I'll kill you," Most Grand warned. "Gimme my money or you a dead man."

"You don't wanna get me mad, Del, 'cause when I hang up this phone that's it. I'ma be on a plane headed somewhere outside the country and here you is some loser ex-con cain't even get no passport."

Bob's facility was amazing. He must have met Mouse at one time or other because he was playing the role perfectly.

There was a span of silence on Delbert's side of the line.

"So if Rose goes with you, you give me the money?" Delbert asked, his anger held in abeyance.

"Naw, mothahfuckah! Shit no! You give me Rose an' I give you one bag. You got to pay sumpin' for takin' my woman and leavin' me up in the mountains to die from my wounds. And don't you even think about arguin' wit' me or I'll cut you down to half a bag."

Bob was following the script just the way Raymond would have; with a flavor of his own.

"All right, all right," the criminal-turned-revolutionary said. "Just tell me where to be."

"Listen, mothahfuckah, I know you thinkin' that you gonna come ovah here an' kill me an' take your money but that ain't about to happen, man. Not nearly. I got four men with guns up in here and you gonna come alone with Rose or I'ma shoot you in the head myself."

Bob gave Delbert the address and warned him again to come only with Rose.

"I'll be there in a hour," Most Grand said. "I'll have Rose an' you bettah have my mothahfuckin' money."

56

The so-called safe house had a six-foot-square raised extension above the third floor. It was like a crow's nest on an old-time sailing ship. There was glass on all four sides maybe eighteen inches high. From that vantage point one could see up and down the street and in the backyard. The house was also wired with intercom speakers in every room. I went up to the crow's nest thinking that the secret existence of houses like that was why Ian Fleming could come up with a character like James Bond.

Our plans were set and yet fluid because we didn't know exactly how it would play out.

"There's a white Impala slowing down in front of the place," I said into a microphone. My words were heard throughout the house.

It had been thirty-seven minutes since the phone call. I had reported on the passage of more than a dozen cars while Redbird, Melvin, and Anatole executed our impromptu plans.

"Anybody out back?" Melvin asked for at least the sixth time. He was waiting at the rear door, ready to move.

"Not that I can see."

Anatole had promised me that the thin band of windows I was watching through were invisible to anyone in the street. I trusted him but I couldn't shake the feeling that my head was a melon at target practice.

The front of the house had two doors. The outer door opened onto a walled-in external vestibule and was seven feet from the proper entrance. It opened easily but was weighted to close immediately and lock, barring either entrance or exit. There was a waist-high trunklike gardener's cabinet to the left on the inside of this entryway. It was secured by a simple padlock. My cohorts had loaded the box with eight pillowcases filled with the contents of one suitcase.

"The car's coming back around," I said.

"How's the back?"

"If I don't say it then there's nobody there, Mel."

The white Impala cruised by a little faster than before. I could tell it was the same car by a small rust spot on the front hood.

New Bob, Anatole, and Redbird were crowded around the front door.

There were four or five possible resolutions to the upcoming encounter. They ranged from very good to acceptable to very bad.

The Impala came around a third time. I told my people that. It pulled to the curb three houses down and Rosemary Goldsmith got out with a black man, not light-skinned Delbert "Most Grand" Underhill.

I used a pair of binoculars and studied the car.

"Rosemary and one other are coming to the door," I said. "I think the rest are all in the car, Mel. You can head out now. And you can make that call, Officer McCourt."

For my part I rushed down the stairs with a pistol in my hand. By the time I had reached the front there was already a conversation going on over the intercom.

"Where the fuck is Delbert?" Bob shouted into the microphone.

He was looking up into a pane of glass over a mirror face that was connected to a periscope-like device used to monitor the inner entrance. The police were taking no chances with bullet-vulnerable peepholes.

The slightly distorted images in the pane were Rosemary Goldsmith and a slender black man in khaki and black. The man pulled out a pistol.

"No, no, no, mothahfuckah," Bob said as if he had lived that role for a lifetime. "Do' is solid steel. You tryin' to shoot through it is the same thing as shootin' yo'self in the head."

Behind me Anatole McCourt was talking softly on the phone.

The slender black man tapped on the door with the muzzle of his gun. We could hear the ring of metal on metal through the intercom and through the door.

"Where is Delbert?" Bob asked again.

"He's in the car, Uhuru," Rose said into the ether.

"Why ain't he here?"

"I don't know," she said but I didn't believe her. I knew, and she did too, that Delbert didn't come because he was afraid that Uhuru-Bob Nolicé wanted vengeance. He was waiting in the car to see if the money made it back to him. If it didn't he was probably planning to go to war.

"You the niggah called Tom, right?" Bob said.

"Yeah," the skinny black drone replied.

"Well, Tom, you need to know some facts. The first thing is that the wood box on your right has eight bags of money in it. The second thing is that the door behind you is locked by bolts. You might shoot the lock off the box but you won't make it past that door before me an' my boys shoot you through our holes in this door. So I want you to put the gun down on the floor, stand with your back to that door, and let Rose stay by the front." I noticed then that sweat was pouring down Bob's face. He was working harder than he ever had in his brawling years in the ring.

"That's right," he said when Thomas had completed the instructions. "No, no, Rose. You stay by my door.

"Now up above your head, Tom, there's a ledge. On the ledge is the key to the money box."

When Thomas turned to reach for the key I yanked open the front door and Redbird grabbed Rosemary, pulling her into the house. She yelped in protest but Redbird was fast and strong. Thomas turned to help his comrade but I slammed the door shut.

"Forget the girl, man," Bob said. He was wilting from the strain of the role. "Take the key an' get yo' money. After that we through here."

"Redbird," Rose said. Something in her voice had changed from one room to the next.

"Miss Goldsmith," the last known surviving member of the Taaqtam said.

I could see Thomas fiddling with the lock, lifting the lid, and then grabbing at three pillowcases. Anatole hit a lever that unlocked the outer door. Thomas managed to gather up a fourth bag in his arms before scuttling out to the street.

Bob was sitting on the floor against the wall, sweat dripping down from his forehead.

Rose was staring into her mother's agent's eyes.

"I was doing it for your people," she said.

He said nothing. When she began to cry he embraced her.

"I'm gonna break down this mothahfuckin' door!" This shout was broadcast through the intercom.

In the mirror I could see Most Grand Delbert holding an M1 rifle. Two of his minions, a white man and Thomas, were behind him.

"You could try," I said through the speaker system. "But you know we called the cops already. How much you wanna bet that their guns are bigger and better than yours?"

He battered the butt of the rifle against the door a few times. When this had no effect he grabbed a bag of money and his two men took the rest.

Less than half a minute later, before they could have pulled away from the curb, there came the weedy and plaintive sound of police sirens—lots of them.

"I'm sorry, Mr. Mantle," Officer McCourt said, "but I'm going to have to put you in handcuffs. I'm doing it because I want them to know that you're my prisoner."

Bob sighed, nodded, and staggered to his feet. There was a spot of blood on the floor from his bullet wound.

"Hold up a minute, man," Bob said. He took off the emerald and platinum ring and handed it to me. "I'ma give you this back, Mr. Rawlins. Thanks for givin' it to me but I never wanna to go through no shit like that ever again."

57

"What happened after all that?" Mouse asked me three weeks later.

We were sitting in my living room at around eleven a.m. on a Tuesday morning. Feather had been back for ten days and was attending her first full week at Ivy Prep. The room was still pretty bare—I'd been too busy fixing up my rental properties to shop for furniture.

Raymond had come over to visit my new home. His right arm was in a sling but that didn't weaken him; my friend, among his many other talents, was ambidextrous.

"Melvin had cut out through the back with the rest of the cash," I said. "Redbird went after him to bring Rosemary to her mother at the Dumbarton. When the cops got there McCourt said that he'd been called by Melvin and apprised of the situation. He told them that because he didn't know who he could trust in the department he drafted me into service. Again, Melvin had vouched for my honesty."

"I heard about the shootout with Delbert and them," Mouse said. "Papers say that they went down in a hail of gunfire."

"That was because Frisk had given the kill order."

"He didn't want no contradictions, huh?" Mouse said.

"No, but he didn't know that we had Willy and Sheila locked up in their car."

"And you got half the money?"

"Split it five ways."

"Five?"

"Me, Melvin, his friend Anatole, Redbird of course, and then there was Bob's family."

"His family?"

"Lenore Goldsmith helped us to set up a kind of trust fund for Belle and the mother of his son, Sister. Lenore sent her lawyer to talk to the Chinese liquor store clerk—he had serious memory loss after that. Then, when McCourt convinced the police that Bob was innocent, we got him enrolled in this drama school up in Portland. His mom is paying for it."

"Damn. But why the rich lady wanna help you?"

"It tickled her that we stole her husband's money. And Redbird told her that it was my plan that saved her daughter."

"Damn, man," Mouse said. "You got luck so strong it's likely to get you killed."

"What happened to your arm, Ray?"

"Mothahfuckin' guard that sold us the information about the armored car decided to try an' double-cross us. We had to shoot our way outta there. Shit, here I only get seventy-five thousand and you make more and never even have to fire a gun."

"Lucky me."

"The cops after the girl?" Mouse asked.

"No. As far as the cops were concerned she was a kidnap victim and she had the missing finger to prove it.

"Melvin went to Parker and his staff and laid out a story. He told them about Tout Manning and Roger Frisk; about the cops in cahoots with the drug dealers. They arrested Manning for conspiracy, fired Frisk, reinstated Suggs, and now I hear that he's in line for Frisk's job."

"No shit?" Raymond said. It was one of the few times I had seen him impressed with my machinations. "You mean now you got a friend in Chief Parker's office? Damn! That's better than any money."

"Yeah," I said. "I mean Mel still has that bent girlfriend but maybe it'll work out. McCourt will be his new Tout Manning. I wouldn't want to be Light Lambert or Art Sugar right now. Suggs and McCourt said that the girl was innocent."

"Was she?" Mouse asked, his gray eyes in mine.

"No, I don't think so. I mean she had to allow Delbert to cut off her finger. I don't know if she was party to the murders of Youri Kidd and Deirdre Melbourne, that girl in Studio City. Delbert was a crazy motherfucker who believed that everybody was tryin' to betray him. That's what everybody that knew him said. But it was Rose who planned to extort and embarrass her father, I'm sure of that.

"Melvin made a deal with Willy Buckingham and Sheila Yamagata. He worked it out with the prosecutor for reduced charges and they testified against their dead friends and claimed that Rose was a prisoner the whole time. The police thought that the half million in the getaway car was the whole amount that Stony paid and he never said any different. His lawyers won't even let the cops talk to him."

"What I don't get is why the girl's father agreed to pay at all," Mouse said. "He must'a suspected that she was workin' with them."

"Lenore found out," I said, "and Redbird told me. They sent only the finger to Stony first. There was a ransom note but no details on how to pay. Later that day they had Rose call him on his private line. She cried and screamed and begged him to save her. No matter what he thought, he really did love his daughter and she played him like a violin."

It was good to be able to talk to Mouse. He'd never divulge my secrets, nor would he judge me.

After he left I drove downtown for lunch with Jackson Blue at the Proxy Nine cafeteria. Jackson liked going down to the basement lunchroom to eat among the rank and file of the international insurance company.

We sat at a little table for two in a corner. On his red plastic tray he had carrot soup and fried rice. I was eating pastrami on rye with mustard and onions.

For twenty minutes or so we talked about Ayn Rand and her Objectivist philosophy.

"But she ain't really no real philosopher," Jackson said at last.

"She writes philosophy," I argued.

"Yeah but really it's just ideas that's alive in the air," he said. "She pluck out them concepts and act like they were her own. But you know a real philosopher tells you what's comin'. 'Cause you know the world always gonna change an' the genuine thinker give you some warnin' 'bout things nobody else even suspects."

I stopped arguing after that. I had learned over time that even if Jackson was wrong he could still talk circles around me.

"So why you invite me up here to lunch, Jackson?"

"I wanna thank you, Easy. Jewelle came up all sheepish to me and said that she had give Percy Bidwell three hundred dollars and he used that to move back east. She said that he went to talk to you and then called her and asked for the loan. She said that she didn't want me to think that she was throwin' away our money but she did give it to him. I know that was you, Easy, and I wanted to say thanks."

"No problem, Jackson."

"So what now?" he asked.

"What do you mean?"

"You saved that rich girl, right?"

"Yeah."

"So her parents must have paid you."

"In a way they did."

"So you still gonna run the streets and risk your life for peanuts or you gonna try and change up? You know Jean-Pierre still got that security job open."

He was talking about a kind of metaphysical Moving Day.

"Thanks for that but I'ma have to say no. I got other plans."

"Like what?"

"I think I'll move my office downtown," I said. "And maybe . . . maybe I'll take on a few agents. Maybe I'll even try and bring in a partner so I can take some time off now and then."

"You mean like a detective agency?"

"Yeah," I said, nodding to some other place and time. "Maybe it's time I learn to count my blessings."